I0555907

The Marquess Who Loved Me

A MUSES OF MAYFAIR NOVEL

Sara Ramsey

For [censored] —

the best brother I could ask for.

CHAPTER ONE

Surrey, 11 February 1813

Nicholas Claiborne was not a sentimental man. And yet even he thought it would be pleasant to feel something better than anger upon seeing his ancestral estate for the first time.

"Damn her," he muttered. "She *would* be hosting a party tonight."

Did Ellie remember this date, this night, as he did? Or was her party a grating coincidence?

When Nick's will had failed him over the last decade — more often than he cared to admit — he dreamed of seeing her again. Sometimes, his fantasy Ellie ran into his arms. Sometimes, she was so caught up in someone else that she didn't notice him. But in every vision of his homecoming, he had forgotten an important point.

He couldn't find his own house.

It was embarrassing, that. The pub owner in the last village, only a mile from Folkestone's entrance gates, had assured him that he couldn't possibly miss the estate. He might have done so more smugly had he known Nick was the long-absent owner rather than one of an endless stream of guests. But Nick hadn't shared his real name — not in the village, not upon arrival at the East India Docks, and not at the London hotel he'd used for the past five days. If the attempts on his life in Madras had been ordered from London — or Folkestone — he wouldn't make it easy for his assailants by announcing his return.

The date of his return was a coincidence. If he weren't tracking a would-be murderer, he might never have returned. But on the eve of Ellie's birthday, he couldn't resist her. When his will finally, inevitably failed him and his compulsion for Ellie had overruled his common sense, he only had a vague sense of where to find his Surrey estate — hardly an auspicious homecoming.

Luckily, the pub owner's directions were sound. The grand wrought iron gates stood open, more inviting than Nick had pictured them when his father had described them to Nick and his brothers. Beyond, some fifty carriages lined the drive. He heard the whinnying of horses and the stamping of hooves, muted masculine laughter and at least one protracted snore. Never mind that it was February — the drivers were accustomed to waiting hours for their employers.

Surely it was the cold that made him shiver, not the gates that waited for him. The colorful coat of arms at their peak was grey in the darkness, but the golden bits glimmered faintly in the moonlight. He had been forced to learn the arms at Eton — lions, unicorns, and roses, remnants of the ancient lines from which his father's side descended.

His lip curled. What would his own arms be? Looms and rifles and tea leaves?

He urged his horse through the gates. If anyone in the house wanted a warning when he arrived, there was no one at the gatehouse to send it. He'd passed no carriages on the road — they likely thought all guests were accounted for and had gone off for a drink. If he were inclined, Nick could seize the gatehouse without firing a single shot.

As an invasion force, he was grossly outnumbered. But then, he held the deed to the property. Ellie's opinions on the matter, like the rest of her, could go to the devil.

The long drive was lined with towering elms, their branches a naked winter canopy. Moonlight filtered through, casting light and shadow on the gravel as he rode. In summer the leaves would be impenetrable. His father, in one of his nostalgic moods, had said the tunnel was a bit of magic, cutting off the view of the main house until the last moment, the better to stun visitors with its grandeur.

The marquesses of Folkestone were supposed to be grand. As the latest in that accursed line, Nick didn't care for appearances. He only cared for what helped him to achieve his ends. If grand hauteur helped, he would use every bit of it he possessed. He had hired a private room at the pub and trussed himself up in the evening suit he'd paid double to have tailored in London that morning. It wouldn't do to show up like a travel-stained beggar, not for what he had planned. He'd left his batman in the village, too — under protest, since Trower thought Nick needed an ally at his back.

Perhaps he did. But this wasn't a Madras back alley, and he'd found no evidence of a threat to his life in London. If Nick faced an attack at Folkestone, it would be more subtle — a cut direct with the eyes, not a saber.

He reached the end of the tunnel. It opened into a wide semicircular carriageway that cut across the acres of lawns and gardens in front of the vast house.

Nick reined in. His breath left him in a gust of frozen mist. The stories his father told had made Folkestone into a prison — Newgate, with fewer inmates and better ventilation.

But tonight, lit up outside with torches and inside with lamps and chandeliers, Folkestone was a shimmering invitation, a mansion seductive in its glory. Perhaps his father had dimmed his descriptions of Folkestone's grandeur for Nick's mother's sake — as though to say that marrying her and being disowned for it had rescued him rather than ruined him.

Nick set his jaw. Folkestone could go to the devil too. He hadn't needed it when he'd unexpectedly inherited it ten years earlier, and he didn't need it now. Besides, he was accustomed to such displays of wealth. The Claibornes had snubbed Nick's mother for no reason other than that she was the daughter of a garrulous Welsh miner-turned-merchant, but the business his maternal grandfather had started could buy Folkestone twenty times over. There was no point in ogling Folkestone like a street urchin.

And he would rather carve out his own eyes than be caught staring at it by someone who was either his servant or his guest.

Or Ellie.

His teeth ground together. He forced his jaw open. It was pointless to order himself not to think of her. He had given himself that order ten thousand times. It was the only place where his discipline failed him. But surely he could be disciplined tonight — if not for his pride, then for the effectiveness of his revenge upon her.

He rode around the courtyard's central fountain. The statues, replicas of Grecian water-bearers, were silent in winter, the water drained to keep from freezing and cracking the stone. At the foot of the house, a wide, shallow staircase beckoned, leading up half a story to the open double doors. He heard hundreds of voices, but no music — the party had not yet begun. But Ellie would have no trouble filling the house with guests. No one would refuse an invitation to such a lavish display, even with the two-hour drive from London.

A handful of grooms watched his approach. The Folkestone grooms typically wore green with gold trim — or at least they had twenty years earlier, when Charles Claiborne, his cousin and unlamented predecessor to the Folkestone title, had stolen all of Nick's clothes and left only a suit of Folkestone livery in Nick's chest at Eton. The hot, furious shame of that moment had faded, but the vivid memory of that green coat where his Eton robes should have been would never leave him.

But the grooms wore sumptuous red and blue tunics with puffed sleeves and hose — livery that would have been more at home at the Tudor court, not a modern country seat. They were all improbably young and impossibly smooth as they bowed to him.

"Welcome to Folkestone, sir," one of them said as Nick slid from his horse. He had the diction of a posh Londoner, not the broad accents of Surrey.

Nick slid off his horse and tossed a guinea to the groom. "Stable him. I'm staying."

That should have startled a look of surprise out of the servant. His face stayed unconcerned, though. He took the reins and led the horse away without a word.

How many other men had said the same thing, to make Ellie's servants so accustomed to his boldness?

One groom ushered him politely toward the steps. The others ignored him. No questions about luggage. No demand to see an invitation. No curiosity about why he had arrived on horseback rather than driving a smart curricle or carriage. Nick wanted to know why they were so lax. He wanted to know why they were dressed as Tudors. He wanted to know why they didn't recognize their master — surely Ellie kept at least one painting of him somewhere in his house? She'd painted him enough times to fill a room — unless she'd painted over him, removing his face from her life as ruthlessly as she'd cut out his heart.

He kept his questions to himself and strode up the steps. But his anger rose. He let it come, preferring rage to thoughts of what might have been — what his life would have been, if he had claimed this house the day he had inherited it. It would have been easy enough to do — take his damned cousin's title and the estate his father had never been allowed to return to.

And his cousin's bride — the woman who should have been his.

His thoughts were consumed by Ellie tonight. But he still had space to examine the house's defenses. If his would-be murderer had followed him from India, it would be absurdly easy to slip onto the estate. In fact, it seemed no slipping was required — Napoleon himself could likely walk into this party unmolested, and perhaps be offered refreshments and a bath before he started hacking away at people.

The tide of his anger swept him up the stairs and warmed his blood. An answering blast of body heat met him at the door. A crush of people milled in the grand foyer, spilling into the public drawing rooms and salons beyond the entryway.

It was a masquerade party — that much was clear immediately. The guests wore even more elaborate Elizabethan garb than the servants. Beneath the perfume of hothouse flowers, he smelled musty cedar. Some of the guests wore costumes that had been stored for decades, if not centuries. The gold and silver threaded clothes and bushels of jewels would do a maharaja proud.

Ellie's birth, as the daughter of a duke absolutely obsessed with bloodlines, had always been high enough to attract a better class than Nick. Her current milieu said she'd found it.

He was tall enough to see over most of them. It had been a consolation years earlier, when they would have had him scraping at their feet. Now, it was merely a convenience. His eyes were already scanning the crowd, looking for red in a sea of blondes and browns and silvers, when someone tapped his elbow.

A servant stood at his side, frowning imperiously. Too young to be a butler — but then, the grooms were young as well. The servants weren't just young, though. They were perfectly formed and immaculately dressed, as though Ellie had hired staff better suited to standing for her paintings than for menial labor.

Nick raised an eyebrow.

"My lady was most specific in the invitation about the preferred costume for this evening. Sir," he added, with just enough doubt to set Nick's teeth on edge.

"My lord," Nick supplied.

The man colored slightly. "My lord," he repeated. "My apologies. But still, the marchioness…"

Nick handed him his greatcoat, hat, and gloves, stripping them off with a predatory efficiency that made the servant flinch. The man almost refused, starting to gesture toward a cloak room. But Nick didn't stop. "Send someone to air out my room. And tell me where to find the marchioness."

"May I have your card, my lord?"

"No."

He'd been in London five days and hadn't ordered calling cards. It was likely an offense grave enough to have him tossed out of the House of Lords — but they would have half a dozen other reasons not to welcome him before they even reached matters of etiquette.

The servant swallowed. "If you would be so good as to wait just a moment, my lord, her ladyship will welcome all of her guests soon."

He had stayed away from her for ten years. Part of him wished for another ten. Another part of him didn't want to wait ten seconds. But he shrugged, let just enough displeasure show in his eyes to make the servant wince again, and waved a magnanimous hand. "Very well. I will find her myself after she's greeted the guests."

"Would you care for a mask, my lord? Not that you must take one, of course," he added hastily, when Nick's eyebrow slowly rose again.

He looked out over the crowd. Nearly all of the others wore costumes, not masks. Few would recognize him — few had known him, other than his fellows at Eton, and he'd seen none of them in over a decade. But if the servants were too dense to realize who he was, he would save the surprise for Ellie herself.

Maybe he would see something on her face to repay him for everything she'd done.

He turned back to the servant and took the mask he offered. He pulled on his formal gloves, obeying that social rule even if he cared for none of the others. And then he strode through the crowd, ignoring muttered huffs of protest as he elbowed toward the closed double doors on one side of the foyer.

If the house map his father had once drawn for him wasn't an exaggeration built on years of exile, a massive ballroom lay beyond those doors. He had just reached a prime vantage point when the doors were flung open. Everyone turned *en masse*, chattering excitedly.

"Do you think she's topped her Roman bacchanal?" a woman near him whispered to her companion.

"I do hope she's brought back the opera dancers," a man said, laughing at his wife's mock censure.

"Of course her costume will be splendid. But I came for her chef's efforts…"

Nick stopped hearing the people around him. They were drowned out by a sudden crashing in his ears, a roar that came from somewhere in the vicinity of his heart. Through the doors, he saw a throne. And on the throne, a queen.

Ellie.

Not a queen. An angel.

A devil.

His eyes blurred.

The servant who had greeted him before — perhaps the butler after all, despite his youth — cleared his throat. "The Marchioness of Folkestone welcomes you," he announced, in a voice that wasn't a shout but still somehow carried through the crowd.

Nick looked across the distance between them, over the heads of those who already moved down the carpet to greet her. The last time he'd seen her, she had worn orange blossoms in her red hair, his bloody cousin's ring on her finger, and a smile that would have driven him to gut her if he hadn't noticed, from where he lurked uninvited in the cathedral's shadows, her downcast eyes and the uncertain tilt to her chin.

There was no smile now, but no uncertainty either. She wore a crown instead of orange blossoms and a golden velvet gown instead of sweet, innocent muslin. She looked regal, serene, just a little bored — a perfect match to her costume.

She hadn't seen him yet, just as she hadn't seen him at her wedding.

He smiled under his mask.

Tonight, she had no choice but to see him. And then...

And then he didn't know, exactly, what would happen.

But this time, he would win.

CHAPTER TWO

Elinor Claiborne, the widowed Marchioness of Folkestone, didn't see her doom when the ballroom doors opened. She didn't even suspect that someone might thwart her plans. This night, for reasons that were a mystery to everyone else, was hers to command. Her guests saw it as a lively entertainment. But for her, it was a living painting, one in which all the players bowed to her artistic vision.

She was still confident in the spectacle she had created, even if her heart wasn't entirely satisfied. The Folkestone ballroom was freshly decorated, redone for the fifth time in her tenure as marchioness. The walls were a light blue this time, with plaster half-columns and elaborate scrollwork to mirror the shape of the French doors on the wall behind her. The Tudor era guards were her addition — actors hired from the West End to look as perfect as possible with their pikes and helmets. And the guests who entered, two hundred lords and ladies from the highest reaches of the ton, were a river of jewel-toned velvet unleashed at her command.

Ellie sat perfectly still on her throne, slipping into her role — cool, unaffected, with a hint of steel. She usually enjoyed parties — and was grateful that she did, since there was precious little else to engage her time — but tonight she was on edge.

Her annual masquerade ball, coming at the start of a large,

weeklong house party, would be Ellie's last public display as the Marchioness of Folkestone. If she were cursed to bear the title and couldn't bring herself to marry anyone else just to be rid of it, then surely it would be easier to bear it on some distant shore — somewhere with no memories left to torment her.

Her father's sister Sophronia, the Dowager Duchess of Harwich, was at the head of the line, moving across the ballroom to greet Ellie with a speed that neither her age nor her extravagant gown could slow. "I trust you aren't seeking a husband with this sudden display of respectability?" Sophronia demanded as she approached the throne.

Those who came to Folkestone this year expecting scarcely-clothed opera dancers or venues for tacitly approved rendezvouses would be disappointed — not due to some sudden change in Ellie's morals, but to the presence of her less debauched siblings. Ellie drummed her fingers on the arm of her throne. "Did the Virgin Queen ever seek a husband?"

"Good," Sophronia said. "I'll grant you, I would be pleased to see you behave yourself after all this time. But I knew you had more sense than to relinquish the advantages of widowhood."

She slid away before Ellie could answer. Ellie's brother Ferguson, the Duke of Rothwell, and his wife stepped up to take Sophronia's place. "Are there to be monkeys released into the crowd this year?" he asked. "Or have you hired some company to play Francis Drake and his band of pirates?"

She sighed as he kissed her hand. "I do not repeat myself, so no monkeys. They made a dreadful mess anyway."

"A shame — when I heard of them in Scotland years ago, I almost begged Father's forgiveness just so I could return to England and attend your parties. Tell me there shall be pirates, at least."

"No pirates. Be glad, brother — at my usual parties, you might have seen your wife stolen away for the evening."

Madeleine, his new duchess, grinned beneath her elaborate Elizabethan hairstyle. "I am quite happy with my lot, wretched as Ferguson is. But if there *were* to be pirates…"

She trailed off with a laugh as Ferguson whispered in her ear and dragged her away. Ellie resolutely turned back to the receiving line. But Madeleine's laughter was a distracting hum under her perfect show of calm.

Ellie had always thought she wanted a carefree, unencumbered life — one she lived on her own terms, not her father's or husband's or anyone else's. She hadn't felt grief when her husband had died.

She'd felt relief.

But there was freedom…and then there was solitude. She liked to be alone. She didn't need to surround herself with admirers to stay entertained, even if she did enjoy the social amusements London offered. The walls she'd thrown up had preserved her freedom perfectly, keeping her detached and untouched even when her house and calendar were full.

The cost, though…

Her eyes found Ferguson and Madeleine again. They stood a bit apart, sipping champagne — an island around which the crowd broke. There was no mistaking how united they were, even from this distance.

Ferguson's hand slipped possessively to his wife's waist. Madeleine smiled up at him, then leaned in to whisper in his ear. He laughed. Heads turned toward them, but he was too busy whispering back to care what others thought. He brushed a hand over Madeleine's headdress and she swatted at him. They were complete together, somehow more than just the simple sum of two people.

She wanted *that*, with a harsh, bitter jealousy that poisoned her every time she saw Ferguson and Madeleine together. Her fingers curled on her throne. Something ugly seethed inside her, clawing at her, reminding her.

She had once had what they had. She could have kept it, if she'd been strong enough — if she had recognized the truth of what she felt for Nick rather than the illusion of approval her father had offered.

And it was her fault that she would never have it again.

Ellie turned back to the next guest, her jaw firm. It all felt wrong, somehow. Not the dire wrong of an omen — she still didn't know what waited in her foyer. But she had to find a way to silence all that regret. She had to stop.

Stop. Stop throwing parties like the noise could drown out her memories.

Stop throwing *this* party, every single bloody year without ever giving herself peace, on an anniversary no one remembered but her. The night that had once, long ago, seemed like a pure beginning, full of promise and light — but ultimately was the beginning of the end.

Did Nick remember tonight as she did, in whatever ancient bazaar or Mughal palace he was striding through right now? Or had he forgotten her so thoroughly that he didn't even remember her enough to curse her name?

The receiving line stopped before her thoughts did, of course. Wasn't that how it always happened? The musicians in the hidden gallery above the ballroom started the closing flourish of the processional they'd played during her guests' entrances. She took a deep breath. No one had ever guessed that, beneath her reputation as the merriest widow in England, she hid a heart of ice. She wouldn't let them see it tonight, either.

She would dance like she was made of fire. She would indulge in her annual cry at the end of the party, a harsh jag of emotion that, once a year, she couldn't contain.

And then she would wake up, play the perfect hostess for the forty or so friends and family she already regretted inviting, and then shut up Folkestone and leave for the Continent. If she couldn't stop the memories, she could at least change the pattern of them.

The ballroom doors began to close. This wasn't Almack's, but Ellie demanded punctuality at this party and was formidable enough to receive it. But just before the door shut, a man shouldered it open.

Her eyes narrowed. He wore a plain mask that her servants kept for rulebreakers. His impeccably tailored evening suit was stark black and white — a shocking declaration in a crowd of people wearing the velvet and brocade she'd prescribed. He strode down her carpet like he owned it — not a penitent apologizing for tardiness, or even a green youth too exuberant to see the danger he was in, but a man who simply didn't give a damn what her invitation said.

If there was purpose in his stride, though, his speed was almost leisurely. William the Conqueror might have walked to his coronation like that, already king by destiny if not by law. Ellie leaned back in her throne, feigning indolence even though her stomach flipped and her heart sped up. Later she wondered if she'd known, then, that her doom was upon her...

But she didn't. She was a woman, not an oracle. All she felt was irritation that someone might dare to ruin her perfectly-planned display — and the tiniest, unacknowledged interest in finding someone who didn't yet toe her line.

When he reached her throne, she extended her hand. "You're

late," she said.

"Later than you know." He crossed his arms. Her hand became an embarrassing relic between them. "The Virgin Queen suits you, Lady Folkestone. Even if we both know the adjective doesn't apply."

She dropped her hand. Dressing as Queen Elizabeth was her own private joke; there were always suitors in the wings, but she never intended to marry again. But her voice still turned to ice. "There's no place for you at this party if you've only come to give insults."

His lips were savage under his mask, so sharply defined that she might have cut them there with a palette knife. "Oh, there will be a place for me. You should have trained your staff better, Ellie my love. Once the Trojan horse is inside the gates, there's no stopping it."

Her mind fired wildly when she heard the old endearment, the one she'd never thought to hear again. The caress, the dark promise in his voice sounded like something she'd heard a decade earlier from a mouth not yet reforged by hate. She leaned forward, her control breaking under the onslaught of memory. "Who are you?" she demanded.

He pulled off his mask and flung it at her feet.

The last time he'd flung something there, it had been a bouquet of flowers.

She looked down, expecting to see roses where the mask was — dead, brittle roses, the ones she'd kept until they'd crumbled to dust.

"Don't say you still can't bear to look at me," he said.

"Nick," she whispered.

Ellie never whispered.

She cleared her throat and forced herself to look at his face. He'd put on at least a stone of muscle in the last decade. It was little wonder she hadn't seen the lean boy he'd been when he walked down her — *his* — carpet. But his face was taut and sculpted, with the same cheekbones and stubborn chin she'd painted any number of times. And his eyes were still a vivid, startling blue under the inky slash of his eyebrows — eyes that held darkness lurking within them now, even though he smiled.

Could it be called a smile, when all she saw was malice? The lips were in the right position and his teeth gleamed behind them — but more like a wolf about to take its prey than an old friend greeting her again. Ellie wished that the only reason he fascinated her was because capturing his feral appeal in paint would be a challenge. But her sudden flush, and all the heat building in her belly, had nothing to do with art.

She forced herself to take a breath. The musicians had, quite awkwardly, started another round of the processional. She was still aware enough of the crowd to notice the murmurs rippling across the ballroom as everyone turned toward her unknown guest. She smiled coolly, searching for the grace that had seemed unassailable moments earlier.

"I am sorry it took so long to recognize you, my lord." Her voice was strong again. She would do anything before she showed how much it cost her to stay on that throne. "I had so nearly forgotten you, after all."

"'My lord,'" he repeated. "I heard in London that your father died a year ago. Pity. I would have liked to watch him as I took my place in the Lords."

In another world, she might have liked it too.

"Why are you here?" she asked. "You vowed not to return until you had forgotten me, and yet you still seem to remember my name."

"It would have been better if we had both forgotten."

"You can forget me just as well here as anywhere else. Welcome to your home, Lord Folkestone," she said, calling him by his title for the first time. She was gratified to see him flinch. "I'll remove myself to London in the morning. If you've anything to say, please direct it to my solicitors."

She stood, ready to descend to the dancing floor. She saw Lord Norbury hovering nearby — the escort she'd requested for the first dance, since he was attending without his wife and needed a partner. But Nick took her elbow before she could walk away.

"We have unfinished business between us, Ellie. Whatever else you may have forgotten, I assume you remember why I left. You owe me a conversation."

He hadn't come all the way from India to converse with her. The very idea was preposterous. And if anything, *he* owed *her* a conversation — or at least a chance to explain herself.

She couldn't do it here, not in the middle of her — *his* — ballroom. He wanted something from her — something she would not like, if she correctly read the menace in his tone. But whatever he wanted, she couldn't consider it when her heart still raced from his return. Changing the battlefield and giving herself time to regroup would at least put her on better footing.

She nodded, pretending that she was entirely unaffected by his touch on her arm. "The servants will see to it that you have a room and whatever accoutrements you require. Shall we adjourn until morning, my lord?"

He stepped closer, destroying the distance her words had attempted to create. For a dizzy moment she thought he would kiss her. His eyes looked the same as they had before past kisses — suddenly warm, intent, focused on her and only her. He leaned in, his lips almost touching hers. Hers parted of their own accord, ready physically even though she knew it was the worst thing that could possibly happen to her.

He wouldn't — he *couldn't* — kiss her in front of half the ton.

As it turned out, he didn't kiss her. Her lips were impertinent enough to be disappointed. Instead, he turned and whispered in her ear. "I don't wait for you — not anymore. Entertain your guests, but we will be having our conversation tonight."

He was gone before she could protest, striding back up the carpet to the double doors. He didn't leave, though. He leaned against a pillar beside them, as though guarding the room — or preventing her escape.

She shivered.

Norbury was at her side an instant later. "Is that man bothering you?" he asked. "I will ask the guards to see him out."

Ellie shook her head. The final notes of the processional sounded again. She stepped over the mask that lay at her feet and gave her hand to Norbury. "It's Folkestone," she said briefly. "We've no cause to remove him, and even if he could be gotten rid of, I doubt those ornamental guards are up to the task. Shall we begin?"

Norbury was startled. It was evident from the sudden tightening of his grip on her hand and the chill in his voice as he said, "I thought he planned to remain in India."

Ellie shrugged. "Didn't we all?"

She feigned boredom, so well that Norbury didn't press. He never pressed, at least not with her. They had never been lovers, but they had been friends for half a decade — and anyone who remained her friend knew when to leave well enough alone.

As the music started, she felt Nick watching, and frowning, from the opposite side of the room. She let her mind go blank. Her thoughts flowed away like water, as she had trained herself to do in those awful months after her wedding and sudden widowhood. She would dance the country dance, then a waltz, then a reel — every dance she had the stamina for, if it kept Nick away.

He would come, though. And when he did, she would find a way to be so calm, so remote, that he couldn't possibly affect her again.

CHAPTER THREE

How was she more beautiful than he remembered? She'd been pretty at seventeen, even lovelier at nineteen — the toast of the season in '02, when her father had belatedly, begrudgingly brought her out in a bid to make her forget Nick. She'd vowed that nothing could induce her to marry someone else. But by the end of the season, she was married to — and, three days later, widowed by — his cousin. And Nick was somewhere in the Atlantic, wishing he could drown his love for her as effectively as she had suffocated her love for him.

She had been beautiful that season, even on the day when she'd tossed him aside for a title. But beautiful wasn't quite the right word now. She was too fierce for mere beauty. Her hair was down, shockingly so — an homage to the famous portrait of Queen Elizabeth, surely. He knew it was a coincidence that it was exactly the way he liked it. As she navigated the turns and dips of the first country dance, her hair flared around her like a curtain of fire. She was pale, though. Paler than she had been before he removed his mask.

The Virgin Queen would not show weakness. But he'd seen the first tiny cracks in her armor.

Ellie — beautiful, traitorous bitch that she was — hadn't forgotten him.

Nick leaned against the pillar, searching for a comfortable angle.

20

Women had frequently danced for his pleasure when he visited the Hyderabadi court. This dance wasn't for him. None of it was for him, unless Ellie's memory for dates was as good as his. But it was somehow more seductive than anything he'd seen with bells and scarves. Ellie moved through the patterns perfectly, effortlessly, tantalizing him every time she disappeared behind another couple.

Tormenting him every time she smiled at the prig who was her partner.

Those who didn't dance gave Nick a wide berth. He heard the whispers, though, and knew they guessed his identity. Whether they avoided him because they hadn't been introduced or because of his heavy involvement in trade didn't matter — he didn't mind their aversion, at least not tonight. The less others disturbed him, the more he could look his fill.

One guest, though, found him almost immediately. The man, two inches shorter and much slimmer than Nick, wore an elaborately embroidered doublet and breeches that would have done a young Henry VIII proud, and the disbelieving look of one who has seen a ghost.

"I should kill you for coming back without so much as a warning letter," his brother Marcus said, clapping him on the shoulder.

"You know the vagaries of communication," he replied. An exact account of why Nick had returned now, and the possible threat he faced, could wait until morning. Instead, he offered a more innocuous reason for his return. "I trust that with Grandfather Corwyn's death last year, you'll be happy to have me back at home despite my lack of notice."

Marcus laughed. "Of course I'm happy to have you home. Rupert would be happy too, if he weren't still in the West Indies. With you here, perhaps I can finally take a holiday."

Marcus was Nick's middle brother, and had managed the London office of Corwyn, Claiborne and Sons, Ltd., with their maternal grandfather while Nick focused on their India operations and their youngest brother, Rupert, concentrated on the Caribbean trade. But after their grandfather's death the previous year, the burdens on Marcus would have increased substantially.

"Take all the holiday you want, if it makes you happy," Nick said. "But when have the Corwyns — or Claibornes, for that matter — ever been satisfied with idleness?"

"Never in my memory," Marcus said. "But I would be more satisfied if we could have this conversation in my office — or rather, your office — and I wasn't dressed like a prime fool. Come have a drink with me and escape this nonsense."

The lure of a drink with his brother, after years of inferior libations taken alone, was strong. Ellie's pull was stronger. "You're not the only one the marchioness has turned into a fool," Nick said, gesturing at the dancers.

"I would say the same, but I doubt for the same reasons."

Nick's gaze had unerringly found Ellie, but he pulled back to look at his brother. "Gone over to the enemy, have we?"

Marcus adjusted the ruffled lace at his neck. "My vow to you comes first — always has. But at least she was here the last decade."

Nick's eyes slid back to Ellie. "You never told me she'd become such a...topic of conversation in London."

The whispers he'd heard about her in London over the past five days had made her into an almost legendary figure — a goddess with the beauty of Aphrodite and the appetites of a female Dionysus. He'd been disbelieving enough — and angry enough — that he had to see for himself.

He wasn't disbelieving anymore.

Marcus sighed. "You left me here to manage your estate, but I won't spread tales about people."

"How many of them are true?"

"Ask her yourself. You might not like the answer, though."

Nick's anger flared again as he watched her dance through all her admiring, worshipful guests. He hadn't been this angry in years. On the ship, he had even thought he might be able to see her again without betraying any feeling at all. But knowing that she had been here, in his house, holding court while he had rotted in India alone…

He turned back to Marcus. "Tell me you still kept to our plan."

It wasn't a question. Marcus sighed. "Yes. But Nick…"

He trailed off. Ten years, and the responsibilities for their grandfather's shipping empire and Nick's Claiborne estates, had stripped away the boy his brother used to be. If Marcus still laughed as much as he had as a boy, there was no sign of it. He was somber now, and slightly wary, as though Nick's homecoming was something he had looked forward to until he had realized what it might mean.

Nick sighed. "I didn't come seeking revenge tonight. Let's talk of something else. I'd rather hear about you than her after all this time."

It was partly true. He'd returned from India to determine whether someone wanted him dead, not to take his long overdue revenge on Ellie. He'd even told himself he wouldn't follow through with the plan he'd hatched with Marcus, in a fit of madness, on the way to the docks a decade earlier.

But seeing Ellie now — a jaded, rich, indolent aristocrat, with the title she'd left him for and a cold, fickle heart that refused to give him satisfaction — made him itch to break her.

Marcus's eyes narrowed. "You wouldn't rather hear about me. Don't pretend you're not here for revenge. I think everyone in the ballroom sensed your intentions."

"I haven't decided what I will do yet," Nick hedged.

"You have. If you hadn't, you would have warned her you were coming. Warned *me* that you were coming. You couldn't risk that I'd tell her and she would flee, could you?"

Nick hadn't warned him because there was no time to warn him — he'd taken the first ship out of Madras after realizing that the attacks on him and his interests were not coincidences. But Marcus's tone sounded uncomfortably like censure.

Nick leaned in, speaking low, but forceful enough to make himself understood. "She brought this upon herself. I can't take away the title she spurned me for, but I can take everything else that marriage gave her."

Marcus held his gaze for a long time, longer than anyone did. Whatever he saw there made his forehead crease.

"At least talk to her first. She's changed, Nick. We all have. Perhaps not for the better…"

"I vow she hasn't changed for the better," Nick interjected. "The Ellie I knew never cared for spectacles such as these."

"The Ellie you knew is dead," Marcus shot back. "If you need proof of it, look at yourself. You aren't the same man who waved goodbye to me on the docks."

He wasn't the same man. He still remembered the docks — a mercilessly cheerful June sky, when all he wanted was rain. And Marcus, who didn't beg him to stay even though he seemed inclined to. Marcus had been the one who was supposed to go to India at the tender age of twenty, while Nick should have stayed to manage the

London office. But Nick couldn't stay, not when Ellie had married Charles — and especially not when she had been widowed three days later, since he might have begged her to take him back.

So he'd gone to India, leaving Marcus to set in motion the revenge that Nick one day intended to finish. The revenge Ellie deserved, even if Marcus now thought otherwise.

Nick shook his head. "When did you become so forgiving, little brother?"

Marcus smiled thinly. "I'm not forgiving. But being present makes me more qualified to play the judge."

Nick couldn't recall a single time that Marcus had sneered at him in quite that way. He'd boasted, teased, bedeviled — but never sneered.

"What would you have me do?" Nick asked. "Beg forgiveness?"

"Talk to her, see if she..."

Nick cut him off again. "Begging her forgiveness isn't on the table. I meant your forgiveness."

Marcus's laugh was harsh, surprised — a blast of sound escaping before he regained control of his throat. He colored slightly, looking around him — a reminder that he might care for the opinions of the guests where Nick did not.

"There's nothing for which I want to forgive you," he finally replied.

Nick raised an eyebrow. "That's a diplomatic answer."

Marcus shrugged. "Take it how you will. I am glad you're home. But I wish you would choose an easier path."

Nick turned back to watch the dance. Ellie and her partner were coming down the line a final time. When they linked arms at the end, she smiled at her partner with something that looked like genuine affection. Not love — not if he could still read her — but something close to that, a brief quirk of the lips and a happy light in her eyes.

He scowled. She chose that moment to glance toward him. All that lovely light froze on her face.

She turned away immediately, expressionless. The set of her shoulders reminded him of a man he'd known in India, just before a surgeon debrided a leg wound to prevent gangrene. At least the man had been fortunate enough to pass out after the first few cuts.

Ellie wasn't the fainting type.

But Nick wasn't the type to put away his knives.

"Who is that?" he asked.

Marcus knew where Nick's focus was. "Lord Norbury. He inherited a viscountcy a few years ago."

Nick recognized the name from the months-old newspapers he had read in Madras. "Is he attempting to win Ellie?"

"No. He's been married for years. They are merely friends."

"'Friends' is still reason enough for me to dislike him."

Marcus laughed again. This time, there was humor in his tone. "It's good to see you haven't changed."

He shrugged. "The ton doesn't care for me. I see no reason to care for it."

"You could have the ton eating out of your hand if you tried, you know. Richest marquessate in the country, all the intrigue over where you've been, your eligible bachelor status — the women will be tripping over themselves to gain your attendance at their parties this season."

Nick didn't respond.

"If you're still here during the season, of course," Marcus added, in a tone that said he knew his previous advice would go unheeded.

The country dance ended with Ellie on the opposite side of the ballroom. Nick took a step away from the door, his heart already quickening.

Marcus grabbed his arm. "At least give her tonight," he said urgently. "Don't humiliate her in front of her guests — if not for her sake, then for your business interests."

As children, the altruistic, selfless arguments were the ones that won Nick over. He hadn't thought of himself as noble since Ellie had disabused him of those romantic delusions. She hadn't called him noble when she'd broken their engagement. She'd called him a peasant.

But no peasant could afford the price Nick would pay to have his revenge.

Still, Marcus's cool appeal to Nick's avarice cut deep. And it cut even deeper because he was right — Nick saw all the guests between him and Ellie as possible investors, customers, or fools who would easily spend their money on the goods Nick provided.

"I've give her a few hours," he said, brushing aside Marcus's hand. "But I will begin tonight."

Marcus sighed. "Send for me when you come to your senses."

Nick resumed his place by the door as his brother left. He took a glass of champagne from a passing footman and settled in to wait. He let his anticipation build slowly, tasting it with every sip of his drink — savoring it all the more because he knew that tonight, finally, he would have satisfaction.

The beginning of the end. By the time he finished with Ellie, he would have his revenge.

And then, surely, he could find a way to forget her.

CHAPTER FOUR

Nick didn't dance. He didn't go in to supper. Beyond the one conversation she saw him have with Marcus, he didn't speak to anyone at all.

The man was unnerving her. Ellie knew that was his intention. His actions were laughably transparent, but she couldn't fight the effect he had on her. When she thought of being alone with him — for the first time since that awful conversation she'd wished, endlessly, to take back — her breath turned shallow and her hands went slick with sweat.

So she didn't think of it, even though his dark presence on the edge of her vision wouldn't let her forget.

She had painted him as Hades once. His pose now, with his arms crossed and his jaw set, matched the painting. The doors between the ballroom and the rest of the house replaced the gates of hell, separating the life she knew from the afterlife that awaited her.

He stood ready, waiting to take her there. Once the party ended, once she crossed that threshold, he'd have her.

Your hysterics are unbecoming, Elinor. She heard her father's voice in her head, as clear and inescapable as the great bells of St. Paul's on her wedding day. Her father — now *there* was a man she could hate and love safely, without worrying he'd one day reappear in her

28

ballroom. Perhaps he should have encouraged hysterics in his children — if her brother Richard could have belly-ached over their father's demands like a normal man, rather than snapping and shooting him, her father would still be alive.

Still, she didn't like hysterics any more than he had. She straightened her shoulders. She couldn't avoid Nick — but Ellie didn't avoid anyone.

She'd made a critical error. She should have attacked, not retreated.

Most of the local gentry had left, taking advantage of the last of the moon to drive home. Some guests would leave in the morning; the rest would stay another week. It was the tamest affair she'd given since she had stopped mourning her husband — if mourning was the right word for cloistered celebration. But even among these guests, they wouldn't miss her as long as the wine flowed.

So when her next dancing partner, Alex Staunton, the Earl of Salford, came to claim her, she demurred. "Lord Folkestone has returned. I should see him settled," she said.

Salford cast a sidelong glance at the door. "Do you think he'd bed down there if you gave him a pallet? He seems to like the spot."

She stifled a laugh. She had known Salford for years, but their acquaintance had deepened after his cousin Madeleine had married her brother. Salford was stuffy to some, but their mutual interests in art and antiquities had brought them close enough that she saw beneath his honor-bound façade. Tonight, his sly humor was a bit of balm that soothed her rupturing scars.

"Folkestone isn't easily led," she said. "But I'll find a room for him."

The servants wouldn't have to air his room, if she gave him the master suite despite the door that connected it to hers. On her orders, they had aired it every day for a decade. But Salford didn't know of her past, or how well she knew the man who had been her husband's cousin and heir.

He eyed Nick, who watched them darkly. "I don't believe he likes me, Lady Folkestone," he mused. "Any idea why that would be?"

"None," Ellie lied. "But he's a strange man, to have stayed in India so long when Folkestone was his. Who knows what he's thinking?"

"Shall we experiment?" Salford asked. He brought Ellie's hand to his lips. It was an empty gesture — there was about as much romantic feeling between them as between a pair of coffee spoons. But Ellie saw Nick's arms tighten, saw him draw a breath — saw the laughter in Salford's eyes as he dropped her hand.

"The marquess seems taken with you, my lady. Your effect remains undimmed."

"I've no idea why," she said with a shrug.

Salford sobered. "If he looked at Madeleine or my sister like he looks at you, I'd have his head. But you've never wanted a champion, have you?"

Salford was too perceptive by half. "Thank you, my lord, but I can manage the marquess."

"Promise me — if you can't manage him, promise you'll tell me."

She nodded once. The gesture was a lie. Salford probably knew it was, but he didn't call her on it.

She walked toward the doors, taking as direct a line as she could through the dwindling dancers. Nick leaned against a pillar, calm again — lounging ever more obviously by the second as she approached. He wouldn't admit jealousy, just as she wouldn't admit discomfort.

But his eyes burned even as his body relaxed.

When she reached him, she dropped into a curtsey, made even more grand by the way her heavy skirts pooled dramatically around her. "My lord," she murmured.

"Lady Folkestone," he drawled. "Never thought I'd see you curtsey to me."

"I hope you enjoyed it," she said, coming to her full height. "I shan't do it again."

"No?" he asked. "Then I'm glad you wore that dress for it. Your breasts are wonderful in it. Especially when you bend to offer them to me."

Her pulse quickened. "I assure you — if I were offering them, you'd know it."

He smiled, that cruel smile she hadn't seen before tonight. "Save your offerings for someone else. If I want what you have, I'll be taking it whether you offer or not."

She raised an eyebrow. "Has no one in the last decade explained nobility to you? You are a peer of the realm, not a feudal baron. There's no *droit du seigneur* that allows you to take any woman you want."

Nick shrugged. He was dressed more modernly than any of her guests, by over three hundred years — but his devastating face belonged on a battlement, not a ballroom. "You know I wasn't born to this. But I will take what belongs to me."

This was quickly turning into a rout — and Ellie was not the victor. She stopped bantering. "Take your estate, then. I meant it when I said I will be gone in the morning."

"And I meant it when I said you owe me. Shall the repayment start now, or do you wish to hide for another hour?"

The certainty in his voice confused her. Beyond their broken engagement, there were no other debts between them. "I owe you nothing. And I wasn't hiding."

"Don't lie. Aren't we beyond that?"

God, his voice was cold. When had it become something that could freeze her so ruthlessly? He must have had the seeds of this when she knew him, but he'd never used it on her.

But he wasn't the only one who had hardened. She would match him, cut for cut, until he left her alone.

"I wasn't hiding," she repeated. "I was letting you stew. You've had a decade to stew, I know. But it's ever so much more entertaining when I can watch."

That was the final shove that broke through his ice. He grabbed her arm, his fingers turning to fire on her flesh. "Now," he ground out, already propelling her through the door. "We talk now."

She was right. Hell surely awaited her. Perhaps she shouldn't have pushed him, tried to force a reaction out of him. She'd gotten what she wanted, though — a glimpse of his temper and, beneath that, the stubborn, passionate man she'd loved.

The man she'd loved and thrown away, when she was young and stupid and desperate for her father's approval.

She'd waited forever for him to come back, wishing he would give her a chance to make amends. But now that he was here, she wasn't sure she could stand seeing him again.

He dragged her through the foyer and past the servants she'd trained to stay out of her affairs. No one tried to save her. He pulled her up the stairs by instinct, but when he reached the landing, he paused.

"Left," she said. "Third door from the end is my salon. No one will disturb us there."

"Father always said this house was a rabbit warren," Nick said.

Were it not for his unbreakable grip on her arm and the thrum of tension in his voice, he might have been any visitor receiving a tour of the estate.

"It was. The servants' domains in the attics and basements could still lose you for a week. But your brother and I renovated the public rooms and bedchambers in a more modern style. You never seemed partial to older modes of living."

"How thoughtful of you," he murmured.

"Yes, well, I hope you enjoy it as I have. It's a good house, Nick."

He spun her into her salon and let go of her arm, not responding to her inane ramblings. The room usually soothed her. Even more so than the rest of the house, every decoration, every scrap of fabric, was chosen to suit her. The large, overstuffed chaise-longue, identical in shape and size to one she kept in her house in London, was upholstered in rich navy velvet. Two chairs stood across from it, complementing the velvet with a gold fleur-de-lis pattern across their seats. Books of prints and engravings lined the shelves, interspersed with objets d'art from her collection.

It was a small, lush room that no one used but her. And it was exactly the opposite of the room where they'd had their last conversation, when she had told Nick, for the second time, that she could no longer marry him, and then insulted him to make sure he got the message. In her memory, everything in that room, one of her father's cold, cavernous drawing rooms, was white — white walls, white upholstery, white hothouse flowers, her white gloves clenched in the lap of her white dress, Nick's white face as his blood leached away while she cut into him. Only Nick's flowers had been red, as though it was his heart he'd flung at her instead of his roses.

She shivered. This was not that room. She was twenty-nine, not nineteen — and her father wasn't here to remind her of propriety and bloodlines. She walked straight toward the row of decanters on a shelf in the corner, not waiting for Nick to follow. She would rather have wine, but she hadn't thought to send her butler for a bottle, and she wasn't of a mind to wait. "Brandy or whisky?" she asked over her shoulder.

"Whisky." He locked the door. The sound was a warning shot. Her hand shook as she tilted the decanter toward a glass, and she splashed liquor on the tray beneath it. She bit the inside of her cheek, hard, striving for control.

She poured a generous amount of whisky into his glass, then poured herself the same amount. Turning, she discovered that he was closer than she thought he was — close enough to reach out and take the glass from her hand. His eyes were hooded under his brows. She couldn't read the expression there.

She used to be able to read every expression on his face. The fact that she couldn't now, even though she shouldn't have expected to, hurt. She thought she had felt every pain over him that it was possible for one to feel, but she discovered a new one — the pain of realizing that she no longer knew him quite so well as she thought she did.

It felt like a death. Ellie raised her glass to him, silent, one hand still holding the shelf behind her as though it could keep her upright.

He raised his glass as well. "To old friends," he said.

"To old friends," she echoed. Perhaps he felt what she did — the shock of knowing that ten years had passed, even though when their eyes connected over the rims of their glasses, it felt like nothing at all had come between them.

She sipped her whisky, welcoming the burn of alcohol as it slid over her tongue. It no longer made her cough. He raised an eyebrow.

"I never thought to see you drink whisky so easily, Ellie."

"There are many things I do easily now," she said, pushing off from the shelf and sliding past him to her chaise. "I'm no longer nineteen."

"No, you're not," Nick said, turning to watch as she took her seat. She regretted it immediately — alone, she would have lounged against the sensuously curved arm. She couldn't relax like that in front of him, though. And the chaise was backless, which meant she would have to sit ramrod straight, as though she awaited his favor.

He felt no such constraint about his posture. He flung himself down into one of her chairs, facing her, his long legs spread out in front of him like he was at his club rather than in a gently-bred woman's home.

Then again, he probably didn't have a club. No club would have had him before he left, when he had obscene wealth but refused to bow to all the indigent lords who thought themselves above him. He hadn't been back long enough to use his title to gain entrance. And he was in his own house, not hers.

Ellie sipped her whisky again, too quickly. Her thoughts kept scattering, bouncing between present and past. She tried to anchor herself to the present and the question of why he was home.

Nick didn't say a word. In her dainty chair, sipping whisky out of her delicate tumbler, he still managed to look like a predatory animal. He watched her, though, as though considering what to do with her — whether to toy with her or kill her swiftly, perhaps?

She inhaled sharply and told herself to stop being dramatic. She couldn't let him unnerve her again, or she might never regain control.

After three minutes of silence, three minutes of him staring at her and her looking at some point over his shoulder, her patience flared out. She tossed the rest of her whisky down her throat, standing before the burn reached her belly. "If you won't talk, I have guests to see to. Perhaps in another ten years we can repeat this charming scene. Until then, I wish you very happy."

She leaned down to set the glass on the small table between them. His hand shot out to grab her wrist. He kept her pinned there, bent awkwardly at the waist, her face mere inches from his.

"This isn't the conversation you promised me," he said. "And this time, I won't let you leave until we've had it."

CHAPTER FIVE

Ellie felt all the questions, all the anger, all the tears of the last ten years eating their way out of the secret places where she had buried them. His silent judgment had affected her more than she realized. She damned him for it. She tried to pull her hand away, but now that he was in a position to claim something of her, he didn't seem willing to relinquish it. She couldn't match him for strength.

But she would never let him see her cry.

"What good is conversation?" she asked, her voice bitter. "I broke our engagement and married your cousin. You inherited when he died, yet chose to stay on the other side of the world. I think we've made our intentions to each other quite clear."

"And yet," he said. His fingers tightened on her wrist. "And yet the fact that I haven't forgiven you means that I haven't forgotten you, either."

She dipped her head, unable to look in his eyes anymore. She could have said the same to him. She had imagined saying it on any number of nights, when she had lain awake and wondered if he would ever return, if he dreamed of her as she dreamed of him.

His free hand came up and brushed a lock of hair out of her eyes, tucking it behind her ear. He had done that frequently when they were younger, during their secret courtship, when they'd rambled the countryside unchaperoned and her hair had turned to shambles in the wind.

If only he'd eloped with her when she had begged him to, before she went to London and was lost to the social whirl. If only she'd eloped with him at the end of that season, rather than giving in to her father's threats and promises.

She raised her head. His hand slid naturally to the curve of her cheek. She waited just a moment too long to tilt her face away, but she didn't examine her reasons. "Let me go, Nick."

She heard the pleading note in her voice and hated herself for it. If he heard her desperation, though, it spurred him on. He released her wrist — but only long enough to sweep the table away with his foot, sending it crashing to the floor.

Ellie stumbled backward, the sudden violence surprising her. Her whisky tumbler missed the soft landing of the thick Axminster carpet and shattered against the nearby hearth, covering the stones with glistening shards of glass. She saw the damage in an instant, then turned back to Nick. His eyes matched the wreckage, with the warmth of a fire and the cruel edge of a razor.

She should have been frightened as he uncoiled from the chair, a cobra about to strike. And maybe she was frightened — but it wasn't the intensity in his eyes that scared her. She feared the hot swirl of emotion rising up within her. She'd learned how to control it all, locked it away where it could never hurt her again. But it only took a few minutes with Nick to sweep the first of those barriers away.

She wouldn't survive if her barriers disappeared entirely.

So when he touched her cheek again, she jerked away like his hand was a brand. "I cannot do this, Nick," she said, forcing the words out through clenched teeth.

"Marcus said you'd given up on me coming home. Are you looking for another Charles amongst our guests?"

Ellie frowned. "Did you come back because you thought I might marry again?"

He laughed, dark and dangerous. "Marry as many men as you like. I'm not here to leg-shackle myself to you."

She pretended, even to herself, that his statement didn't disappoint her. "Then why are you here?"

"Business, of course. I'm still the merchant you threw over for a marquess, even if I have the title now."

He brushed a kiss across her forehead. It was leagues away from the chill in his words. She leaned in, letting herself be seduced by what she knew lurked beneath all their feints and insults...

Then he whispered in her ear. "I am in the market for a mistress, though. And I'd take you whether you are married or not."

She snapped her head back. How did she keep fooling herself into thinking that he wasn't utterly ruthless?

"If you've come to find a mistress, you're in the wrong room."

He clucked his tongue, as though correcting a headstrong pupil. "I'm in the only room I want to be in. And I *will* have you, Ellie — depend upon it."

And then, as his lips descended on hers, she realized he intended to prove it.

*   *   *

When he had first kissed Ellie, twelve years earlier, she had tasted of berries. They had been picking blackberries together in the hot August sun, far from the lax guardianship of Ellie's governess and the nearby country cottage where Nick's mother was in the final throes of her last illness. Ellie had taken her gloves off, heedless of freckles and thorns, and her fingers were stained purple with juice. She laughed at one of his jests, and her lips were purple, too. She freed her glorious red hair from her hat, and strands of it whipped around her face.

He had reached out to smooth the hair away from her mouth. Something in her blue eyes, the hopeful tilt to her smile, urged him forward before his better self could dissuade him. He was gentle, so gentle, not wanting to hurt her, feeling like he'd somehow stumbled across a princess who had been waiting for him to rescue her. She'd grown up alone, left in the countryside by her uncaring father, and Nick wanted to be the one who showed her happiness. She tasted of berries, of innocence, and as her hands clasped hesitantly around his neck, he had lost himself.

Tonight, in the house he owned but she inhabited, she had the fierceness of a queen, not the hesitating dreaminess of a cloistered princess. He had thought he could do this coldly, emotionlessly, cruelly — as cruelly as she had destroyed him. But there never should have been cruelty between them.

He claimed her mouth. This time, her lips were pale and her mouth tasted of whisky. He'd never tasted alcohol on her before, but the intoxicant somehow fit the woman she'd become. There was no innocence between them anymore.

He couldn't be gentle, and he refused to be kind — but he had just enough control to keep from throwing her to the floor and taking her like a beast. All he wanted, all he could handle, was a kiss. A single taste of her, before he remembered why he had lost her.

Before he put his long-dormant plan into action and ruined her happiness as comprehensively as she had ruined his.

He wrapped his arm around her back and crushed her against his chest. She whimpered against his mouth. The sound almost brought him to his senses. But then her mouth parted, and the dim corner of his brain that could still think knew that whimper for what it was.

She wanted him in spite of herself.

That knowledge was dangerous, adding the barest trace of triumph to his growing need. Ellie might not love him, but he could still make her want him.

Her hands came up around him. She was no longer a tentative girl. She knew what she wanted, and she made it clear in the way she pulled him down to her, in the way she opened her mouth and welcomed his plunging tongue. Her fingers were rough, digging into his scalp as she anchored herself in his hair. Her arms dragged his shoulders down, adding sweet pressure to the need he already felt for her.

He hadn't thought he cared whether she wanted him — for his plans, it was almost better if she didn't. But as she flared to life around him, his own desire exploded. How had he thought that a kiss could be enough? They would both be bruised in the morning if he didn't pull back, but that dark need for her urged him on. He'd never wanted to mark a woman before, but he needed every man in the house to take one look at her and know that she was his.

The warning bells started up at that thought, but he ignored them. He could never keep her without wondering if she accepted him because he had inherited a title. But if he was careful, he could have her again without getting his heart involved.

Just as he decided to kiss her senseless, perhaps take her hard and fast against the wall as he'd dreamed of any number of times — perhaps ignore his revenge until morning — she pulled back.

"Nick…I can't."

All those years ago, kissing her amongst the blackberries, he was the one who had stopped first, too cautious for her sake to risk more than a kiss. She wanted him just as badly now as she had wanted him then — perhaps more, now that she knew exactly the pleasure that their kisses would lead to. But even though her body screamed for him, her voice broke. He could kiss her again, try to coax her…

Her eyes, though, stopped him cold. He had never seen her cry before — not when they had started their secret engagement, and certainly not when she had thrown him over for his cousin. But the tears were there now, threatening to spill over her lashes, turning her blue eyes into fathomless pools.

This wasn't his plan. The Ellie he knew wouldn't come undone over a mere kiss. He wanted her tears — or thought he did. But he wanted to wring them from her in a way that left no doubt he'd won.

She blinked furiously. All her armor slammed down over her like a prison gate. When she looked at him again, the tears had turned to glaciers.

She walked toward the door, saying nothing as she reached for it. He caught her in two strides and slapped his palm against the wood.

"I'm not done," he said.

She stiffened her shoulders. In a different mood he might have admired how she turned to face him. Another woman would have fainted, or at least cried, at the menace in his tone. But Ellie didn't flinch.

"Your actions over the past decade say you're done," she said. "Why else would you have stayed in India all this time? Unless you knew you couldn't see me without changing your mind?"

He couldn't answer that. She reached up to stroke his face. Not a greedy, full-palmed caress — more a whisper, one fingertip trailing down the line of his jaw. Her nail scraped against his skin, and he shuddered.

"Why are you not done, Nick?" she asked. Her hand dropped to his chest, unerringly flattening against the rapid crescendo of his heart. "Have you come back for me?"

Yes. His heart screamed yes. Did her skin soak in that scream? Did her blood carry it to her heart, her mouth, her soul?

His heart screamed yes.

But his mouth and soul were liars.

"I've come back to take what you owe me."

She dropped her eyes to his chest, to where her hand curled into a fist before falling away. Her mouth tightened — confused that his words contradicted what she felt?

"What do you think I owe you? If you want an apology, I'll give it," she said.

Her voice was soft but resolute. Ellie would apologize, just as she had apologized the first time she'd broken their engagement. But when he had found out who she would marry and came back to dissuade her — she hadn't apologized then.

Even if she did now, even if he could believe an apology from her, it wouldn't be enough.

Only revenge would be enough.

"You owe me more than an apology. You can pay me on your back, or on your knees — but you'll start tonight."

CHAPTER SIX

She almost wished he'd slapped her. A bruise would fade. But those words, cruel and implacable, would run endlessly through her dreams.

She sucked in a breath. His heart had beat for her. She was sure of it. But his eyes denied it. That brutal look was back. His mouth — the mouth that kissed her like he'd never left her — was an uncompromising line, a weapon he would use to eviscerate her.

Ellie forced her fists to open, forced herself to settle back onto her heels. She'd come to her toes as though the added height could help her. The darkness in his voice told her to run. But the images already playing in her mind, the memories of all the ways they had loved each other back when she had thought that love conquered all, made her heart race and her palms dampen.

As revenges went, there were worse fates in the world than sharing a bed with Nick.

Still, she'd pleased and placated men before, and always, *always* regretted it. Nick, her father, Charles — different men, to be sure, but they had all, in some way, wanted her as a possession.

If any man were to own her, she should have chosen Nick. But now that no one owned her, she couldn't let him try again. She wouldn't let herself be seduced by the idea of what might have been —

or give herself away for less than she deserved.

When she thought she could speak without betraying herself, she said, "I understand your hatred. But I won't be your whore."

"This has nothing to do with what happened between us. It's a business transaction, nothing more."

She laughed bitterly. "I don't know what you've heard of my reputation, but any lovers I've had were for pleasure, not lucre."

"Then you failed to earn what you're worth, but that's not something I'll take the blame for. Do take your experience into account when you negotiate your fee with me — you're surely better than you were the first time I had you."

The first time. Eleven years ago tonight — her birthday present from him. She treasured that memory, the way he'd touched her, how he'd tried so hard not to hurt her. It hadn't been perfect. They'd tried again, as often as they could over the next four months, until it was. But it was one of her most perfect memories.

He tarnished that memory now, like fetid air settling on precious silver.

"How dare you come into my house and insult me like this?" she snapped.

"Ah, 'your house.' Now we come to the crux of it," he said. He finally stepped back. She might have escaped the room, but he stole the key from the lock before crossing the room and pouring whisky into a fresh glass.

"Not going to offer me any?" she asked, knowing she sounded churlish rather than confident.

"I will, if you want to add to your debt."

He sat without waiting for her — a breech of etiquette that twisted the knife he'd already embedded in her gut. He took her chaise without asking, lounging on it as she couldn't do earlier. He braced an arm against the rolled cushion and sipped his whisky as he watched her. Caesar might have looked the same, waiting for Cleopatra, a queen brought low, to pleasure him.

But Cleopatra had had her own agenda. Ellie let her hips sway as she walked toward him — a sway made more pronounced by the tight, dropped waist of her old-fashioned gown. His eyes were drawn to the movement. His Adam's apple bobbed as he swallowed, hard — and it wasn't whisky in his throat when he swallowed again.

"And what, pray, is my debt to you?" she asked as she drew nearer.

His eyes slid back to her face. The question seemed to confuse him momentarily — long enough for her to see something haunted, more like a trapped animal than a ruthless hunter.

Then Caesar was back in command. "Forty thousand pounds, give or take. I suppose a glass of whisky is negligible."

"Impossible," she said flatly.

She veered off toward the whisky anyway. He stayed silent while she pulled out the stopper and poured. It was only when she turned to face him that he smiled.

"I have the receipts to prove it. Tell me, Ellie my love — how many nights will it take to repay that debt?"

She went hot, then cold — a nerveless, spineless dread. Whisky would make it worse, but the glass was already in her hand. Drinking it was better than dwelling on that question.

When she thought she might be able to speak, she said, "How can I possibly owe you forty thousand pounds?"

"Servants, dresses, paints, canvases, parties such as tonight's — you spend far beyond your means, my dear. I'll grant that it took you longer to reach this sum than I thought it would, back when Charles died and I inherited. If only you liked gaming hells."

"I know I spend your money on servants — it's your estate, damn you, and Marcus said you specifically invited me to live here as long as I liked. But the rest comes from the income from my marriage settlements."

"Sadly, you are mistaken." His eyes weren't sad — they were triumphant. Then they widened, the picture of innocence. "Surely Marcus explained that you were borrowing money from my estate?"

The floor dropped out from under her. All these years, she'd thought she'd been on solid, albeit unhappy, ground. But he yanked it from her, leaving her in a murky swamp of betrayal.

She shook her head. "Marcus wouldn't do that. I trusted him — *trust* him — to handle my financial affairs."

"He worked for me before he worked for you. If it's any consolation, he says you are quite disciplined with the funds you are allocated. I could have beggared you long ago if you weren't so good at managing your household."

It was no consolation, and he knew it. *Marcus.* Clever, treacherous man — calling a truce after Nick left, offering to deal with her father's and husband's solicitors to make sure she got every penny owed her when her father would have forced her to marry again. She'd been too grateful to spurn Marcus's offer, even when she knew he blamed her for Nick's absence. And he was so helpful, for so many years, that she never hired someone to replace him.

Never asked how he had invested her monies so well that she could consistently take more than five percent of the capital every year.

Never thought to check his books.

"Marcus doesn't work for me. He's my friend," she said, clinging to what she'd believed rather than what Nick would make her see.

Nick tossed back the dregs of his whisky. Since he'd already thrown the table aside, he set the tumbler on the floor and leaned back. The bastard was enjoying himself — and suddenly she hated him for coming back, more than she ever had for leaving.

"You should have read your Machiavelli," he said. "The fact remains that you signed quarterly receipts from Marcus, on behalf of my estate, for monies approaching nearly six thousand pounds a year. He was most scrupulous in using the income from your settlements and properties to repay what he could — you would owe another twenty thousand if he hadn't treated you fairly. I'm sure he can show you the accounts if you're curious."

Ellie wanted to vomit. It was a harsh, uncharacteristic feeling. She never lost control like this. But she knew what he'd left unsaid.

The forty thousand pounds from her marriage settlement were invested in an unbreakable trust. She could live off the interest, but no one — not Nick, not Marcus, and certainly not her — could touch the principal.

And if she only had two thousand pounds a year, she couldn't possibly pay him back.

"Why?" she asked. "Why this? And why now?"

"Isn't it obvious? You married Charles for the title, this estate, and so you didn't have to share a bed with a peasant like me. I can't take your title, alas. But I can ruin you so comprehensively that you cannot afford the circles it lets you move in. As for the rest — you can surely deduce it while I plow you like the peasant I am."

She kept her face expressionless, even though she couldn't control her angry flush. "And why now?"

He shrugged. "You aren't getting any younger — no sense delaying the harvest."

He watched her face as he insulted her. Did he hope for begging? Tears? Some sort of display that would prove he'd hurt her?

She tossed her hair back, downed her whisky, and threw the glass across the room to shatter in the same spot where he'd thrown her first one. He didn't flinch — just raised an eyebrow.

"You are unbelievable, Nick. Only an out and out villain would spend ten years plotting this. Why didn't you just have me murdered? It would have been quicker, and it certainly wouldn't have cost you forty thousand pounds."

"I don't know what the going rate for murder is. But I find your display worth the price."

"I'm sure murder is trivial," she said. "I will gladly find someone to do the job on you since you didn't think to do it on me."

He grinned, a flash of real humor that was gone almost before she registered it. "Wouldn't you rather murder me yourself? You're resourceful enough."

"Blood is so very hard to clean up. But I'll sacrifice a carpet or two if you push me."

He waved a hand magnanimously. "If you have a better offer for how to repay me, I'll entertain it. I am a man of business, not a monster."

His eyes dropped, blatantly, to her breasts. She crossed her arms over her chest, seeing red again. "You're a beast. And I don't need to become your mistress. There are men who will marry me, and then my husband can repay you."

"Men who will take a soiled twenty-nine-year-old widow with thousands of pounds of debt?" Then he made a show of glancing behind him to the clock on the mantel, which read a bit past two in the morning. "Excuse me, a soiled *thirty*-year-old widow. Many happy returns on your birthday, love."

"You can go to hell and take your happy returns with you."

He laughed. "Already been there. I'm afraid the devil's bored with me and cut me loose. I await your offer."

He was serious. He couldn't be serious — couldn't have planned this, couldn't want what he'd asked for. That brief kiss earlier, before she'd broken it off, had been a taste of the old Nick, even if he was rougher than he used to be with her.

For a moment, she thought he'd forgiven her, even if he wouldn't say the words. She thought he'd come back for her, ready to fight for her the way she wished she'd fought for him.

She was sure he'd felt something for her — for a moment, at least, even if the moment died.

Which meant that this wasn't cold revenge. It was methodical, and it was most definitely cruel. But she'd felt the heat behind it.

As long as he felt passion for her, she had at least one advantage. She just needed to keep her own passion in check.

"One week," she said abruptly.

His gaze roved over her body — her soiled body, as he called it. She gritted her teeth.

"That is nearly six thousand pounds a night. You won't like what I would make you do for that, especially not when you have houseguests."

She didn't think she'd ever blushed as fast and hot as she did when his drawl broke over her. "Then what is your offer?"

"Come to me and I'll tell you."

His eyes dared her to run. But he held the key to the door — and everything else. And anyway, if this was about humiliating her, she wouldn't give him an ounce of satisfaction.

So she walked with her head held high. When she reached his side, she looked down into his eyes, as vivid as any sea she'd tried to paint. There was triumph there, yes — but lust predominated.

She should have left Folkestone when she had had the chance, gone someplace where she could have pretended, forever, that he would have forgiven her if he'd known where to find her.

But that chance was gone. She brushed her hand through his hair. "Don't do this, Nick," she said, knowing as she said it that he wouldn't hear her warning. "If not for me, then don't do it to yourself. There are sins that are unforgivable. Don't damn yourself as I have."

His hand slid to her waist and pulled her down into his arms. "I'm already damned."

She sighed. "Then tell me what you want so we can get on with it."

His hand rose to her breast. She didn't flinch — barely felt it anyway through all her heavy brocade.

"Four months," he said, silky smooth despite the subject matter. "You'll do whatever I ask, in bed or out, for four months. And at the end of it, your debt will be forgiven."

He ran his thumb across her collarbone. Her body warmed under his touch even as her heart turned to ice.

"Can I guess the date you'll release me?"

He smiled. "The thirteenth of June, of course. Consider it a belated wedding gift."

"The thirteenth of June," she repeated. She braced herself against his shoulders and scanned his face. "How long have you been planning these dates?"

"The duration — always. But it's merely a convenient coincidence that I came home in time to start tonight. Don't flatter yourself into thinking I returned just for this. I've other business in London, but I may as well collect from you since I have four months to spare for the task."

Four months. It was obscene, a dark reversal of their ruined courtship. The dates were exact — from the anniversary of their first coupling, to the day she had married Charles instead of him. And again, she knew that whatever the temperature of his voice, his anger was too hot to be passionless.

"I want it in writing," she said, ignoring his fingers as they slid through her hair. "Marcus has proven himself a poor witness, but he and my maid will do — I don't want to take any more people into our confidence than necessary."

"Done."

She worried at her lip, considering the unforgiving notes in his voice. "No violence, either. If we were married you could beat me legally, I suppose, but do remember that we're not."

Nick's eyes went dark. "As though I could forget that you threw me over. But I won't beat you."

She nodded crisply. She knew he wouldn't have, but she was glad he didn't leave it hanging over her head as a threat. Then she thought of another point. "And I will not do everything you ask outside of your bed. Inside your bed is enough."

That seemed to break his patience. He wrapped his fist in her hair, winding it until she had to bend toward his lips. "You're not in a position to negotiate," he said.

Then he kissed her. Or rather, took her.

As a boy, he'd worshipped her.

As a man, he possessed her.

His fist held her in place. His other arm caught around her waist, making his claim unmistakable. She sighed as she opened her mouth to him. He swallowed her sigh and pulled her closer, until she was crushed against him. Acres of brocade still protected her, but beneath that armor she quivered. The ache she'd nursed for a decade exploded into a demand so sharp, so potent, that she couldn't stay cold and passionless despite her plans.

She'd obsessed over him for ten years. She'd hated him for ten minutes. The coldly rational Ellie who had grown up after his departure was shrieking at her to stop — to remember her dignity, if nothing else.

But that voice echoed her father's. *You will not embarrass your family with that peasant, Elinor.*

She moaned against Nick's mouth. His kiss was a fire that could, just maybe, burn away all her thoughts. She met his tongue eagerly, breathed through her nose, and hoped the heat and air were enough to make herself ignite.

Ultimately, though, her wardrobe thwarted her efforts to forget. When his hand dropped to her bodice, he couldn't unlace her — her costume was too elaborate, and her maid had sewn her into it to achieve a perfect fit.

She moved to straddle him. "There are other ways," she murmured, reaching for the buttons that would undo his breeches.

He grabbed her hand. "I'm aware, love. But shouldn't I get to see what I bargained for?"

Damn him. He wouldn't let her forget. She sat back, and he winced as she placed weight on his knees. "You'll have four months — I'm sure you'll get around to ogling my breasts some other night."

"Every night."

The coldly rational Ellie who had grown up without him wanted to gut him.

The Ellie who had missed him forever wanted to shred her dress just to feel his gaze on her skin.

Her better half won that round. She rolled off him before he could grab for her, standing beside him and smoothing her skirts as though she'd come off a horse rather than a thwarted lover.

"Shall we postpone our...union, then? You cannot remove this dress without a maid. And anyway, you agreed to four months — but the dates you gave me are four months and two days. I won't be cheated any more than I already have been by the Claiborne men."

Nick leaned up. She stepped back in case he tried to reach for her again. Her slippers crunched over broken glass and she stepped to the side, glad she still had her shoes.

He might have come after her, but the sound of glass stopped him. He looked down at her feet, then back up to her face. She knew she was flushed — he always brought out a flush in her, and it was worse now that he was being an utter blackguard. But perhaps that flush saved her — made him take pity on her, even if she'd never asked for anyone's pity.

"Very well. We'll start on the thirteenth. Four months, Ellie. Enjoy tomorrow — you won't get another reprieve."

He said it the way a monarch might condemn a traitor. *Four months.*

"You will rot in hell for this, Nicholas Claiborne."

"I know."

She took the key and left. She briefly considered using it to lock him in, but she didn't have time for petty pleasures. She tossed it on the carpet instead, and admired her own restraint when she returned to the ballroom rather than searching the house for a gun.

Nick could take his revenge. Knowing her traitorous heart, she might even enjoy it.

But Ellie would keep her freedom — no matter what it cost her to win it.

CHAPTER SEVEN

The next morning, Ellie's maid rummaged through the pots and boxes atop Ellie's dressing table. "Perhaps the white lead, my lady," Lucia said. She held up a small porcelain vessel. "Nothing else will conceal the shadows."

Ellie sat in front of the mirror, wearing a dark blue dressing gown that only added to her pallor. "There isn't a potion in England that will make me look like less of a hag. I look wretched if I haven't slept."

The fine lines starting to crinkle around her eyes drew attention to the dark circles beneath them. She hadn't indulged in her annual cry the previous night, but she had barely slept. She couldn't stop thinking of Nick — both the Nick who touched her like he loved her, and the Nick who intended to take every bit of vengeance he could wring from her flesh.

But the fragile winter sunlight brought unwelcome clarity. The part of her that craved his seduction was thoroughly browbeaten by the part that raged at his villainy. Hadn't she vowed to stop being obsessed with him? Wasn't she ready to leave England and all her desperate dreams of him behind?

She was in command of herself again. She knew what Nick wanted now, and she wouldn't be tricked into betraying what she felt for him. She could manage him until she raised enough money to buy her escape.

Or at least she could lie to herself.

Lucia tapped her on the shoulder. "White lead?" she asked, with all the patience of a nurse talking to an invalid.

"No. We're going to London for business, not pleasure. I trust my face won't scare the men at Rundell and Bridge too terribly."

"They may give you a better price for your jewels if you terrify them," Lucia mused.

Ellie laughed. "I should have asked you to manage my estate instead of Marcus. You're ruthless enough for it."

Lucia didn't smile. "Mr. Claiborne will regret what he's done to you, my lady."

Her words sounded like a vow. The maid's relationship with Marcus had always been prickly. Lucia had once been a gentleman's daughter, although Ellie had never asked how she'd fallen from grace and landed on the Theatre Royal stage where Ellie had discovered her. She had been in Ellie's employ for over two years, since the day Ellie had asked her to sit for a painting and then impulsively asked her to stay on as her lady's maid.

Lucia's bold dark hair and dreamy grey eyes made her look enchanted — a Celtic witch, perhaps, rather than a household drudge. She was far too striking to be safe as a servant in most houses. But Lucia knew how to take care of herself. She kept every man, and particularly Marcus, at arm's length. They still called each other Mrs. Grafton and Mr. Claiborne, although Ellie suspected Marcus wanted more from Lucia than the cool disregard she offered him.

Today, Lucia's voice finally held a thread of emotion toward him. Ellie wanted to grin, but she kept her face solemn. "Leave Marcus ungutted until he explains exactly where the money went. After that, you may have him."

Lucia made a noncommittal sniff before disappearing into the dressing room. She was usually as quiet as a church mouse, but this morning she slammed through every drawer as she selected Ellie's attire. She returned with a fresh chemise, stockings, and stays. She had just helped Ellie into her undergarments and fastened the corset when a knock on the door interrupted them.

Ellie glanced at the clock on the mantel. It was a few moments after eight. She nodded at Lucia, who answered the door as Ellie shrugged into her dressing gown again.

"This is the earliest I have ever known you to be out of bed," Madeleine said as she walked into Ellie's chamber. "When we were in Scotland last autumn, I swear I never saw you before ten at the earliest."

Ellie accepted her sister-in-law's kiss. "Desperate times and all that. I am sorry to have sent for you and Prudence so early."

Behind them, Miss Prudence Etchingham entered, followed by a servant bearing a tray with tea and chocolate. "This isn't early by my standards," Prudence said. "Lady Salford is an early riser, and I am up even earlier so that I may have an hour to myself before attending her. But I will gladly sacrifice that hour if the story you want to share is as delicious as I expect it to be."

"I don't have anything delicious to share, unfortunately. You will have to settle for tea."

Prudence arched an eyebrow at Ellie's evasion. "That's not what I would have guessed after last night. Even Lady Salford remarked on how taken Lord Folkestone was with you. If he had accidentally strayed near the chairs where the dowagers and companions sat, they might have flayed him alive with their curiosity."

Prudence was a companion to Madeleine's aunt and Alex Staunton's mother, the widowed Lady Salford. Lady Salford had taken Prudence in several months earlier, an arrangement that had freed Prudence from her overbearing, impoverished mother.

But for all that Prudence was grateful, Ellie saw the tightness around her mouth. A future as an older lady's companion was not one that any woman with Prudence's mind would embrace wholeheartedly, even if Lady Salford was easier than most. Ellie had planned to take Prudence with her to Europe for a few months…but Nick's return had changed all that.

Ellie gestured the ladies into comfortable chairs by the fire. Prudence dismissed the servant and offered to pour. Lucia returned to the dressing room for Ellie's carriage dress, but Ellie stayed standing. With all her shields in tatters after Nick's arrival, she needed to feel like she had troops to command — even if those troops were friends who now viewed her as the finest bit of entertainment they'd had in ages.

As Prudence passed around their cups, Ellie considered how to phrase her request. If this were one of their normal meetings, they might have discussed Prudence's new historical treatise or heard a dramatic reading from Madeleine's latest play. Madeleine and Prudence had been friends for years, while Ellie had only joined their circle the previous summer. They had invited her to join their secret artistic club, the Muses of Mayfair, when they had discovered that she was a painter during Madeleine and Ferguson's courtship. The only member missing was Madeleine's cousin Amelia, the newly married Countess of Carnach, who had stayed in Scotland with her husband rather than attending Ellie's house party.

But while Ellie usually guided them into talking about themselves instead of her, Lord Folkestone's return was so momentous that none of them could forget it. Prudence started the inquisition. "I was concerned for your health when Folkestone dragged you from the ballroom last night. Is everything well?"

"I hope it's well," Madeleine added. "Thank goodness Ferguson and I retired early. If he had seen what Prue described to me, he might have murdered the man."

"I don't need my brother to protect me," Ellie said.

Her tone was mild, but her feelings weren't. Ferguson had been missing from her life for years. They were on much better terms now that he had returned from the exile their father had sent him to, but his newfound protectiveness occasionally rankled.

Madeleine smiled. "You know Ferguson. If he decides to protect someone, he will do it whether she wants to be protected or not."

Ellie tried not to hate the dreamy look in Madeleine's eyes. "Well, don't let him decide to protect me. I already have a plan."

Lucia came out of the dressing room with one of Ellie's carriage dresses — a gorgeous grey that made her think of a Scottish sky in winter. Prudence's eyes flickered from the dress to Ellie's face. "Don't say you're leaving us?" she asked.

Ellie set aside her chocolate and removed her robe so that Lucia could help her into the dress. "That's why I asked you to attend me so early this morning. I have pressing business in London that cannot wait, and I need someone to act as hostess and entertain the ladies until I return. The men can mostly take care of themselves, particularly if Lord Folkestone chooses to play the host…"

"Unlikely," Prudence said, interrupting her. "Lady Salford's maid helped me to dress, and she heard that Lord Folkestone had already left for London. Not that I gossiped with the servants, of course — but they can be useful."

Madeleine grinned. "Planning a rendezvous in the capital? How shocking of you, Lady Folkestone."

Ellie sucked in a breath that had nothing to do with Lucia's sharp tug on the back of her dress. She hadn't known that Nick was going to London, but she couldn't delay her trip just to avoid him. "What that scoundrel does is no concern of mine," she said sharply.

She knew her mistake immediately — both of her friends went from interested to *very* interested. "So he's a scoundrel now?" Madeleine asked. "Was he a scoundrel before or after he moved into the room next to yours?"

"I didn't put him in the room next to mine," Ellie said smugly. "The only room left, other than the master's chamber, was a small bachelor's room in the old wing of the house. He may freeze to death there, but it would save me the trouble of finding a new residence."

Prudence and Madeleine both looked into their cups at the same time.

"What are you not telling me?" she asked.

"I must have made a mistake," Madeleine said, in a voice that didn't allow for mistakes. "But I saw him leaving this hallway when your maid requested that I join you for tea. Since I knew all the other rooms on this floor were occupied, I assumed he was in the master's chamber. Unless he was in here with you?"

She sounded so guileless that her innocence somehow wrapped around itself and became an insinuation. "Yes, you made a mistake," Ellie said firmly. "I'm sure he stayed where I put him. But that is neither here nor there. All I need is for you to keep my guests entertained until dinner so that I may deal with an urgent matter in the City. I'm sorry if you came to my room expecting a grand story of reunited lovers, but there's no world in which that story is going to happen."

"Do you really believe that?" Prudence asked. "From the way he watched you in the ballroom, he looked more than a little interested in a reunion."

"And I do like a reunited lovers story," Madeleine said. "Almost enough that I wish Ferguson would go away for a bit so that I may have him back."

Ellie and Prudence exchanged a long-suffering look. Madeleine's love for her husband was nearly sickening in its perfection. But Ellie caught herself and shrugged. "No reunited lovers. There are enough men in the ton that I don't need to repeat myself."

Lucia ordered her to hold still as she shoved pins into Ellie's unruly curls. Prudence looked at Ellie wistfully. "You truly don't want him? Not even a little?"

Ellie had pondered that question all night, in between snatches of fitful sleep, and she was no closer to an answer than she had been when she had peeled herself off Nick and left the salon. The memory told her what her body wanted — it wanted Nick, as hard and often as possible, until it was sated enough to let him go.

She knew herself well enough to know she would have seduced him eventually. She hadn't taken a lover in over three years, but she wanted Nick as she wanted no one else. He had merely beaten her to the seduction, albeit with a cruelty that still stunned her. That didn't mean she wouldn't enjoy herself.

But the stinging tears that had threatened to overwhelm her as she had lain in the dark told her what her mind wanted.

It wanted to escape before the floodgates crumbled, before everything she had done to rebuild herself into an inviolable fortress collapsed at her feet. Her body didn't want to let him go, and her heart was torn between the two — but her mind knew she wouldn't survive losing him again.

"There's no going back, Prudence," she said, after a pause that was a bit too long. "Staying now will only make it harder when we part ways again."

"So you *do* want him," Prudence said triumphantly.

Madeleine and Prudence both looked up at her with identical expressions of inquisitive delight. She knew they cared about her. They wanted her to be happy. They wanted to share in her emotion. Their friendship was still new to her, but it was what Ellie had dreamed of as a child, all alone on the country estate where her father had abandoned her. She had been exiled, raised by a series of nursemaids and governesses, for the crime of looking too much like the wife he'd adored and lost. With Ferguson similarly exiled at Eton and her other half-siblings in London, she had dreamed of having friends to play with, to laugh with, to share secrets with...

But she hadn't realized then that secrets held a dark, dangerous kind of power. What danger had her secrets posed when no one cared about them but her? It was a lesson she'd learned, and learned hard, during her first season in London, when she had finally found other women her own age to talk to.

Suddenly, it wasn't Madeleine and Prudence in front of her. Annabel and Clarabel Claiborne had been eighteen and seventeen during Ellie's debut, while Ellie was already nineteen, but they were kind and cheerful — easygoing, charming girls whom Ellie's father approved of her knowing. She wanted her father's approval badly enough that she would have been friends with a lamppost if it had possessed the right pedigree and fortune. If the girls' charm was a bit shallow, it was made up for by how nicely they tittered at her conversational gambits.

And so when they had asked her one night, when they'd all had too much champagne, whether she had found a man to pin her hopes on, Ellie had told the truth. She'd been giddy with the truth, sure of her own heart, confident that once the season was over, her father would let her marry Nick. He'd promised to let them marry, after all; Ellie just had to finish the season without marrying someone else.

So she had shown Annabel and Clarabel her heart. Wasn't that what friends were supposed to do?

Friends in the ton knew better. Annabel and Clarabel hadn't intended to hurt her — perhaps they never even knew that a word was enough to change the course of Ellie's life. But they went off and whispered to their brother that his despised cousin had tricked a duke's daughter into falling in love with him. And when Charles Claiborne, a marquess rather than a merchant, came asking the duke for Ellie's hand...

Ellie shook her head. Madeleine and Prudence weren't Charles's sisters. She wanted to tell them what Nick had done. She wanted to show them how he'd hurt her, how confused she was, how much she still wanted him.

But when she opened her mouth, the words wouldn't come out.

"Are you feeling well?" Madeleine asked, suddenly concerned. "Perhaps you should rest rather than going to London today."

"I shall be fine in London. As for the rest of it..."

Ellie paused again. Prudence finally took pity on her. She stood and linked arms with Madeleine, pulling the duchess out of her chair when Madeleine looked ready to stay and pursue her questioning. "There's no need to know your feelings today," Prudence said. "But we are here should you need our help."

It was a nice gesture. If Ellie were nineteen, perhaps she even would have accepted it — perhaps she would have been grateful for it, rather than immediately dismissing it. But she was thirty now, on a birthday no one other than Nick would acknowledge since she hadn't told them the date. She knew the limits of her friendships.

And she knew the truth — no one could help her with Nick.

As soon as they left, she let Lucia pin her hat to her hair and took up her swansdown-trimmed grey pelisse before descending to the front hall. A drive to London was hardly relaxing, given the state of the roads and traffic, but at least she would have a few hours to herself. She needed to explore all the options that would buy her freedom, repair her shields before she saw Nick again — and somehow find the courage to leave him a second time.

CHAPTER EIGHT

Nick loved the City. India had held its own unique charms, and he had enjoyed it enough to stay years longer than he had intended. But no matter how long he lived in Madras, he sensed that he would never quite feel at home there. The Indian men whom he dealt most closely with were anxious to prove their loyalties, and so never shared their culture with him. The ones he didn't deal with viewed him with suspicion bordering on hostility.

He was no stranger to hostility. The upper classes in London hadn't liked him either. But he couldn't entirely blame the Indian populace for hating him, or for wishing the British would leave.

But this corner of London, wedged between the City and the East End, felt like home. The mix of shops and warehouses drew laborers from the east and bankers and merchants from the west, and was ideally suited to supply the whole metropolis with the staples and luxuries the people demanded. Still, he knew most peers would rather die than soil their Hessians by setting foot inside a warehouse.

With his father's breeding and his mother's money, Nick could afford to spend his days somewhere far more salubrious. But salubrious climes required socializing with the people who could afford those climes. Nick wasn't in the mood to be social.

Then again, he also wasn't in the mood to investigate his own potential demise. But if he wanted to make progress, he needed to see if any threats materialized around his London offices.

And he couldn't sit idle at Folkestone all day without breaking his promise to give Ellie a reprieve.

Marcus, walking next to him as they left one of the Corwyn, Claiborne and Sons warehouses, took a deep breath. Then he coughed. "The countryside always makes my lungs soft," he complained when he'd regained his breath. "I am surprised you can stand the city air after six months on the ocean."

Nick inhaled. London, and particularly this quarter of London, was an unholy potpourri of unwashed bodies, manures of both horse and human variety, coal fires, and cooking pots. The stench was almost a physical attack.

"The ocean is more pleasant, I'll grant you that," he said. "But by the fourth month aboard, when the foodstuffs are maggoty and there is only salt water for bathing, London seems wholesome by comparison."

"For all that I'm jealous of what you and Rupert have seen abroad, I consider myself fortunate to have been the brother who stayed behind," Marcus said. "There are advantages to a stolid life in the cleaner areas of the capital."

Nick hailed his batman, who had lounged near the street watching the passing traffic. They waited near the curb as Trower fetched their driver. Their newest warehouse, only recently completed, was a temple to modern industry, with an imposing marble façade designed to impress buyers who came to purchase their imports. But its purpose was given away by its lack of street-facing windows. With the value of the indigo and spices stored in that warehouse, it had been made as impregnable as any fortress.

For all the abuse the higher classes heaped upon the trade, Nick thought there was nothing more exciting than seeking out new products and making risky deals, whether in the far-off reaches of the empire or in the trading rooms of the City. "Your London life never sounded stolid in your letters," he said to Marcus.

"Utterly stolid, I assure you. Wouldn't want our grandfather to think I was shirking my duties."

Nick laughed. Their maternal grandfather had remained very much in command of most of the London operations until his death a year and a half earlier, but Marcus was no idle gentleman. "You had the old man in your pocket from your first steps. And he was hardly a Puritan. I doubt you'd be half so debauched without his influence."

"It is a shame you weren't more often in London to partake of Grandfather's generosity as a youth. The fair ladies at Madame Patrice's were worth any number of hours spent counting tea chests."

Nick had gone to Eton, as his father had before him. But unlike his father, who had been perfectly aristocratic until he fell in love with the wrong girl, Nick was mocked from the start for his ties to the trade. It might not have been so bad — there were other, lower born boys who took the brunt of the bullying — but Nick and his cousin Charles, who was two years older and already the Marquess of Folkestone, hated each other on sight. And even the youngest boys knew to side with a marquess over a merchant's son.

Nick had refused to back down and hadn't left despite their years-long conflict, but his parents hadn't made the same mistake with Marcus and Rupert. Where Nick had grimly survived Eton, his brothers had stayed in London, learning the trade from their father and grandfather. Little wonder they were inveterate rakes. Nick sometimes felt like a brooding monk by comparison.

He shrugged. "I've had my share of pleasure without needing Grandfather to be my procurer."

Marcus snorted. "Grandfather never had to procure for me, brother." Then he cast Nick a sidelong glance. "If you want me to point you toward some prime houses, though..."

"No need," Nick said.

There was a finality in his voice that would have warned off lesser men. But he and his brothers had been raised as equals. The Folkestone title had seemed destined to stay in Charles's line, and primogeniture did not apply to their shared inheritance from their grandfather. Marcus wouldn't yield to him just because Nick now outranked him.

"Please don't say you went through with your revenge last night," Marcus said.

They had avoided talk of Ellie for five hours — longer than Nick had expected Marcus to refrain from the subject. "She's not my mistress yet," Nick said, sharing a truth that, at midnight, would be a lie.

Their carriage pulled up and Trower jumped down to open the door for them while the driver held the horses. Marcus waited until they were seated and the carriage was in motion before saying, "Your lack of compassion with her surprises me."

"It shouldn't."

Again, Marcus plunged past the warning in Nick's voice. "After everything you've done for me and Rupert? Granted, I'd begun to accustom myself to the idea that you would never come home, but you gave me more room to make decisions than most men would have. Hard to believe you could be so kind to us and so...unkind to her."

Nick had lain awake the previous night, in the giant bed that had once been his cousin's, separated from Ellie by a locked connecting door and ten years of regret. She had tried to stuff him into a small room as far from her as possible, but he'd taken a single look at the lumpy mattress and ordered the butler to put him in the master's chamber instead. At the moment, disregarding her wishes had given him a visceral kick of satisfaction.

But in the dark, the question of kindness had haunted him. He had always been kind to those who depended upon him — it was his duty and privilege as a gentleman, even moreso when hundreds of people relied upon him for their livelihoods.

And he had always been kind to Ellie. Even on the day she had destroyed him, he hadn't done what he wanted to do — couldn't toss her onto his horse and ruin her publicly just to keep her. When his rational self had considered his revenge on the ship home from India, he had thought that he couldn't do it. The Ellie in his head was still, always, nineteen, all meek adoration and pretty, fragile need. She'd hurt him badly, irredeemably, and he wanted to do the same to her — but he hadn't been sure that he could follow through. Ten years was more than long enough for his anger to cool, and while he still hated her for what she had done, destroying a woman was beneath him.

The Ellie in his house, though — she wasn't the Ellie he had remembered. He had been so shocked by the transformation that he hadn't even fully grasped it before the feral, maddened beast within him had marked her as an opponent deserving of his revenge.

Now, though, he wondered. Did she deserve it? Or was he pursuing her because he had realized, on some level, that she could take it?

Such considerations could only lead to madness.

Marcus coughed. "I thought having you in London would make

for faster communication, but it feels like I've been waiting months for you to answer me."

"If you were so concerned about whether I would be kind to Ellie, why did you follow through with our plan?" Nick asked.

Marcus's face turned grim. "Misplaced loyalty, brother."

Nick had never heard that tone in Marcus's voice. But then, Marcus hadn't been in a position to judge him in person before. Nick leaned forward. "What do you mean by that?"

Marcus didn't waver. "Ellie's paid for her sins. What you're doing now — that's a new sin, and one I'll pay for as well. I would have stopped long ago, but I suppose I'm just as much a sinner as you are."

"How so?"

This time, Marcus paused. Finally, he said, "Much as I enjoy playing the country lord, I wanted you to come home. And this revenge of yours seemed to be the only thing that would bring you back. But there's still time to change your mind."

Marcus didn't know that time had run out. And he didn't know what had really brought Nick home. Nick was nearly positive that Marcus wasn't behind the attempts in Madras, but "nearly" wasn't good enough — especially not when Marcus stood to inherit a title, another share of their company...and perhaps Ellie, if that's where his inclinations ran. He wouldn't be the first Claiborne to try to ruin Nick's chances with her.

He didn't let any of that flicker across his face. "We've all made our beds. But if you want to play the country lordling, I won't stop you. Once my business here is done, we can discuss the future."

Marcus frowned. Then, abruptly, and without asking Nick's approval, he pounded on the ceiling of the couch and ordered the driver to take them to Folkestone House.

"There's no need to show me everything today," Nick said.

"I know, but we still have an hour or two before we should drive back to the country. And it's in my best interests to show you how much you would enjoy living here, if only so that I'm not stuck managing your holdings forever. If anything will convince you, it's Folkestone House. Ellie may have awful taste in men, but she has an eye for color that rivals anything I've ever seen."

Nick knew Marcus well enough to hear the cheeky insult in his comment, but he let it pass unremarked. As they drove, Nick flicked open a curtain to watch the passing crowds. The pale winter light, too far north and filtered through the smoke from thousands of chimneys, muted the city's dubious charms.

He had looked forward to returning to London, when he could forget the fact that Ellie waited here. Despite how much he loved the subcontinent, India was a harsh mistress — heat so intense that he boiled alive in his proper British morning suits, followed by months of monsoons with torrential downpours that could drown a man in the street. All the Englishmen had lived in fear of disease, and fevers claimed more men than would ever return to Britain alive.

But for a few months, from October to February, it was just dry enough to stop mouldering and just cool enough to be able to breathe. And no matter how difficult things were, there was color — endless varieties of reds, yellows, oranges, and blues, in every house, in every market, draped in silken sari swathes on every woman.

There wasn't enough color in Britain. Ellie, though…Ellie was a streak of red in a grim, grey country.

He couldn't forgive her, but he still wanted her. If she'd influenced the London house as much as she had Folkestone, her touch would be in every room.

And he could look his fill, without her knowing, while trying to remind himself why he had to let her go.

CHAPTER NINE

"You could sell the Canaletto, the Reynolds, and everything by Gainsborough, my lady," Lucia suggested, examining the catalogue she had unearthed from Ellie's private salon in Folkestone House. "They would likely bring a tidy sum above what you paid."

Ellie stood in the very center of Folkestone House's main drawing room. It had been a dull and uninspired room when she had entered it as a bride, filled with dull and uninspired minor works by failed protégés of the Old Masters. She had turned it into one of the finest private displays of art in London. Every painting was perfectly stretched in gilded frames and hung on the walls with more space between them than was currently *en vogue* — an effect that made each shine a bit more brightly, without relegating some paintings to the very edges of the ceiling as was common in other drawing rooms.

She turned in a slow circle. "I could sell all of them. But it could take months — especially if no dealer will take my business."

Merchants were eager to sell to a woman, but not all of them would deal with her. Her anger still burned from her earlier call at her London bank, where she found that the manager would not disburse any funds without Marcus to countersign the order.

But her heart broke at the thought of selling the paintings she had collected so carefully. Some were works so masterful that she had to have them. Others were less showy, but fit perfectly in either color

73

or theme with her decorating scheme for Folkestone House's many rooms. All, though, had spoken to her — often at times when no one and nothing else had.

"I would rather sell my jewels," Ellie continued, musing aloud. Lucia didn't respond. No response was necessary, not after the disastrous interview at Rundell and Bridge. They were entirely solicitous and sympathetic, but they caught the scent of her desperation. They would give her only a fraction of the jewels' worth. And three thousand pounds was not enough to save her.

It wasn't losing access to the house that broke Ellie's heart. She had never loved it. It was that this room, like every other, had been designed with a single purpose — to please Nick, perhaps to win him back. But all the effort, all the soul she had poured into these rooms, was like blood spilled on a distant battleground, in a battle fought before word arrived that a surrender had already occurred. While Ellie had fought, hopelessly, for the day when she might finally atone for her mistake, Nick had plotted to ruin her. And this house, and the money she had spent on it, were the instruments of her defeat.

She straightened her spine. It had been a stupid plan anyway. Nick no longer cared for beauty. He only cared for profit. And she could no longer afford to be sentimental.

She turned back to Lucia. "Gather the catalogues of my collections to take back to Folkestone. We will make a prospective sale list tomorrow. Lord Salford knows the private buying sphere as well as anyone. He may have some thoughts on how to liquidate everything without letting my financial difficulties slip."

Lucia was better suited to be an aide de camp than a lady's maid, and was more than competent for the task at hand. She also understood the stakes. "It may be possible to sell some items without arousing suspicion," she said slowly. She was calmer and more methodical than Ellie; where Ellie's voice sometimes tripped a rapid staccato in its attempt to keep up with her own thoughts, Lucia's voice had the feel of a deep, mysterious lake, with currents rippling across it only after she had considered all the possibilities. "But the provenance of your collection is well known to any major buyers. And with Lord Folkestone's return...there will be rumors no matter how discreet you are."

"What would you have me do?" Ellie demanded. "I can only live for free at my brother's house or at the Folkestone dower house — and since my mother-in-law still clings to it, you can be sure I will avoid that wretched place at all costs. Selling is the only option."

Lucia stood, stiff and formal, the way she always did when she prepared to tell her mistress a truth that Ellie didn't want to hear. "There are two other options, my lady. Accept Lord Folkestone's bargain, distasteful as it is, and keep everything. Or, if I may be so bold, sell your paintings."

"You just said I can't sell my paintings," Ellie said peevishly, ignoring the first option entirely.

"Not these paintings. The paintings you created yourself."

"I couldn't possibly."

Lucia frowned. In these moments, when her logic made her forget herself, she had the assured, confident demeanor of a lady, rather than the subservient class her youthful sins had cast her into. "You have the connections necessary to set up a display in a private gallery, and you have hundreds of canvasses to choose from. You might not raise the entire forty thousand pounds, but you could surely earn enough to shorten the duration of Folkestone's demands."

Ellie turned away from Lucia and looked at the paintings on

the walls. She'd dreamed of showing her paintings publicly when she was younger — might have done it, too, if it could have caused the scandal she needed to prevent her father from finding a second husband for her. But that desire had faded as her painting had turned wilder, as her perfect little landscapes and watercolors turned into fierce, tempestuous fantasies.

Ellie left too much of herself on the canvas. And her real self wasn't fit to be shared with anyone.

"Unthinkable. I'd sooner stay with Nick than whore my paintings like that."

She couldn't see Lucia, but she sensed her maid's disapproval. "It's the world's loss," Lucia said. "If you weren't so precious about your work, I am convinced you could rival any of your contemporaries."

Ellie's voice turned cold. "See to the catalogues. I want to be in the carriage in less than a quarter of an hour."

She heard Lucia leave; the maid was wise enough to know when Ellie's limits had been reached.

If only Ellie knew her own limits. She hugged her arms around herself. The caretaker had lit a fire for Ellie when she had returned unexpectedly, but a single fire wasn't enough to banish the chill of a house that had been empty for a week.

She heard steps in the hallway — heavy, masculine steps, not Lucia's lighter gait. More than one man, if she heard correctly. One moved faster than the others, faster than dignity would usually allow. She turned to the door just as it burst open. One of her footmen — the youngest one, hired for his blond hair rather than his ability to serve — rushed across the threshold. "Lord Folkestone, my lady," he gasped.

Her arms dropped to her sides. Her hand itched for a paint brush.

She suddenly saw the footman in Athens — not a glittering Adonis, but a winded Pheidippides, the messenger who had run twenty-six miles to give news of the victory at Marathon before dropping dead at her feet.

Stop being dramatic.

But there was no time to stop. Nick rounded the door behind him and the footman had just enough sense left to slide out of Nick's path before any of them discovered whether Nick would have pushed him aside. "Lady Folkestone," Nick said. "What a delightful surprise."

"Lovely to see you, I'm sure," she said. "Welcome to Folkestone House."

He bowed, a match for her insincerity. "Don't say you've decided to return to London and abandon your guests?"

She knew there was only one 'guest' he cared about — and it had more to do with revenge than hospitality. "I did think that today was the only day I might get away."

His eyes narrowed at her reference to the reprieve she'd won from him. "And what business might bring you to the capital?"

"Oh, you know how flighty I can be," she said, waving a hand. "One never knows when my attention might turn to something else."

It was a dangerous game. Nick was no longer the kind, gracious boy who would let her tease him, but she wasn't ready for him to know that she sought a different means of repaying him. He took the bait, though — she'd known from his clenched jaw and brooding, hooded eyes that he would be quick to anger.

And even quicker to action. "Get out," he growled at the footman, who still wheezed near the door. The man squeaked his agreement and left without even checking to make sure that Ellie would be safe.

She really needed to start hiring staff who were capable of

guarding her, not just men who might look good draped in classical linen.

Beyond the door, she saw Lucia. But her maid was too busy hissing accusations at an extremely uncomfortable Marcus to save her. And then it was too late — Nick slammed the door and turned the key in the lock, leaving them alone to confront each other.

"We really must stop meeting like this," she said. "I cannot afford to fix any broken door frames."

Nick snorted. "This house seems as sturdy as any I've seen. Unless you introduced dry rot as part of your spending campaign?"

"Would that I had thought of that," Ellie retorted. "What are you doing here, Nick?"

"It's my house."

She'd thought she hated his coldness — but smugness was worse. "Ah, how silly of me to forget. Will you be staying here tonight, then?"

She knew she sounded too expectant. He didn't even bother to answer her question. "Tell me what you were doing here," he demanded.

"I owe you money, not explanations, my lord," she said, giving his title all the venom she possessed. "Or anyway, you've shown no desire for them."

He leaned against the door and let his eyes wander over her in a callous, dismissive way. "You can satisfy me in many ways, Ellie my love — and I look forward to discovering even more of them. But I find your explanations wholly uninteresting."

"Your loss," she said, shrugging with a nonchalance her heart didn't feel. "You aren't the first Claiborne in this house to believe I should be seen and not heard."

Mentioning Charles was a spark to a powder keg. Nick gritted his teeth. "I'm not my cousin."

"No, you're not," she agreed. "Charles was the arrogant, annoying prig who married me. You are the arrogant, annoying prig who bought me. Such a difference, that."

She expected an explosion, but Nick just smiled. "I'll give you arrogant and annoying. But I'm no prig."

"No?"

"No." He strode toward her. She held still, not willing to give up ground, and he reached her in four steps. "A prig would be a stickler for what's proper."

He slid a hand to her waist and pulled her close, close enough to whisper in her ear. "A prig would never let a tradesman such as myself soil your pretty skin with my dirty hands."

His other hand stroked her hair, petting her like a prize he'd won at a backwater fair. His voice turned to a growl. "A prig would have known, from the first day that he saw you in that far-off country field, that a lady of your class would never have a man from mine."

She opened her mouth to deny it, but his hand clasped over her mouth — not the tender shushing of a child, but a desperate, overpowering attempt to stop her voice. "I'm not a gentleman. I might have been, once, until you showed me what I really am. So say those words again, my love. Call me a peasant. Hold your nose at how I reek of the shop. Say how much I embarrass you. I don't care anymore — it's all true. But never, *ever* compare me to Charles."

His hand against her mouth was another piece of the wall between them — a wall she couldn't scale, or blast through, or burrow under, because she'd reinforced it just as heavily from her side as he had from his.

But she could shout over it, and hope that he heard the tone of her voice even if he refused to hear the words. When his hand slipped away, she said, "You are many things, Nicholas Claiborne. But you have never been an embarrassment."

He slid a hand up to her hair, tentatively, like Socrates picking up the hemlock cup that would be his death. She tilted her head back and looked up into his face. She saw wariness there, hidden under his cold veneer, and it broke her heart.

His voice softened, but the steel underneath it didn't. "Don't pretend, Ellie. I never wanted to be part of your circles, and until I inherited a bloody title, they never wanted me. On some level you know that. And in your heart, you could never let yourself be with someone like me."

He'd said the same words when she had told him of her father's ultimatum years ago. The old duke had said that she could marry Nick if she spent a season in London and found no one better — a trade she'd been glad to make, never suspecting that her father would push her into marrying someone else.

Nick had known the pressures she would face, even if she hadn't. She hadn't suspected that her father would be that stubborn. She was sure that he, and everyone else, would welcome Nick once they grew accustomed to him.

But Nick had always been convinced that she would ultimately, inevitably, come to her senses and give him up. She opened her lips, started to deny his words, but he spoke before she could. "Don't say anything, Ellie. I can't believe you. And you won't convince me."

The unfairness of it was too much. It was unfair that the world had convinced him of the gulf between them. It was unfair that he wouldn't listen to her.

But she was unfair for expecting him to. She shouldn't have

married Charles.

She especially shouldn't have married Charles when she had still been in love with Nick.

Ellie didn't say any of that, though. She pulled his fingers into hers. "I don't remember your hands being dirty. I remember them being warm, and gentle, and forceful, and devious."

With each word, she kissed one of his fingertips. His knuckles gripped hers with crushing force. She somehow found his strength comforting. As she kissed the last finger, she looked up into his eyes. She was only inches from him. But after ten years and thousands of miles, those last few inches felt like an insurmountable obstacle.

He massaged her neck lightly with his free hand. His thumb found the pressure point at the base of her skull and she tilted her head to the side, offering him a view of her throat.

"God, Ellie," he whispered. The soft cadence of his voice sounded like a lament.

But when his lips met hers, there was no mourning there — only fire.

CHAPTER TEN

She'd loved him when she was nineteen. That hadn't been a lie. And she'd enjoyed him, too. Enjoyed his hands, his mouth, his tongue — all the places where he was hard and she was soft. She used to melt under him like candlewax, and each time she cooled, she had formed back around him, pliant and yielding.

This kiss threatened to melt her again. She moaned as he sealed his lips to hers. He took her breath and she stole it back. She still held his fingers trapped within hers. They became her anchor as her head started to spin.

She knew she should stop him.

But she didn't. She wanted the memories — the memories she'd relived endlessly, obsessively. She wanted them to be real again, not just ghosts that tormented her in the darkness.

Maybe he wanted the memories too. This kiss wasn't reverent, the way he used to kiss her. But it wasn't angry, either. His mouth was gentle — not a brutal conquest, but the renewal of a longstanding claim. His hand lingered at her neck, lightly, light enough that she could break away at any time. But his fingers clasped hers just as fiercely as she did his, until it was no longer clear who was holding whom.

She slid her other arm around him and stepped into the space

82

between his feet. His hand slipped up, teased her ear, caressed her cheek. She did melt then, sighing against his mouth as her body molded to his. It felt right, this kiss, in a way that nothing and no one had quite felt since Nick had left.

The kiss lasted endless minutes — slow, smoldering, a carefully controlled fire. When one quickened, sliding toward a breast or hip, the other slowed, slipping away, changing the angle — keeping things the same, balanced on the edge between memory and reality.

Between who they might have been, and what they really were.

Nick pulled away first. But he didn't step back — he held her against his chest and leaned his chin on her head. She burrowed her face into his jacket. He had held her like that once before, and the lingering ache of memory punched her in the gut.

She had sought him out the day after her first ball, giving her groom all of her pin money so that he would look the other way while she rode with Nick. They had stopped in a far corner of Hyde Park, and she confessed how she had stood, shy and uncertain, on the edge of her first ball — and how much she had wished he could be invited to such events so that she would have someone to dance with.

He had reassured her, told her that she would conquer them all, and pulled her off her horse to dance with her until she could laugh again. Then he had held her like that, just for a moment, in an embrace that had felt like a goodbye even though she hadn't understood it at the time.

She'd gone back to her governess then. Several weeks elapsed between that embrace and the day she had broken their engagement. But in the years that followed, she would have done anything to go back to that moment in the park. She wished she had begged him to run away with her instead of standing aside and letting her slip away.

She was finally back in his arms — just where she'd thought she would never be again. It was different now. He felt different, all muscle and resolve instead of youthful worship.

Her thoughts raced, but her brain was unwilling to pin any of them down for fear of finding a truth she didn't want to confront. Could she pretend that he was a malevolent stranger — that the Nick she had loved wasn't the man who was determined to destroy her?

Or did she want Nick to be real, no matter how he had changed?

She felt him draw a breath. "I missed you, Ellie," he said.

All her racing thoughts crashed into each other. Whatever she really felt was buried under the wreckage. But there was one truth she could share.

"I missed you, too."

*   *   *

She felt right in his arms. He'd held others after her, and even enjoyed most of them. But she was perfect there, curved around him until he didn't know where he ended and she began. He'd missed that in India, more than anything else from home — the feeling that somewhere, somehow, one person in the world knew him, fit him, wanted him.

Wanted *him*, despite everything he was.

Still, he couldn't forget what she'd done.

"I thought you wouldn't want me to return," he said.

"You could have asked, you know. I trust you still remember your letters. Unless you've spent so many hours counting your fortune that you've forgotten how to write?"

She hadn't moved an inch, but he felt the gulf expanding between them, a tide that carried them further apart with every heartbeat. "You could have written just as easily, Ellie my love. Unless you've forgotten your letters with all the men you've let sniff at your skirts?"

She'd tensed when he unintentionally used his old endearment for her, then flinched as his barb struck home. She glared at him. "Don't be crude, Nick. It's beneath you."

"But that's what I am, isn't it? The crude tradesman who can never have you? Good enough for a quick fuck, but not for your breakfast table?"

"You've had me before, and you'll have me again. I wouldn't worry so much about being a tradesman — it seems to have served you well."

He'd wanted to insult her, to draw a reaction from her. But he'd unearthed the weary, jaded woman whom he'd seen the previous night, in the instant before she had recognized him.

Ellie shouldn't be jaded. She should be laughing.

He raked a hand through his hair. "What happened to you, Ellie?"

Her blue eyes were genuinely confused. "What do you mean?"

"You've changed. You used to be all fire. But there's ice now — why?"

She pulled away from him, as though his touch suddenly pained her. "I'm old, Nick. We both are."

"Older, but not old. And that's not what I meant."

She turned, walked toward the window, and peered out over the barren gardens beyond the glass. "Winter always follows summer. Perhaps that's what happened to us."

"You know I don't like riddles."

She laughed darkly but didn't look back at him. "You don't like explanations, either. So if I can't tell you the truth, and I can't speak in riddles, what's left? Runes? Tea leaves?"

"What truth is left to tell me? Your intentions were clear when you broke our engagement."

She leaned her forehead against the glass. Her breath fogged the window, and she pulled back to trace a pattern in it — their entwined initials, the cryptic design she had used to sign her paintings of him.

Then she turned to face him. His heart skipped a beat. His Ellie had been a pretty, well-contained fire, the kind that cheered a man on an autumn evening. This Ellie was a bonfire, burning from within as though her very heart was the fuel. Her eyes were stark, her mouth was tight. In the stormy grey of her dress and the muted light of a winter afternoon, Ellie burned for him.

He'd heard of widows throwing themselves on their husbands' funeral pyres in India, although he'd never seen the *sati* act himself. Ellie was still alive in front of him — but she burned, with an intensity and a depth his Ellie had never shown him.

"Do you want the truth?" she asked. "Or do you want revenge?"

Who *was* she, this woman he'd bought and paid for?

"The truth," he said.

"The truth," she repeated. "I was young, and stupid, and would have done anything for a chance to please my father. You were young and stupid too, and thought it was all about your shortcomings rather than my father's demands. You should have known — you knew how Father browbeat me. And I will go to my grave regretting that I let him."

Then she straightened her shoulders. "But I will also go to my grave before I let another man force me to change just to please him. You can have your revenge. It may even make me feel better to repay you — I've heard atonement helps, although I've never found it so. If it works, I suppose I should thank you for that."

She paused, and he saw the weight of the words she wasn't saying press against her cheeks as she compressed her lips. But those words, when they finally escaped, surprised him. "Just...just don't ask me to fall in love with you again, if revenge is your only reason. Not because I can't feel it for you, but because I can't survive it a second time."

Her fire burned through his resolve more effectively than any tears could have washed it away. This Ellie was stronger, deeper, more mature than the Ellie he had loved — and the Ellie he had loved was dead, in some brutal and final way that he hadn't realized until that moment. But the Ellie in front of him was alive and vibrant in a way that the Ellie who lived in his dreams could never be.

He nodded once. Really, what could he say? That he wouldn't let her fall in love with him? That he would let her go?

He'd asked her for the truth. He couldn't lie in response.

Ellie exhaled, then inhaled, swallowing whatever else she might have said. The moment passed, like a freak thaw in January, and her eyes reverted to ice. "Thank you, my lord. Now if you'll excuse me, I wish to return to Folkestone. I shan't waste my last day of freedom with you when I could enjoy my friends instead."

He kept his hands clenched behind his back, not letting them reach for her. "Enjoy your day, Lady Folkestone."

"Will you return for dinner, or do you plan to stay in London?" she asked.

Dinner — with all those bloody aristocrats. He would rather dine in hell, but he had found no evidence of a threat on his life in London. The threat, if it existed, may have been born at Folkestone. It was his duty to return.

Even he knew that he was making an excuse to stay close to Ellie. But he didn't stop himself. "I've a bit of business to attend to yet, but I shall return for dinner."

"Good. My chef would be displeased if he killed the fatted lamb for nothing. He is very French, and very angry when a plan changes. If you don't come tonight, we will all be eating porridge for a week."

She grinned at him. For just a moment he saw her at eighteen again, vowing to do anything to charm a laugh from him.

He did reach for her then, but she'd already slid away. His hand dropped as she stepped toward the door.

Then she turned back. "I meant it, Nick, when I said I missed you. Despite everything."

She was gone before he could reply. He listened to her steps, slow at first, then gaining intensity as she retreated down the hall. She would have every feature firmly in control before any servant saw her, he was sure of it.

Just as sure as he was that he never should have come back from India. He should have stayed there until the sun burned out every emotion, until the monsoon drowned every memory.

Because even though he couldn't keep her, he wasn't sure he had the strength to leave her again.

CHAPTER ELEVEN

"He is insufferable," Ellie declared. The carriage hit a rut in the frozen road. She reached for a strap to steady herself. "Not a word for ten years, and now he wants to know everything about everyone?"

She'd held her tongue for nearly two hours, but as they neared Folkestone, she finally broke her silence. Lucia didn't open her eyes. Enclosed carriages always made the maid queasy, but it was too damp for her to ride in the open air with the driver.

At least the maid was more comfortable in the larger Folkestone traveling coach. Ellie had used that as an excuse to steal it from Nick and Marcus, even though she knew she was merely being petty. But if Ellie were to spend two hours stewing over Nick's return, she would rather do it in luxury than in the smaller coach she'd been forced to take to London that morning.

"I am sure his lordship knows something of the estate," Lucia said, leaning back into the cushions. "Mr. Claiborne corresponded with him regularly."

"Marcus can go to the devil and take his brother with him. Every man in every generation of this family has been an oaf — or worse. I suppose I should be grateful that Charles didn't give me a child. Can you imagine raising a Claiborne male?"

"Your sparkling personality wouldn't be utterly absent in your

89

offspring, I trust."

Ellie looked at her maid suspiciously. "Do you count that as a blessing or a curse?"

Lucia's mouth curved the tiniest bit. "I'll allow that you are preferable to any Claiborne I've met."

Ellie sniffed. "If you weren't utterly unemployable, I would turn you off and be done with you."

Her maid's smile widened, an odd contrast to the sickly green of her face. "You are too kind, my lady."

"Tell me the truth, Lucia. What should I do about Nick?"

Lucia paused, so long that it seemed she might be sick in earnest. Ellie reached up to pound on the ceiling, but Lucia spoke before she could order a halt.

"Do you want what I think, or what you want to hear?"

Ellie dropped her fist into her lap. "What you think."

"I think you want me to say you should leave."

"That's not what I asked for."

Lucia shrugged. "Then if I say I think you should stay — do you want to hear that?"

"Staying is an awful idea."

"My point precisely, my lady."

"You know what happened between us," Ellie said. She'd shared the details one night, when she'd had far too much claret and was in a maudlin mood as she prepared for bed. Lucia had been good enough not to reference it again, but her mind was a steel trap — she wouldn't have forgotten. "Why wouldn't I run at the first sight of him?"

"For the same reason you've lived in his house all these years, I suspect. And the same reason you haven't married again."

"I'm not in love with him, if that's what you mean."

Lucia opened an eye.

"I'm not," Ellie insisted.

Lucia opened her other eye. In the dim interior of the coach, she suddenly looked deadly serious. "Believe what you will, my lady. But for all the advice you've given me, let me return the favor. You either stayed because you love him, or stayed because you want revenge. I don't know which desire drives you — but either way, the only way to seize it is to stay with Folkestone and see where he leads you."

Love.

Revenge.

Ellie wanted both. But Lucia had missed a crucial piece.

Ellie wanted forgiveness — both from Nick and from herself. And she wanted to believe that, if she ever had the chance to love again, she would be strong enough to hold on to it — and strong enough not to lose herself just for the taste of it.

A crack sounded outside the carriage. Someone shouted. Ellie felt the carriage jerk as the horses tried to bolt, and another jolt as the driver reined them in.

Ellie opened a window covering. Lucia moved to do the same on the other side. The sun, shrouded in clouds, had nearly set — but even in the dimness, Ellie saw the shapes of two masked men on horseback.

And two guns, both aimed at the carriage.

She pulled the curtain closed. The carriage had lost speed. Their driver couldn't evade mounted highwaymen. She could only hope that the robbery would be bloodless. No one had been killed by a highwayman in their neighborhood in ages. It was best to give them something, then send them packing. She had taken descriptions of her jewels to London rather than her entire collection — there was little else for the highwaymen to take.

But it was odd of them to choose daylight, when they could be more easily recognized and their victims were unlikely to be wearing expensive evening finery.

"Do you have your pistol?" she asked Lucia.

The maid held up her reticule.

"Put it between the cushions — they'll take the bag. We will give them what they want, but if they threaten violence, defend yourself."

"Of course." Lucia slid the pistol out and secreted it under the upholstered cushion. Ellie surveyed the rest of the carriage, but unless she wanted to try hitting the men with a lamp, there were no other weapons.

The carriage stopped. Her breath came fast and shallow. She braced herself against the seat — they wouldn't see her tremble.

A second shot fired, closer this time. Lucia's lips compressed in a grim line. Ellie looked up, not sure whether to open the ceiling panel — not sure whether her nerves would hold if the driver was dead above them.

But she couldn't sit idle — not when she might be able to pay the thieves to leave before anyone was harmed. She reached for the door handle and unlatched it.

"Stay here," she ordered Lucia.

Just as she opened the door, someone yanked it from the outside. She stumbled, hitting her head on the doorframe. The sharp explosion of pain made her eyes water.

One man had dismounted. He looked up at her with a leer as he gestured with his pistol. "Now ain't you a prize," he said, staring straight at her breasts.

She ignored him, looking over his head to the man who watched — mounted, masked, and inscrutable. His horse and clothing were of better quality than the man who'd come for her. Some part of her found that odd.

"Call off your lackey and tell me what you want," she demanded.

Behind her, Lucia cursed under her breath. The man who stood at her feet reached for her arm. But her gambit worked. The leader whistled at him, calling him to heel like a dog.

"Who is in your carriage?" the horseman asked.

An unusual question — and another warning bell. The part of her that was neither terrified nor angry knew, suddenly, that this was not an ordinary robbery.

"What if I said I had two footmen, both armed?" she asked.

"Then I'm sure they would have already inserted themselves in this conversation. Tell me now, or I will kill your driver."

She couldn't tell if he was bluffing. And she didn't hear any travelers in the distance who might aid them. She raised a hand in surrender. "My maid and I travel alone."

The second man lifted her out of the doorway before she could protest, dumping her on her derriere in the ditch. Certainly not an ordinary robbery — and she was suddenly cold, shivering on the ground, hoping someone would come before she learned why the highwaymen had stopped her.

At least her driver still lived, even if his face was ashen. He edged forward, very slowly — perhaps hoping to pull a gun from under his seat.

The mounted man noticed and swung his gaze from Ellie to the driver. "You're not the man I want to kill today," he warned, in a voice that might have been pleasant if the words weren't so threatening.

The second man turned back from the carriage door. "The bitch tells the truth. No gents, just a maid."

Ellie expected the demands to start — money, jewels, perhaps even the horses. But she didn't expect the man to close the door to the carriage, leaving Lucia inside.

"What now, sir? He ain't here."

"Perhaps we can find a use for her," the leader mused, staring at Ellie.

Ellie pulled herself to her feet, ignoring the implication, pretending that she didn't feel something ugly twist within her belly at his words. "I've five pounds and a set of gold eardrops. Take them and flee, before someone comes along."

She sounded brave, braver than she felt. She braced herself as the rougher man strode toward her. She knew what the gleam in his eyes promised. This couldn't possibly end well.

Another gunshot sounded, close enough to deafen her. The man stumbled, then fell sideways to the ground.

Her horses bolted. The carriage lurched down the road, picking up speed as the animals panicked. The driver shouted, indistinct under the ringing in her ears. She turned toward the mounted highwayman just as he raised his gun. There was nowhere to run, nothing to protect herself with. She instinctively lifted her arm, shielding her eyes.

Another shot. Something splattered across her skirts. She thought he'd missed. But when she took a step back, she saw the gore.

He'd shot his partner in the face.

She stumbled backward before she could think. Her throat burned, but she didn't register the nausea until she was already retching in the sparse, brittle winter grass. This had nothing to do with how her father had died, but for a moment she saw him lying in the ditch instead, his face mangled and broken.

The man slid off his horse at his colleague's feet. "Turn away," he ordered Ellie, not waiting to see if she obeyed.

She couldn't look away — could prey ever look away from a predator? He flipped the body over with his foot, as though his partner was a bit of rubbish in his way. The body was limp. One of the eyes was gone and the cheek below it was destroyed. The other eye stared sightlessly into the sky.

Then the living highwayman lifted his booted foot and stomped down hard, crushing the skull like it was a softened gourd.

She vomited again.

"My apologies," the highwayman said. She looked up to see him wiping his boot on the grass before mounting his horse. He didn't spare a glance for the body between them. "I will take care not to trouble you again."

His voice was utterly without emotion — surely that wasn't normal? She shuddered, thinking suddenly that all the visions she'd ever had of evil were wrong.

The man veered off into the trees. The hoofbeats faded into the winter silence. She wiped her mouth with her hand and forced herself to breathe. Turning nearly a full circle to her right to avoid seeing the dead man again, she took stock of the road. Her carriage was gone. The dead man's horse grazed, uncaring, in the ditch.

Ellie's breath rasped in her throat. She'd seen death before. She didn't particularly regret this one. But the violence of it, and the way the man's partner had desecrated him, then abandoned him...

She couldn't stay there. She took off at a fast walk, almost a run, cursing her skirts as she hiked them up with one hand. She would have stolen the horse, but she couldn't mount unassisted, and she hadn't ridden a man's saddle since she was in her teens.

So she walked, hoping her carriage would come back for her

before any other travelers found her — hoping the carriage had stayed upright and that the horses didn't kill Lucia or the driver in their panic.

It was nearly five minutes before her carriage returned. "My lady, are you hurt?" the driver cried as he set the brake and leapt from the box.

She shook her head. "Lucia? The horses?"

Lucia opened the carriage door and leapt down without waiting. Her skin was a ghastly shade and her eyes had turned to glass. "Alive, albeit bruised. I shall never ride in a carriage again."

Ellie exhaled. She felt sick again, with her heart pounding furiously and the bile threatening to rise. Her head pounded. She touched her hairline and found a bruise spreading vicious streaks of pain across her scalp. She took a deep breath, then another. But she kept her eyes open, unable to confront the visions painting themselves over and over again in the dark corners of her mind.

"Are you sure you aren't hurt, my lady?" Lucia asked.

"Of course. We won, didn't we?"

Lucia grabbed her shoulders, shaking her lightly, just enough that they both felt how her knees were locked. "You need to sit down, my lady," she said firmly. "Let me…"

If she said anything else, Ellie didn't hear it. Her nausea subsided, but something black rushed to overtake it, and she slid swiftly into the void.

CHAPTER TWELVE

She awoke to pain burrowing relentlessly into her chest. It felt like someone digging into her breastbone in an attempt to steal her heart. She was struggling before she could open her eyes, trying to move away, trying to protest with something other than an incoherent moan.

Her movement stopped the torment. "I'm sorry, Ellie my love," Nick said. "But you must wake up."

She opened her eyes. He knelt on the floor of the carriage — the smaller carriage she had taken to London, not the larger one she had returned in — bending over her with a look that was half worried and half furious, his knuckles still grazing her ribs.

The pain was already fading, but the memory wasn't. "What did you do to me?"

"Chafed your breastbone. You aren't the type to carry a vinaigrette, it seems. But for awakening someone, it's more effective than rubbing your wrists."

Where had he learned that? She shook her head, trying to focus. "What is the urgency? Are we still in danger?"

Nick's lips were a grim line as he shook his head. "I doubt your attacker is still within five leagues of us. Marcus and I were only twenty minutes behind you, but we've no way of knowing where to look for

97

him."

She tried to sit up, but his hands held her down. "Wait a moment. You may be sick."

"Where are Lucia and Marcus?" she asked.

"Lucia refused to ride, but we're less than two miles from Folkestone via the footpaths that cut across the country. She and Marcus are walking back."

"And you let them? Is that safe?"

Nick frowned. "From what Lucia told us, I expect so. I sent my batman with them — Trower was in the army for over a decade, and he can take care of them. But we must decide, before we reach Folkestone, what we plan to say to your guests. I could have decided without you, but..."

"What is there to decide?" she asked, cutting him off. "We must tell the proper authorities. They will want to know there's a dangerous highwayman in the neighborhood."

"What if he's not a highwayman?"

She remembered her own doubts — but how could Nick know of them? "Why would you guess that?"

"What did you see?"

"Before or after he murdered his lackey?"

Nick brushed a piece of hair away from her mouth. "Before. I'll deal with the after."

"He was too well-dressed for a highwayman. He spoke like a gentleman, although that could be an act. The dead one called him 'sir.' And he didn't seem to want our property — he asked who was in the carriage, not what we had."

"Did they say who they expected?"

Ellie shook her head. "They expected a man, though they didn't mention a name. They told the driver he wasn't the man they wanted to kill."

Nick's thumb had been caressing her temple, but he stopped at those words. "You are sure they said they intended to kill someone?"

"I believe so. It was all so fast, but I'm nearly positive of that. Perhaps the driver remembers."

"He is following with your coach. I will question him when we return. Better to do it now, before the details turn hazy."

Ellie tried again to sit up. This time he let her, but he didn't reclaim his seat.

She looked down into his eyes, suddenly curious. "What do you know of investigations?" she asked. "Isn't this a job for the magistrate?"

He didn't respond. He didn't look away — his gaze was as unwavering as ever. But there was darkness there she'd never seen before.

Finally, he said, "I know this was not a random act, if what you remember is true. What I don't know is who is behind it. And that means I don't know whether we can trust the local authorities to investigate properly without making a hash of things."

"Why? The local magistrate is capable enough to bring the man to justice if he can be found. He should hang for what he's done, even if killing his partner might have been good for humanity."

"He didn't kill his partner. A bullet went straight through the man's heart before he was shot in the head. The leader would likely hang anyway, but I care less about him and more about who he's working for."

"My driver killed the highwayman? I didn't think he was such a good shot."

"No doubt he would like to claim responsibility, since he seemed useless as a protector," Nick said, acid lacing through his voice. "But the honors go to your maid."

Ellie gasped. "Lucia killed him? How is she feeling?"

"She's no less calm than you are. She owned up to it like she shoots highwaymen every day, then calmly walked off toward Folkestone without looking back. I'd rather take either of you into battle than the driver, if it comes to that."

His tone sounded like he was joking, but she saw the intensity still lurking in his eyes. "Is this a battle, then?" she asked. "You seem to believe they were trying to kill you, but hardly anyone knows you've returned."

He nodded. "I've been seen in London, but the bulk of people who know I've returned are at Folkestone."

It took no time at all to guess his meaning. She scowled. "You think someone at Folkestone sent those men to murder you."

He held up a placating hand. "I've no proof of that. But they must have been waiting for the Folkestone carriage. It's possible someone in London sent them, but anyone following me in London would have seen that you had taken my coach. It's more likely that someone knew I'd left this morning and seized the opportunity to waylay me."

"And I thought I had no competition in my desire to murder you."

Nick grinned. "I'm sure you were first, if that makes you feel better."

She laughed, but the sound turned into a sigh. "I do hope you're wrong. Both that someone wants to do you violence and that the danger lies on the estate."

Nick glanced out the window, then turned back to Ellie. His frown returned. "We are nearing Folkestone. Do you want to tell everyone what happened? Or can we take a more measured approach?"

She looked down at her skirts. The blood had turned rusty, but it was still visible even in lamplight. "I look a fright. And I'm sure I bruised my head on the carriage."

"It's not visible through your hair. I checked the swelling while you were unconscious. I've already instructed the driver to take us around to the stables. We can avoid the guests, at least. But only if you're comfortable with this."

She could have still been unconscious if he hadn't forced her awake — and then he could have decided for her. "Why do you care what I think?" she asked. "It's your life at stake, if this threat is to be believed."

"It's my life, but I would spare you any further trauma." He took her hands in his. She realized her gloves were missing, and the feel of his skin on hers warmed more than her fingers. "And it's my estate, but you know the people there. If you think they must know, I'll follow your lead."

She tightened her fingers around his. "What happened to the Nick who forced me to become his mistress?"

His grin was mirthless, almost sad. "You will undoubtedly see him again. But this afternoon..."

He trailed off.

"I'm fine, Nick," she said gently.

"You're one woman in a thousand. But even though you can handle yourself doesn't mean I enjoy seeing the aftermath and knowing I deserve the blame."

"You don't deserve the blame," she said. When he started to protest, she overrode him. "You don't, unless everything you've just said is a lie. The blame lies with the attackers — not you, not me, not whatever victim they sought. We still don't know for sure that you are the one in danger. It could have been Marcus they were after, or one of the guests. Or even a different man altogether — perhaps they are only interested in stealing cravat pins and cuff links."

Nick laughed, squeezing her hands. "That's preposterous. But thank you."

She resisted the temptation of that laugh. At least she could still pry one from him, even if she no longer knew what to do with it when she'd won it. Instead, she slipped her hands out of his grasp. "We can keep the highwayman a secret if you prefer. Lucia and the driver — or drivers, since I suppose your driver knows of this as well — won't say a word if I ask them not to."

When she let go of him, he moved to the seat across from hers. "Are you sure?"

His voice was calm, but utterly ruthless.

"Sure of them, or of your plan?" she asked.

"Both, although the plan won't succeed if they fail."

"My servants are discreet. They wouldn't be employed here if they weren't. As for the plan — *do* you have a plan beyond our initial silence?"

He didn't acknowledge the question. "Why are your servants so discreet?"

"I'm a widow, Nick, not a nun. It's best for everyone if my servants don't spread tales."

"And what tales would they spread?"

His jealousy was aroused, even though he had little cause for it. She frowned at how quickly he had changed the subject. "Shouldn't you be more concerned about your potential death than my past sins?"

"I've changed, Ellie my love." His voice dropped, turning into a caress. "Sin interests me more than it used to."

Ellie snorted, breaking the seduction that hovered over her like an executioner's axe. "If you think to lure me into giving you a full confession, you'll have to try harder than that."

He leaned back into the cushions, stretching his legs so that one booted foot stroked her ankle. "I'll find what I want to know in the end. You can depend upon it."

She would have laughed, but seeing the blood on her skirts turned her sober again. "I will help you find the highwayman, no matter what you need of me. But that doesn't change the past."

He didn't respond. He closed his eyes instead, looking like a great general dreaming of battle even though his foot still toyed with hers.

She looked away, staring mostly unseeing out the window until the carriage stopped in front of the Folkestone stables. When she turned from the window, she found Nick watching her again.

He helped her out of the conveyance without a word. When she was on her feet, he looked her over. "Can you walk to your room?" he asked. "You should rest until dinner — Marcus and Lucia won't return in time to discuss everything before then, so we should reconvene tomorrow."

She nodded. "My head hurts, but I can still walk. Are you sure we should wait? I thought you preferred to question people immediately."

"You've been injured — resting will help you more than questions will."

"I'm not an invalid, Nick."

He nodded absently, but didn't let go of her hand. There was a depth to his silence that had nothing to do with the mechanics of an investigation, and a fear in his eyes she had never seen.

Then he brushed his lips across her knuckles. "I meant it too,

Ellie. When I said I missed you."

He strode away, running his hands savagely through his hair like a man who'd narrowly escaped disaster. She sucked in a breath, wishing she knew her own heart, wishing she knew what was possible and what was not.

She hadn't been brave enough at nineteen to explore possibilities. She had been a coward, and a fool, and so desperate for her father's approval that she had believed the story he had told her about familial duty and social responsibilities.

But that past was over. If Ellie hadn't been brave at nineteen, she would make up for it now. And while she had no intention of letting Nick back into her heart, she would make sure he survived his homecoming — whether he ever recognized her actions or not.

CHAPTER THIRTEEN

Dinner that night was not the glittering success Ellie was accustomed to hosting. For one, her head still ached, even though the bruise was smaller than she had expected. It seemed to throb in time with the grating titters of the ladies around her. They hung on Nick's every word like he was a Hottentot curiosity whose kind they had never seen before. They wouldn't snub him — only a fool would snub money *and* a title — but they wouldn't stop examining him, either.

Which meant, of course, that none of them missed the way he watched her, or the way she ignored him. She should have flirted like he was any other male, but she was too raw for flirtation. She flirted with Norbury instead. He was amenable to it, but the concerned look in his eyes said he knew what she was doing.

So by the time Ellie could take refuge in her bed — perhaps her final night alone, if Nick held true to his plan — she was in no mood for sleep. Not a single word had been said about highwaymen at dinner, but she wasn't ready to dream about them. Instead, she let another maid prepare her for bed, since she had ordered Lucia to rest after their ordeal. As soon as the woman was gone, Ellie threw a cloak over her delicate peignoir and nightgown and took the servants' stairs up to the former nursery.

The rooms had once housed the scions of the Claiborne family, including Nick and Marcus's father. But with no children in residence and no plans to produce any, she had taken over. The long windows lining the south wall would have provided ample light for childhood lessons, but they were even better for painting.

Not that she'd painted anything that had pleased her in an age. Nor could she paint tonight, not without lighting every lamp and candle in the house. But she also couldn't sleep — not when she saw the highwayman's ruined skull when she closed her eyes.

She carried a taper with her and lit the lamps that hung on the walls. There had been fires in the grates earlier in the day, as there always were to protect the paintings in the room. But now they were banked, and the snow that had begun to fall outside no longer melted on contact with the windowpanes. She was glad for her cloak now, even though she would inevitably cast it aside, unthinking, as she sketched.

The blank canvas on her easel taunted her. She turned away from it to stand at her work table. There were great sheets of foolscap there, places for her to test her inspirations before committing them to canvas. She chewed on the end of her pencil, considering.

Wasn't she beyond Nick as a subject? After the last time, she'd vowed not to paint him again. But those vows had failed before, and the neat row of canvases leaning against the far wall mocked her. She'd last given in four months earlier — surely she could withstand the temptation.

Temptation. She'd once thought she would be tempted to murder Nick when he came home. One of her first paintings after he left was a shamelessly derivative copy of Jacques-Louis David's "Death of Marat," with Nick taking Marat's place in the bath and Ellie herself, added as a vengeful Fury, wielding the knife.

But there had been whole months when she'd managed to keep him out of her thoughts. It was only the past year, seeing her brother find such happiness with Madeleine, that had brought everything back. She hadn't come to Folkestone since Ferguson's wedding. Painting there, in a room that might have held her children, was enough to make her ache.

She pushed back the tide of memory and sketched. If she took Lucia's advice and tried to make a living from her art, it would have to be more commercial than this. But she would be damned before she painted other families' portraits, even if they sold better than more experimental fare. And thoughts of money could wait until she knew just how far Nick would go in his bid for revenge.

Her pencil flew across the paper in swift, sure strokes, with less hesitation than she'd felt at her work in weeks. She usually preferred working from myths instead of fairy tales, but for some reason, the old French tale of Persinette called to her. On paper, the tower took shape, rising up from a dense and twisted forest. A woman stood in the window at the top of the tower, in profile, her face just barely recognizable. The full moon peeked from behind a shroud of storm clouds to glint off her impossibly long plait of hair.

In pencil, there were no colors, but Ellie knew how she would paint it — dark, and tempestuous, with the woman's red hair as a beacon. Her beauty would lure the prince to her tower, and her hair was the key to her prison. But they were destined to pay a terrible price for their love, wandering apart for years before finding each other again.

She chewed on her pencil again, her hand starting to cramp after half an hour of unrelieved sketching. Nick wasn't in the painting — and yet he *was* the painting. She didn't want it to be an omen. But her art was the one part of her life, other than Nick, that she couldn't fully control.

She heard footsteps outside the door, both too heavy and too hesitant to be a servant. She flipped over the paper, then bowed her head like a child hoping to avoid a storm, leaning forward over her sketch as though compressing her size might keep anyone from violating her private space.

She failed. The door opened. "I thought it might be you," Nick said behind her.

She turned. "Why are you here?"

The door closed. He turned the key in the lock, barring the door as she should have done. "I heard movement up here, but knew it wasn't the servants' quarters — I'd heard nothing last night or this morning to suggest this section was inhabited."

"I would say I'm sorry for disturbing your sleep, but you should have stayed where I put you."

"You knew better than to expect that."

She scowled. "You shouldn't wander alone at night if you're in danger. What if I had been your murderer?"

He held up his walking stick. "I thought of that. This isn't a dandy's affectation."

"And if he had a gun?"

Nick patted his pocket.

"Dare I ask if you have any other weapons? Perhaps a broadsword in your trousers?"

He grinned, slow and satisfied. "You can conduct as thorough a search as you like, my lady."

She blushed. She always meant her innuendoes now, but this one wasn't planned, and it somehow embarrassed her.

"Your…weaponry is no concern of mine."

Her attempt to regain control, to play the jade, fell on deaf ears. He set his walking stick aside and carefully laid his jacket — and the gun it presumably carried — on the chair where she'd thrown aside her cloak in the heat of her drawing. "What are you painting these days? Flowers still, or have you moved on to trees?"

She'd painted endless flowers when she was eighteen, for want of any other models on the estate where her father had dumped her. "I've more varied subjects now," she said, leaning back against her worktable.

She crossed her arms as she watched him walk around her studio. She almost ordered him to leave. She rarely invited anyone inside, except the maids who lit the fires and swept the floors. But the part of her that didn't want his scrutiny couldn't override the part of her that hoped, stupidly, for his praise.

He clasped his hands behind him, his shirtsleeves rippling over the bunched muscles of his back. The first time they had made love, when she had still lived in the country, was after he had sacrificed an entire day to play her model. It had been illicit, exhilarating, and utterly forbidden — but her governess had been sick with pneumonia, and didn't know that Ellie had given up painting flowers in favor of something altogether more dangerous…

She shifted and pressed her nails into her palms. *Forget, forget,* she chanted to herself.

He was quiet as he walked around the room. Some of her paintings hung on the walls, but he gave those only a cursory glance. It was her failed efforts, leaning frameless and unloved against the walls, that drew his gaze.

"What will you do with these?" he asked, craning his neck to examine one that sat on its side.

"Paint over them, if I'm ever in need of canvas."

He kept walking. She forced herself to stay still, to not turn and watch his progress, as though she wasn't trying to read every reaction on his face. She hoped he would keep moving, that his knowledge of mythology would fail him, that he wouldn't see himself in the canvasses where her will had broken and her heart had bled into the paint.

But she knew, somehow, when her hopes were dashed. His steps stopped. A floorboard creaked as he shifted his weight, perhaps to lean forward and see a painting more closely in the dim light. The silence stretched on, endless. She was sure she'd already cut crescents into her skin, but she dug her nails deeper into her arms, feigning oblivion.

"I'd have brought manacles up with me if I'd known you wanted them," he said.

If she had blushed before, this was an inferno. She'd had more suggestive conversations — why should this be any different?

"Artistic folly, nothing more," she said.

"Did Odysseus have to be chained to do Circe's bidding?" he asked. She could almost hear his head tilt to examine the painting from a fresh angle. "If Circe had your hair, I vow Odysseus would have been lost immediately, chains or no."

In the painting, Circe *did* have Ellie's hair. Why had she painted Nick as the legendary hero and herself as the goddess who enslaved him? She should have burned it years ago.

She squeezed her eyes shut. "The painting was an interesting exercise, but I doubt the market would have it."

"I don't know. I find myself quite…moved."

His voice could cast a spell as seductive as anything Circe might have tried. She finally turned to face him. "Why are you here, Nick? I know it's your house — your right. But why now?"

He still looked at the painting. It was too late to burn it, even if her blush could set it alight. In a distant voice, he said, "I came back to find a murderer. I shouldn't have disturbed you tonight, Ellie."

"Haven't we always disturbed each other?"

Her voice was low. His answer was even lower. "Always. The gods could not have devised a more perfect punishment than you."

"Punishment? For what?"

His spine stiffened. "For wanting you. For having you. It never ends well, mortals falling in love with goddesses."

She shivered. "I'm no goddess."

He turned. "To me you were. Are. Still. I thought you'd have fallen to earth by now. But when I walked into your party last night and saw you, even more beautiful than before…"

She curled her fingers on the edge of her worktable. "You know I've fallen to earth. I'm not an innocent anymore."

"It had nothing to do with innocence. Unless you regret losing it?"

"I didn't lose it — I gave it to you," she said. "Do you regret taking it?"

He closed his eyes. His hands were still behind his back. Circe might have held him like that, awaiting her pleasure. Somewhere, swirling through the moment, Ellie felt a bolt of pure, possessive lust. She wanted him to want her, with something savage driving her to make him say it — even if they both might have been happier forgetting.

"I've never regretted it," he said. "Even if losing you was inevitable."

She didn't like that word. It hung between them, frozen and

immutable in the chilled air. She wanted fire, not ice — the present, not the past.

Her hair was wrapped around her head for sleep. She removed the pins, catching Nick's gaze as she did so. She set each pin on the table, but his eyes never left hers. Her braids fell to her waist. She threaded her fingers through the plaits, unraveling them. Her hair would be a riot, messy and bold — the way he liked it.

She had hacked it all off when he left, but she was glad to have it back.

She shook her hair out, and she didn't miss how his mouth tightened. She could have him again. Starting tomorrow, he would demand it — but she could have him tonight, on her terms. She sensed it in the way he watched her, hope battling avoidance. She'd learned that pleasure didn't last — but he tempted her as she hadn't been tempted in years.

"Do you know why I painted you?" she asked, coming around the work table.

He stayed still, his hands behind his back, denying himself as she came to stand in front of him. "Trouble finding models better than me?"

She laughed. The low seduction in his voice thrilled her — told her she could have this. *They* could have this.

"Perhaps." She stroked his arm, felt his muscles jump for her. "You were my first, after all."

"Shall I thank you for the honor?"

Ellie shook her head. "I should thank you. Without you, I might never have known what was…possible from a perfect match."

"You're not talking of painting, are you."

It wasn't a question. She felt the moment start to slip, to veer into territory she wasn't ready to explore.

She sighed. "Are you willing to let me seduce you or not?"

His breath hitched. With his shadow of stubble and his missing cravat, he looked like a man startled out of — or into — a delicious dream.

She almost wanted to hang the seduction and paint him instead. But when he reached for her, life became preferable to art.

Their kiss was something they had been born for. If there was anything inevitable, it was how well they fit together — how even after all this time and anyone else who'd come between them, they still knew exactly how to match each other. There was no awkward misalignment, no accidental scraping of teeth. It was like a ballet arranged just for them. They knew their parts by heart. She was hungry for him, desperately so — hungry for that feeling of perfect symmetry, of two halves brought together in a way that never failed to thrill her artist's soul.

If she was hungry, he was ravenous. His fingers dug into her hair, changed the angle of their kiss. She skimmed hers down his torso, resting them on his slim hips, her thumbs seeking the indentations in his pelvis.

"This isn't a good idea," he murmured against her lips when they came up for air.

She untied his shirt and pushed it up, until he was forced to pull it over his head. "Then why did you come here?"

He brushed his hands across her shoulders and pushed her sleeves down her arms. Her peignoir fell around the sash at her waist. "Don't remember. Doesn't matter."

"Then forget that this is ill-advised. I already have."

He picked her up suddenly. She laughed into his chest, her

sleeves trailing behind them. "The only bit I regret is that we aren't near a bed," he said.

"You know we don't need a bed. But I do wish it were warmer."

He kissed the top of her hair. "Care to risk a dash to my chamber?"

She paused. The moment started to slip again, threatened like a bubble that would be destroyed by the merest brush with reality. She wanted to stay inside it, where everything was perfectly iridescent. There was no way this could end well.

Forget, she told herself.

"There's a cushioned bench near the far fireplace," she said. "I'll trust you to keep me warm."

The room was long enough for two fireplaces, but the other half, where she hadn't lit any lamps, was full of shadows. He carried her there easily, as though for all her height she weighed nothing.

But when he set her down, she heard the same hesitation in his voice that threatened to break her. "Are you sure you want this?" he asked. "I won't be offended if your head hurts or you're too...cold to continue."

It sounded like part hope, part dare. She pulled him toward the backless couch. "I want this. And so do you."

CHAPTER FOURTEEN

They were the words she'd used a lifetime ago, just before his control had finally broken — before he'd lost himself in her, in a fit of what he'd thought was momentary madness but he later learned was permanent affliction. He couldn't deny her then, all that fragile hope in her voice and unwavering yearning in her eyes.

Now, with her delicate jasmine perfume and oil paints mingling again in the air, he was just as lost. When she nudged him toward the bench, he sat on the edge of it, oddly uncomfortable to be seated while she still stood. But she put her hands on his shoulders, keeping him there.

"You always worshipped me, didn't you?" she asked.

The candles from the other side of the room lit her from behind. Her hair was a corona of flame brighter than any golden-haloed icons he'd seen in his travels. She untied her sash and let her peignoir slip to her feet. Her white nightgown, primly diaphanous, was nearly transparent in the light. He ached for her already, even though worshipping her was madness, even though taking her again — without revenge as a cloak over his desires — would ultimately drive another dagger through his heart.

He should say that he hadn't worshipped her. The lie was tripping its way down his tongue, ready to part his lips so it could slip out and

115

slap her. But the memory of her bloodied skirts stopped him.

What if this was the last night they ever had? He'd thought they had already had their last real night, without threats or regrets, a lifetime ago, but now that another presented itself...what if they never had another? If the man who wanted him dead found them — if Nick survived and she did not — could he forgive himself if their last moments were tainted by lies?

That thought was enough to overcome all the times he'd told himself, on the rickshaws, ships, and horses between his faraway life and her present beauty, that he would resist her. Need and memory flooded into the empty places in his heart where all his resolve had vanished.

"Yes," he said. "I always worshipped you."

Ellie sighed. Then she kissed him on the forehead, a sweet benediction. "Did you know I worshipped you, too?"

He clasped her hands in his. "You thought you worshipped me. It happens, the first time..."

She curled her fingers into fists within his grasp. "Let me show you how I felt. Then tell me whether you'd call it worship or something else."

"I don't want your worship. I never did."

She sighed. There was something fragile in that sound, like a hidden flaw in a stone — outwardly unbreakable, but easy to crack with just a touch in the wrong place.

"I never wanted your worship either," she said. She stepped into the space between his feet and cradled his face in her hands, her thumbs brushing his temples. "But I can't stop wanting you, even if I know it's suicide."

They'd both feinted, hesitated, tried to give the other the chance to leave — but when her mouth met his, their kiss sealed all the exits, burnt all the bridges between what they should have done and what they chose to do instead. Or maybe it wasn't a choice. Nick didn't think he believed in reincarnation, but if he did, he knew he was born to love Ellie over and over again...

...and born to lose her. He put a hand on the back of her head, leaned up to kiss her more thoroughly, let her soft moan drown out his dark thoughts of loss. He knew what they were destined for — but tonight he could pretend otherwise.

Once that decision was made, it was easy to kiss her, to want her, to worship her. Her hair tumbled through his fingers, a blissful tangle of silk. Her lips molded to his. Her jasmine perfume enveloped him. In the thousands of days he'd spent in Indian marketplaces, she'd haunted him — one whiff of the flower and he'd half expect to see her.

Now that he had her, he broke away from the kiss and pulled her down into his lap. She wrapped her arms around him, tried to kiss him again, but he pulled away and inhaled.

"God, Ellie, I still want you," he said. "Even after everything you've done."

Her eager hands, which had been burning a path down his sides to the waistband of his trousers, came up to his face. When he retreated from her hair to look into her eyes, he was struck by the ferocity there — a depth of resolve that gave the lie to proclamations that women were the weaker sex.

"You can do anything you want with your anger tomorrow," she said. "You bought that right with your financial games. But tonight — if you want tonight — we don't talk of the past."

The past. Ellie was the past, a past that obsessed him and consumed him. He couldn't forgive her.

But she wasn't asking for a future, or even a better tomorrow than the one he threatened to give her. She was asking for the present.

And his body was more than ready to oblige.

Ellie felt the moment when he honored her request, even before he voiced it. Some desire in his blue eyes flared, a hunger that matched her own. But there was strain, too — as though the idea of ignoring the past, even for a night, was so foreign to him that he didn't know how to start.

But where he had mastered the art of obsession, Ellie had become an expert at oblivion.

"Close your eyes, Nick. Pretend we met at a masquerade, both masked. Not everything has to be about us."

He didn't respond. But even though he didn't throw the past in her face and say that it *was* all about them, she sensed his disagreement.

Stubborn man. "Stop thinking," she urged. "I promise you, it works."

She kissed him again before she could take back the lie. She'd never learned how to put away her memories and regrets forever, just ways to silence them. Endless painting sessions, extravagant parties, a handful of lovers — nothing had healed her, but she'd taken the snippets of peace they'd offered.

He growled as he pulled away. "You're thinking too. I know when you're distracted."

That surprised a laugh out of her. "I'll stop if you kiss me again."

He reached down to the floor, groping for something. She realized what he wanted the instant before he found it — the long, wide green sash from her peignoir.

She arched a brow. "Want to play Odysseus to my Circe?"

Nick snorted. "Some other lifetime, darling." He pulled the sash tight, testing its strength. "There's only one way this will work."

"Death by strangulation is not how I envisioned my end."

"If I strangle you, I'll use my hands. But we can't look into each other's eyes without remembering who we are."

She reached for the sash. "I wanted to show you how I worshipped you — even easier if I make you feel it rather than seeing it."

He dodged her and had the first length wrapped around her eyes before she could stop him. "Not tonight. You have four months to pleasure me. Take my generosity tonight and let me pleasure you."

Four months to pleasure him. Those words left her part ashamed, part enthralled. Not ashamed that he'd tricked her into it — ashamed that, for all that she was looking to save her soul from him, her body wanted to stay.

"You're right," she said, her fingers scrabbling to pull the sash away from her face. "This won't work."

"Shh," he said, pulling the silk tight and tying it behind her head. "Don't think. It's good advice, even if you lied about the ease of taking it."

The darkness heightened her hearing. She detected a note of humor in his voice, like a secret spice in a rich sauce, adding balance to something that might otherwise have overwhelmed her. It wasn't lost on her that she would look something like Lady Justice — another painting she'd done, on another night when her will had failed. Did Nick see her as a judge? Or a supplicant for his favor?

He'd have four months to treat her as a supplicant. She crossed her arms and wished she could stare him down. "Make this good, Claiborne."

He laughed. "Always."

His breath grazed her ear. His lips pressed against her throat.

She arched away, her usual sensitivity enhanced by the imbalance of not knowing what he planned. His hands slid down her arms and his calluses caught on her gooseflesh. But she wasn't cold, despite the chilled air. She was a fire he had stoked, suddenly, to life — all the coals she had banked when he'd left her suddenly flared, ready to ignite them both.

His leg swung out from under her and he shifted her off his lap. "On your knees, darling."

She felt the chaise shift as he moved away, heard the creak of floorboards as he stood beside her. The image her mind painted, replacing what she couldn't see, was dark and erotic — a harem girl kneeling, serving a sultan who stood before her like a god.

She shivered as she came to her knees on the bench. These weren't the games she played with her lovers. She was always the goddess, and they were always the mortals she deigned to spend an evening with.

"Cold?" he asked, his voice losing that erotic thread as concern replaced it.

She clenched her hands into fists. "No, not cold. Are you going to do this, or should I go to bed alone?"

Another creak of ancient wood. His hand took her fist and brought her fingers up to his mouth. They uncurled reflexively as he kissed her knuckles. "Patience," he murmured.

Oblivion didn't allow for patience. Her fist curled again, but with his fingers still holding hers, it became a gesture of tenderness instead of aggression.

His free hand brushed her hair to the side. He kissed her neck, right where it met her shoulder. She heard him inhale, and there was something sharp about the way he breathed her in. He dropped her hand, then slid the sleeve of her nightrail down her arm, as far as it would go without removing it entirely. He trailed kisses across the newly revealed expanse of skin, wrapping her hair around his fist to hold her still as his mouth explored. He was slow — achingly, frustratingly slow. She wanted everything, but his pace made it too easy to remember.

"Damn your patience, Nick," she said, reaching for the sash that blinded her. "You don't have to take your time anymore. I know what comes next now."

His grip on her hair tightened, but he didn't rise to the bait. "If you take it off, we are done."

She hesitated. He dropped a hand to her breast, a sudden assault that made her suck in a breath. She fit perfectly in his palm. Her nipple tightened and she squirmed beneath him, wanting him to drop her hair and take her other breast, wanting the perfect symmetry of his touch to envelop her.

But he denied her. His other hand stayed firmly in her hair, a treasure he couldn't part with. The hand that roved, seeking more, abandoned her bosom and skimmed over her ribs. His arm wrapped around her waist, catching her firmly up against him.

This time, he angled her head and his lips found her mouth — another move she hadn't anticipated. It was a kiss she could drown in, a kiss that awoke her body and the fast-beating, treacherous heart she'd locked away so well. His lips knew her. His hands, in her hair, on her body, sculpted the contours of her soul rather than mere bits of flesh. With others, she was cool, remote — a guarded citadel. With him, every touch was lightning, every stroke of his tongue bringing the thunder of her own heart as her walls tumbled down.

"Nick," she murmured as he pulled away.

"Still want to stop?"

She'd forgotten his ultimatum. "No. Just...don't make me wait forever."

He chuckled as he smoothed a bit of hair away from her face. "I can't even if I wanted to."

His hands had left her as he said this. She mourned the fading imprint of his hand on her torso and the disappearing sensation of his fingers pulling through her hair.

But he didn't leave her alone in the dark. Something unfurled in her belly as he caught her up, his arm snaking under her derriere to lift her slightly off the bench. He dropped her again an instant later, but he had rearranged her nightgown, and her bare knees made direct contact with the subtly textured cushion.

She groped for his waist, tracing her fingers along his skin until she found the fastenings of his trousers. But as before, he stopped her. "Stop rushing, darling," he said.

Then he dropped to his knees. Her hands, which moments before had nearly grazed his erection, came to rest on his shoulders instead. His palms slid up her thighs, pulling her nightgown up.

The painting in her mind remade itself. The serving girl became a queen; the sultan, a captive king, brought in to pay obeisance.

"Are you sure you aren't Odysseus?" she asked, her voice shaky as his hands reached her waist. He could see all of her, laid bare before him, while she could see nothing of the thoughts on his face.

His thumbs caressed her, tracing a path to her navel. "Only if you're Penelope, not Circe. Now hush, or you'll miss the best part."

She wanted to be his Penelope, the woman he'd fought the world to come home to. But she was no faithful wife. And his craftiness was Odyssean in its brilliance — but aimed toward revenge, not love.

He kissed her belly. "Stop thinking." Then he kissed her inner thigh. The shadowed stubble of his cheek rubbed against her skin and made her shiver.

He kissed her other thigh. "Give in, Ellie. For five minutes, if you can't give me an entire night."

His words bound her to him, to the moment — to a world of darkness and brocade and his clever, clever mouth.

"Yes," she whispered. She bowed her head as though to look at him, and her hair fell over her breasts. "Always yes."

His mouth found her most private place, a dark echo of every kiss he'd given her in every lifetime that had come before. She pressed against him, wanting it, wanting him — wanting to see the contrast of his black hair against her pale skin. But in the dark, all she could have was the feel of his tongue and the heat of his mouth.

Surely he would burn her with it. He'd never done this to her before, not all those years ago when he treated her like a fragile statue he feared breaking. She gasped as he licked her — gasped again as he sucked the bud where all her pleasure was centered. Her hands found his head, burying themselves in his hair — part demand, part plea.

He responded in kind, wrapping an arm around her thighs, trapping her against him so she couldn't move away. Every stroke of his tongue was a welcome torture. She throbbed as though her heart beat for him between her legs. She leaned back, not to escape — to admit that here, now, all that mattered was the point where their hungers fused them together.

Nick knew, somehow, what she needed — remembered the tempo she craved, even if he'd used his hands instead of his tongue when he'd taken her in the past. His strokes were sure, slowly building in speed; his arm was an iron band, as inescapable as any dream she'd had of him. She leaned even further back, until the strain in her thighs added to her need, until her hair fell free behind her. She couldn't see, couldn't analyze light and shadow and color.

Couldn't search for darkness in Nick's eyes.

Her mind gave her what her eyes could not — a swirl of color threaded through with the heat of his mouth and the texture of brocade. Her fingers tightened in his hair as her need approached pain. But he held her just on the edge of the pinnacle he'd built for her, turning all that pleasure he'd offered her into a brand that scorched her soul.

"Nick — please," she moaned, trying to urge him on.

His arm tightened around her, and for a breathtaking moment she thought he would stop. But even his revenge wasn't that cold. His free hand found her derriere, caressing her, pulling her closer — tilting her just an inch, just enough to give him a fresh angle.

She came apart then. Everything disintegrated in a violent blast of heat. Her heart shuddered; her legs trembled. Without his arm around her thighs, she might have fallen. Her mouth fell open, but she swallowed her scream as he'd taught her, back when they were young and she still had chaperones.

As she fell from the peak, as her legs stopped quivering and her pulse slowed, the past caught up with her. She reached for her blindfold, wanting to see Nick as he was now — wanting to see whether there was any emotion in his eyes that matched the beat of her damnable heart.

"Not yet," he murmured, breaking away from her skin to catch her hand.

He swept her off her knees and onto her back. The old Nick would have checked her comfort, touched her softly, kissed her slowly — made sure she was ready.

The new Nick didn't ask permission. He plunged into her

moments later, and she gasped as the force of it rocked her back against the bench. His trousers, softer than the brocade beneath her, brushed against her thighs. He'd waited only long enough to free himself before taking her.

The depth of his need for her shocked her — a depth she couldn't anticipate when all she'd felt was the deliberate, calculated seduction of his tongue. But he wasn't deliberate now. He surged again. She slid a hand down his back, under the waistband of his trousers, settling on the firm muscle of his backside to urge him on. He found her breast with a heavy hand, more conquest than caress. She moaned under him as he sank into her — moaned again as he took her free hand in his. She might have found the gesture sweet if their fingers twined together. But he grabbed her wrist instead, pinning her arm above her head as he sunk into her again.

He was claiming her, not loving her.

And she would damn herself later for letting him — but at that moment, she didn't care.

He leaned in to her ear. His unshaved cheek rasped against hers. "Beg me, Ellie."

He withdrew his cock as she hesitated, until only the tip remained. "Tell me you want me," he whispered, flicking his thumb across her linen-covered nipple. "Tell me you've always wanted me."

She arched up to him, wanting him to fill her. "Nick — it was always you. Please…please, Nick. Don't leave me again."

His hand crushed her wrist as she said more than he'd asked for — more than she wanted to reveal. Her words fell apart as he rewarded her, driving into her with a force that could make her believe he was just as lost as she was. Three more strokes and she came again, her body rising off the couch like she was possessed. But she couldn't move far, not when he still held her pinned. The torment of wanting to touch him, to see him, when he denied her, added an edge to her climax, sending her faster and harder into the void.

She sensed, as she slowly returned to her body, that he was about to join her. She felt the tension in his back where she still stroked him — heard his harsh breathing as he fought for control. But he didn't bury himself — didn't succumb to temptation as she clenched around him. He withdrew with a groan that went straight to her heart and spent himself on her belly.

Ellie squeezed her eyes shut beneath her sash as he collapsed, half on her, half on the couch. She told herself she didn't care — he almost always withdrew, a wise precaution. He had only spilled inside her once before — when they'd first made love, before her father denied his proposal. Still, as his seed cooled on her skin, she felt deflated, somehow — like the dream he'd given her in the dark could only turn sordid in the light.

By the time Nick could breathe again, he'd already lost her to her thoughts. He knew it from the way she tensed under him — a small, defenseless thing retracting into its shell. Ellie would skewer anyone who saw her as defenseless, and even among the Amazons she wouldn't be small. But his old protective instincts rushed forth, wanting to save her, to make things good for her.

Even though it went against all his plans for her. And even though he was the greatest danger she faced.

He tried to remind himself to be ruthless, as ruthless as she had been when she broke their engagement. But he couldn't quite bring himself to leave her lying there alone. His mouth refused to utter some callous quip meant to wound her. Instead, he pulled the sash away from her eyes.

She looked up at him. All the emotions he'd wanted to wring from her were there, reflected in sapphire. Desperation. Need. Regret. Fathomless pools of regret, so deep that he knew, then, how much she'd missed him — how deep she'd excavated into the core of her own heart, letting the acid of memory eat away everything else.

Did his eyes look the same? Had he given away as much as she had — shown anything beyond the ruthlessness he wanted her to see?

Don't leave me again. She didn't repeat the words, but they hung between them as though the sound had turned to resin, trapping them within it like flies in amber. He'd made her beg — and taken a fierce, visceral satisfaction from hearing his name break on her lips — but he hadn't expected that.

They couldn't stay preserved in this moment forever, though. If she'd taught him anything, it was that nothing lasted — not promises, not love, and certainly not a perfect half hour of pleasure.

He rolled off the couch and stood beside her. He adjusted himself and refastened his trousers, but she stayed still, unashamed, her gown hiked up to her ribs and her legs splayed as though closing them would prove the moment was over. He wanted her again already — might have damned his revenge and made love to her, slower this time, the way she used to like it — but she shivered. The room was still cold, even though he hadn't noticed while he was inside her.

"Stay there," he ordered. He strode across the studio and retrieved her cloak, along with the handkerchief in his coat pocket. She sat up when he returned, looking dazed, but he nudged her back down and used his cloth to clean his seed from her skin.

"Apologies for that," he said as he dropped his handkerchief and helped her stand. "Next time I'll be ready with a cloth."

Her nightgown falling back into place cut the final thread of their dream. Her eyes narrowed and annoyance layered over her regret until he could almost believe she'd never cared for him at all. "Thank you for reminding me of my debt," she said. "I'm sure my comfort was not part of our agreement."

If she wanted cold, he'd give it to her. "I'm a man of business. You will perform better if you are well fed, well rested, well groomed, and put through your paces at appropriate intervals."

She'd been twisting her hair into a messy knot, but she dropped it and glared at him. "I'm not a racehorse, Nick."

He scooped her peignoir up from the floor and handed it to her. "You cost more than one. Don't be surprised that I feel a bit proprietary."

"If I could throw you right now, I vow I would," she muttered, slipping her arms into her robe and finding her sash to tie it shut.

"I'm sure you'll be too tame to throw me by the time your debt is repaid."

Ellie glared at him, but took her cloak from his hand like he was a gentleman rather than a scoundrel. "Thank you for deigning to pleasure me tonight. If no woman will marry you — and really, who would? — I'm sure there's a whole host of widows who would pay for that tongue of yours."

She was trying to shock him. He smiled thinly. "If you want to keep paying for it after you've settled your debt, I'll entertain your offer. But let's not get ahead of ourselves, darling."

She tossed her hair back. "Unlike you, I've never had to pay for a bed partner. Now, if you're quite done insulting me, I shall take my leave. You can show yourself out, if you know your house well enough to find your way."

She swept out, her slippers dampening the rage he heard in her steps. He waited until he no longer heard her, until the house was silent around him — or as silent as an old house could be, creaking and shuddering as the temperature fell and an icy wind beat against the windowpanes. It was too cold to stay there, when a featherbed and a warming pan waited for him downstairs. His blood no longer found joy in winter, not after an endless summer in India.

But he put on his shirt, shrugged into his jacket, and returned to the paintings that lined the walls. Ellie confused him at every turn — one moment making him think she'd always loved him, the next claiming that she could never love anyone at all. Not that he blamed her; his thoughts were just as confused. Perhaps, in this life, there would never be clarity between them.

But after tonight, he realized there were two places where he might glimpse the real truth, the one she hid even from herself: in her paintings, made when she never expected him to return, and in his arms as she came undone.

He'd have endless time to exploit her weakness for him in bed. But her paintings — she might move or destroy them, especially after he'd recognized himself in her painting of Odysseus.

So in the candlelight, alone, he explored her.

And hoped that somehow, on some canvas, he might discover why she had given him up.

CHAPTER FIFTEEN

The next morning, at an unfashionably early hour, Nick asked one of the footmen where to find his study. He had arranged to meet Ellie, Marcus, and Ellie's maid in hopes that they might solve the issue of the highwayman discreetly and with minimal bloodshed. Not that he wanted to see Ellie in such circumstances — not after the pleasure, and confusion, of the previous night. But when Nick found his study, he wished he hadn't.

"Bloody hell," he muttered as he came to a sudden stop in the center of the doorway. Studies were supposed to be male preserves, all dark wood and handsomely-bound leather books. This was...this was...

"Do you like it?" Ellie said as she came up the hall behind him. "I redecorated last year."

"It's..."

There were no words.

She slipped past where he stood rooted to the floor and claimed the seat behind the desk. Then she gasped, hugely and artificially, with a hand pressed to her heart as though she were an untrained Covent Garden actress. "Oh my, this is your desk now, isn't it, Lord Folkestone? How tactless of me."

But she didn't stand to give way. And he didn't want her to.

The study was an affront to everything masculine — but she was somehow even more beautiful when her blue eyes were lit up with smug satisfaction. And they were certainly lit up now, as he reacted to what she had done to the room. Even her own salon, the one where he had proposed their unholy bargain on his first night in the house, was more masculine than this. His father had told him that the study, at least when it had belonged to Nick's paternal grandfather, had held hunting trophies, ancient furnishings, and comfortable leather chairs for reading.

There were no comfortable chairs now — just a few tufted hassocks in varying shades of lavender. He walked into the room, pretending it wasn't utterly ridiculous. The walls were hung with a soft pink damask. The desk was white and gold, with curved legs better suited to a French boudoir than an English gentleman's retreat. The only welcome sight was the whisky decanter on one shelf — even Ellie's hatred of him wouldn't make her banish spirits from the room.

"I will say, Lady Folkestone, your color choices surprise me. I believe I prefer the palette you used in your painting of Circe — even with the chains."

He couldn't tell if she blushed or if the pinkness of the room had blinded him. Either way, she smiled. "I hope you're always so approving of my artistic efforts."

It was only when her eyes flickered toward the fireplace that he took a closer look at the painting above the mantel. It was the first canvas she'd ever painted of him, if he was not mistaken — and he had always hoped that the silly, besotted look on his face was due to her previous inexperience with human models, not because he actually looked at her like that.

But the painting was different than he remembered. Before, he'd held a book, half-falling from his hand in a negligible pose. Now, the hand still stretched down — to pet a poodle with a giant pink bow that perfectly matched the wall hangings.

"A poodle?" he choked out

"Shall I ring for tea?" she asked, ignoring him. "Lucia should be down momentarily. I can only assume your brother will do your bidding as he always does."

"I detest poodles."

She stood and tugged the frilly lavender cord that served as a bellpull. "Again, an artist's license. If you had given word that you were coming home, I would have replaced it. Perhaps I could have you pat Marcus's head instead? Or does he work for gold, not affection?"

Marcus strode into the study in time to hear her words. "Ellie, I am truly sorry," he said, with the resigned voice of a man who knew his apology would go unheard.

She waved a hand. "It was my fault for forgetting you were a Claiborne. I should have expected you to bring me to grief."

Nick watched her sit again. She was prickly this morning, with all her armor in place. In this mood, with those blue eyes sparking instead of softening, he could almost believe that the previous night had been another one of his dreams.

But this wasn't the woman he dreamed of. A footman arrived and she sent him for tea, then turned her daggered gaze back on Nick and Marcus. "If you don't mind, let us postpone any more words until my poor maid arrives. I am sure she is just as eager to know why she was forced to kill a man as I am."

"And as I am," Marcus said, shooting a dark look at Nick. "Mrs. Grafton should never have been in such danger."

"Should I have been?" Ellie asked.

Marcus colored slightly. "Of course not. But Mrs. Grafton deserves better."

Nick sighed. Ellie looked like she wanted to draw blood, but he needed his brother and his — whatever Ellie was to him — to stay away from each other's throats. "Let us take Ellie's suggestion," he interjected. "The explanation should wait until we are all assembled."

He didn't understand why Ellie had insisted on her maid's presence. It was nearly as unusual as Marcus's concern for the woman. But then, Lucia *had* shot a man, and it was likely Nick's fault she had been forced to do it.

The silence turned uncomfortable immediately. Ellie folded her hands in her lap and stared straight ahead. Marcus leaned against the mantel, not looking at anyone, and wound his watch with the slow, methodical grace of an assassin awaiting an opportunity. Nick eyed the whisky decanter. But even in that room, with two people who might wish him just as dead as his unknown enemy did, Nick still thought it was too early for a drink.

And so he was relieved when Lucia and the tea cart arrived at the same time. "I am sorry for keeping you waiting, my lady," Lucia said. "I had to finish the task you gave me."

She didn't apologize to the men — didn't even acknowledge them as she walked directly to Ellie and handed her two sheets of paper. Ellie nodded as she took the papers. "Of course, Mrs. Grafton. You haven't inconvenienced us at all. Please, do be seated."

Nick's eyebrows rose. Lucia was graceful, direct, and perfectly serene — more gentlewoman than servant, and nothing like what he had expected. She had been calm the previous day, in the few minutes he had seen her before Marcus had taken her away, but he had assumed that was due to the shock she'd had. She should have been more affected, like any raw recruit who had killed in battle for the first time. But she was still calm — and when she met his eyes, the direct look in hers said she would welcome the opportunity to take a shot at him as well.

Make that three people in the study who wanted him dead.

As soon as the footman had left, Marcus clicked his watch shut. "You've evaded us long enough, Nick. What the devil are you mixed up in?"

"I'm not evading. We couldn't discuss this last night, not if we didn't want everyone in the house to know."

"Shouldn't they know?" Ellie asked, setting aside the papers Lucia had given her. "I know you said you have a plan, but I don't want my guests to be harmed."

"You are welcome to ask them to leave, if you are so eager to be alone with me."

They hadn't acknowledged the previous night at all. But if Ellie had enjoyed it — and he knew she had — she was currently more likely to stab him than seduce him. Her eyes narrowed as she said, "We shall address our agreement momentarily. But let us start with why a highwayman wanted to kill you."

"If I knew why, I wouldn't be here," Nick said. He walked over to Lucia and took the cup of tea she had poured for him, then leaned against the wall opposite from where Marcus stood by the fire. "Your guess as to motive is as good as mine."

Ellie looked at Marcus, who didn't meet her gaze — he was too busy staring at Lucia. Ellie turned back to Nick. "Between us, we could likely guess a dozen reasons. Where shall we begin?"

"Villains always come to bad ends," Lucia said, rising and taking Ellie's cup to her. "If his lordship is no longer in a position to harm you, does the 'how' of it matter, my lady?"

"It does if their ends might harm the rest of us," Ellie mused. She didn't seem concerned that Lucia saw Nick as the villain in this story — in fact, if Nick hadn't heard a different note in Ellie's voice the previous night, he might suspect she agreed with her maid.

He cleared his throat. "Let me share the details. Then you may decide whether I am the villain."

He started with the three attempts on his life in Madras. The warehouse fire that would have trapped him in his office had he not left half an hour earlier than he always did. The shot during a hunt that had grazed his shoulder — any closer and he might have lost the limb, if not his life, to infection. And the assailant who had come after him with a knife in a Madras bazaar. Trower had stopped that attempt, after tailing Nick without asking permission to guard him.

"Did none of them say who they represented?" Marcus asked.

"There were no witnesses to the warehouse fire or the shot. I didn't look hard, though. I was still half sure they were accidents. As for the knife-wielder, Trower killed him before he could talk. He appeared to be a Maratha mercenary, though. He would have worked for anyone who paid enough."

"And those were the only events? Over how much time?" Ellie asked.

She was pale, but her tone was purely business. "Three events over a fortnight," Nick answered. "Trower and I took the next ship out of Madras a week after the would-be stabbing. Trower didn't let me out of his sight that whole time, and he hired a dozen men to guard us."

"Did anything happen aboard your ship, my lord?" Lucia asked. "Or were you guarded there as well?"

"No suspicious events at sea, nor during the week we spent taking on supplies at St. Helena. We had no additional guards, but I own the ship. The captain was most diligent about keeping me alive."

"As he should be," Marcus said. "Your connections in India have captured more of the private trade in that country than we had any right to expect a decade ago. If he lost you, his career would be finished. Do you trust the other men in our employ there?"

Nick had considered every single man in the India operation on the long voyage back to England. He nodded once. "There were always a handful whom I had to let go for one reason or another. But the ones currently there — for the most part, I trust them. And I can't see what any of them would stand to gain by murdering me."

Ellie pulled out a fresh sheet of paper from the desk, as well as a pen and ink. "Should we discuss who stands to gain something?" she suggested. "Or is that a delicate subject, when those who would gain the most are in the room with you?"

Nick waved an expansive hand. "Please, start. I'm curious to hear who you think my enemies are."

He watched her write her own name at the top of the sheet in graceful, looping cursive. He laughed. "Is that a confession?"

"Of course not. This is a list of people who might want you dead — not a list of people who likely ordered it." Then she smiled. "But to save myself forty thousand pounds and the irritation of your return, murder does look cheap."

"True. But it's not you. Who is the next suspect?"

She pointed her pen at Marcus, who nearly choked on his tea.

"You cannot seriously think I want to kill Nick," Marcus spluttered, once he had recovered from his coughing fit.

She wrote his name on the list. "Again, not likely. But you stand the most to gain — the Folkestone title, for one, not to mention whatever share of Corwyn, Claiborne and Sons is left to you in Nick's will. Nick's return changes everything for you, does it not?"

He didn't look at her. He looked at Lucia instead. "Perhaps it does. But I would rather have more time, not more responsibility. Nick is welcome to take over his estate any day he pleases."

Nick believed him. Perhaps he shouldn't. Ellie was correct, after all. Marcus would gain more than anyone if Nick died without another heir. But even as a youth, Marcus hadn't cared for power. Stuck in the middle between Nick and Rupert, he had played the peacemaker rather than the rabble-rouser.

That brought another thought uncomfortably close to the surface. He hesitated, and Ellie sensed it. "Who would you add?" she asked.

He kept his eyes on Marcus. "I have another brother who would stand to gain."

"Rupert?" Marcus asked, turning toward him. "That is even more unreasonable than suspecting me. Next I suppose you'll accuse the Prince Regent?"

"Of course not. But Rupert always wanted to build something of his own. And I don't think we see eye to eye on our business dealings, although sending a letter from India to the Caribbean and back takes so long that I hear from him far less than I do from you. Perhaps he was tired of trying to change my mind about business issues."

"I assure you that Rupert is not a murderer," Marcus said. "I've seen him several times in the last decade — whatever his sins, fratricide is not among them."

Ellie intervened. "We are merely listing suspects, not sending anyone to the gallows. And I agree with Nick — Rupert has a hot head, and a motive. He stays on the list, even if he's not likely."

Lucia coughed delicately. "Is there anyone else, my lady? Or do all his lordship's enemies share his last name?"

Nick felt a stab of remorse at that. He didn't think any of the three were likely to kill him, but he should be bothered by the fact that they topped the list. "We've listed all the Claibornes — let us move on to more likely candidates."

Ellie frowned at that. "We did miss a Claiborne, actually. The dowager marchioness still lives on the estate, although we are no longer on speaking terms. But it drove her absolutely mad that a man with your background inherited her precious son's title. Perhaps she hired someone?"

"That seems unlikely," Marcus scoffed. "Even if her anger hasn't subsided, how would she arrange it? She never leaves Surrey, as best as I can tell."

Nick agreed. "There are more likely options, and they are all related to my business interests. The East India Company tops the list."

"Shall I write 'the Company'?" Ellie asked sarcastically. "Or do you have names?"

"Marcus knows the directors better than I do. They are all based in London."

Marcus handed his cup back to Lucia to be filled again. As she poured, he pushed his hand through his hair. "I find it unlikely that the Company is behind this, Nick. True, you are driving our business in India — but if you died there and I pulled us out of the India trade as a result, they would face a dire shortage of ships. You know they can't haul all their goods on their own. With the discussions in Parliament about their monopoly, they can ill afford a loss in profits."

Marcus had told Nick all about the debates in the carriage the day before. The East India Company already wasn't quite a monopoly; private traders accounted for almost ten percent of the goods imported to Britain from India. The Claibornes had made a tidy profit off even that sliver of trade, not counting the contracts they had to transport Company goods on their ships. But if the Company lost their monopoly entirely…

"Perhaps another trader, then?" Nick asked. "With me gone from India, other ventures are better suited to take advantage of whatever happens to the Company's share of the India trade."

Ellie tapped her nose with her pen. "But that doesn't explain how someone knew to find you here, or why they still wish to harm you in England. If it were purely a matter of driving you away from the subcontinent, they wouldn't need to send a highwayman after you here. As much as it displeases me to say it, we could likely narrow our search by looking at my houseguests."

Lucia frowned. "The man I shot wasn't one of your guests or servants — I didn't recognize him at all. And I am nearly certain the same can be said for the other highwayman."

"I didn't recognize them either," Ellie said. "But that doesn't mean they weren't hired by someone we know."

"Then tell me, Ellie — among your guests, who is a likely culprit?" Nick asked.

"Beyond the people in this room?" she responded. She turned to Marcus. "They are my friends — I may not be able to stay unbiased. What is your assessment?"

"So you want my opinion now?" he asked.

She scowled. "Only if it helps find who wants to kill Nick. Once that is settled, I can get on with murdering him myself."

Marcus and Nick both laughed, but Marcus sobered first. "I

don't see any of them as likely. As best as I know, none of them are involved in the East India Company. Perhaps among your servants… but even they are rather too artistic to be bloodthirsty."

"Even the most artistic people can be bloodthirsty when provoked, Mr. Claiborne," Lucia said.

He nearly stammered as he apologized. "Forgive me, Mrs. Grafton. I did not mean to remind you of yesterday."

She looked just as startled as he sounded. "That wasn't what I meant at all. Just that artists shouldn't be overlooked."

Nick couldn't agree more. Ellie had the soul of an artist — but she had the brain of a general, and the steely look in her eyes was more suited to a war room than a studio. She cut off Lucia and Marcus without a moment of hesitation. "Enough. None of my servants, as far as I know, have ever gone to sea. I doubt that they'd even know how to arrange the murder of someone half a world away. We can still consider them, but I don't see the use of it." She turned back to Nick. "Is there really no one else?"

Nick paused, then shook his head. "Just the occasional junior secretary or hanger-on who was unhappy to be sent packing back to England. But would any of them try to murder me on two continents?"

"Nick is correct," Marcus said. "In all the time I've been in London, only one man came in to complain that Nick had sent him back to England. He wasn't pleased when I refused to help him find another job. But he was too pleasant about it to be a murderer."

"Was it Edgewood?" Nick asked. "He was always pleasant, even when he was embezzling everything in sight."

Marcus shrugged. "I believe so, although I could be mistaken. He didn't make a scene, and I never saw him again. Seems unlikely he would want to kill you when there's nothing to gain out of it."

Nick considered their other options. "Perhaps none of the guests are directly tied to the Company. But what of their investments?"

Ellie's hand hovered over the paper. "I know Norbury is heavily invested in the Company."

Marcus's nose wrinkled. "His estate is leveraged — he would be made uncomfortable if the Company's fortunes change."

"Still, I don't see him as a murderer," Ellie said, with a note of finality in her voice. She didn't add him to the list.

Nick didn't push it. "So our only official suspects are Ellie, Marcus, Rupert, the dowager marchioness, and the East India Company. If one of you would confess, it would make this all much easier."

"It will have to be Marcus," Ellie said. "I've no intention of confessing my sins."

He remembered how he'd promised to learn her sins in the carriage the day before — but this wasn't the time or the place, even if their agreement was now in full force. Instead, he gave her a loaded glance. "Someday you will, my dear."

She leaned back in her chair, but her eyes didn't give an inch. "Unlikely. But if this is the best we can do for a list, so be it. Do you have a plan for it?"

"Trower is working to identify the dead highwayman. Perhaps that will give us a clue. Beyond that, I plan to talk to your houseguests. If one of them is behind this, I will ferret it out."

Ellie nodded. "I shall see what I can learn from our guests as well. Lucia knows how to pry information from visiting ladies' maids and valets. If any visitor has a secret, we stand a good chance of learning it."

Marcus drained his second cup of tea. "I can talk to the tenants and see if anyone has noticed a stranger in the area."

"I will come with you, if you want to leave now," Nick said. It was too early to talk to most of the guests, but country farmers kept different hours. "Not a word of this to anyone, though. Our only advantage lies in keeping everyone here, and making the killer nervous about why we haven't reported the highwayman. If the party disperses, we'll be no closer to finding an answer."

Ellie stood up, leaning over the desk to hand Nick one of the pieces of paper Lucia had brought her. "Before you go off looking for danger, sign this. If you demand that the party stay intact, we need some rules for our…other agreement."

He took the sheet. It was their agreement — brief, direct, and in writing. It stated that if Ellie did as Nick wished until the thirteenth of June, her debt would be forgiven. But Ellie had added an addendum: no one could find out about their arrangement. If gossip started to spread, he would let her go immediately.

He looked up and met her eyes. "This is not what we agreed to."

"No, but if you don't agree to this, I vow I will murder you myself."

She wasn't teasing him. "Why is the gossip so important to you? From what I've heard, gossip has never bothered you."

"Gossip has never bothered me because I was always able to control what they said. But I cannot control you, can I?"

Nick snorted. "I'm sure you'll try. You didn't answer my question, though."

"It would be obvious, if you knew anything of the ton."

That was a statement that should have insulted him, but he considered it a clue, not a barb. Realization dawned fast. "Your sisters."

"My friends as well. And my servants, if you want all of it. They are so discreet because they know I can procure jobs for them anywhere they like — but if my reputation goes, so go those opportunities, and so goes their loyalty. I could risk any scandal I wanted at nineteen…"

"…Except for eloping with a merchant's son," Nick interjected.

She ignored him. "But I have other responsibilities now. I'll give you what you think I owe you — as I said, perhaps atonement will help me. But if you are seeking to humiliate me in public, and ruin other lives along with mine, you're not the man I once loved."

The man she once loved. She said it so matter-of-factly — both the love and the dead, past-tense nature of it. He didn't want her love to be dead. He didn't want everything between them to be the past.

But she was right about one thing. If he ruined her in public, it would ruin his honor along with it. And as much as he had dreamed of her groveling at his feet in the middle of Almack's, a public revenge wasn't worth the cost.

He stole the pen from her hand and signed both sheets with a bold, scrawling stroke — feeling almost like Faustus making a deal with the devil, but he was in too deep to stop himself. Public revenge was off the table — but private revenge, and all the ways he'd imagined taking her, were still open to him.

He handed her the pen. "Sign, my love."

Her fingers brushed his. There was no hesitation, no fear, no regret in her touch. Her eyes were stark again, but if she saw visions of hell, they didn't stop her from signing her name.

It was done. He ignored Marcus and Lucia, who both coughed at the same time, and went around the desk to kiss Ellie on the top of the head. "Tonight," he murmured into her hair. "I will send you instructions later."

She didn't betray any curiosity. "Just don't interfere with dinner."

"I wouldn't dream of it. There's no need to add your chef to the list of suspects."

Ellie grinned at that, just barely. Her amusement should have piqued him. He should have been annoyed that she was spiking his guns with her acceptance of his revenge — she almost seemed to want it, in a way that he had never predicted when he had imagined it before.

But he found he didn't mind. Now that he knew she wanted him on some level, even if she denied it, he couldn't imagine having her any other way.

Just as he couldn't imagine how he was going to leave her at the end of it.

CHAPTER SIXTEEN

With every aspect of Nick's arrival — from how he'd loved her the night before to the danger he now faced, plus all the uncertainty she felt toward him — Ellie was in no mood to trouble herself with her guests. After leaving the study with the contract they'd both signed, she evaded everyone during the breakfast hour.

She couldn't be fully alone. For one, she needed to settle the menus with her housekeeper, which she did over tea in her salon. She couldn't avoid her guests for a second full day, though. They would speculate that she was avoiding Nick. And that wasn't a rumor she wanted to start.

But Ellie knew how to manage them. Give a group something unexpected and no one noticed anything but the spectacle.

"Are you ready, Maria?" she asked her younger half-sister.

Maria nodded. She lifted the bow and fitted the arrow against the string.

"A shilling says you can't hit the target," Maria's twin, Kate, said behind them.

"Two shillings say you can't do better," Maria retorted, taking aim.

She let the arrow fly. It sailed down the portrait gallery, past all the generations of Claibornes who would be horrified to see such reckless

145

hoydens in their house. The arrow hit the target with a satisfying thud, lodging halfway between the edge of the target and the red circle at its center.

The guests assembled behind Maria clapped. Sir Percival Pickett, perhaps the most eccentric of Ellie's guests, was particularly effusive. "Brava, Lady Maria!" he exclaimed. "I vow a Grecian goddess couldn't have done better."

"She didn't hit the center," Kate scoffed, taking the bow from her sister. "It would be a poor goddess who couldn't do that."

She stepped up, took an arrow from the waiting footman, and fired. Where Maria had missed left, Kate missed right — by exactly the same amount, according to the servant they sent down the gallery to measure it.

The ribbing continued, good-naturedly, as Kate promised Maria three shillings out of her pin money. Ferguson teased that he would cut off their allowances for gambling. Sebastian Staunton offered them lessons — an offer that made the twins glow and Ferguson glower. Sir Percy stared off into space, no doubt casting the twins as heroines in his next epic poem.

Ellie smiled. The snows had finally stopped, but they'd received nearly seven inches the previous night. Setting up an archery contest in the portrait gallery when they couldn't be outdoors had been inspired. Her younger guests were enthused. Her older guests were equal parts charmed and titillated. Archery was one of the few sports open to women, and something that both sexes could enjoy together. It was only the indoor nature of their contest that any gossips might find shocking, and they would have to be the utmost prudes to condemn her for it.

The long, narrow gallery on the floor above the ballroom was perfect for shooting, especially with a footman stationed on the other side of the far door to prevent accidental entry. And if a wayward arrow hit a painting or a window — well, it was Nick's house, not hers.

Madeleine stepped up to the line they'd agreed to shoot from. Ferguson stood close behind her — whether to give his duchess pointers or to look down the bodice of her gown was unclear. Ellie ignored them and waved the twins over to a quiet alcove near the door.

"Are you enjoying yourselves?" she asked.

"Of course," Kate said, as though the question was too obvious to be asked.

"Especially when I am winning," Maria added.

Ellie couldn't help but smile. The twins had seemed like a single unit the year before, when they had lived with their father and never saw anyone but each other. But since they'd come out into Society and moved in with Ferguson and Madeleine, they had become individuals — still close, but more likely to compete with each other than to unite against the world.

Kate wouldn't concede defeat. "You aren't a better shot, Maria, just a better gambler. And there are still other games to be won."

Their eyes slid simultaneously to Sebastian, who had lost interest in the archery and was looking out the high, narrow windows to the snow-covered lawn. He had lighter brown hair than his brother Alex, with appealing brown eyes in a face tanned by the Caribbean sun. Why he was still in England, Ellie didn't know. He had a plantation in Bermuda, but had been in England since November — the longest time he'd spent on this side of the Atlantic in years.

"Be careful, my dears," Ellie said in a low voice. "If you catch a man like that, you won't know what to do with him."

"I have some ideas," Maria whispered.

Kate giggled as Ellie sighed. "Why the concern, Ellie?" Kate asked. "We are merely flirting. By the time you were our age, you were already married, widowed, and well on your way to bedding half the ton."

"It wasn't half the ton," Ellie protested with a laugh. "Whoever told you that was mistaken."

"Father did tend to exaggerate when he was angry," Kate said, pausing to clap too enthusiastically when Madeleine hit the wainscoting behind the target. "But still, you can't begrudge us a bit of excitement after all the years he kept us locked away."

Ellie didn't begrudge them. She'd only taken four lovers since her marriage — not the regiment her father had assumed, although she'd worked hard to cultivate her dissolute reputation to keep him from setting her up with another husband. And she hadn't regretted them — they were all rakes with secret sweet sides who kept their own counsel and expected nothing from her. None of them had equaled Nick — but then, she hadn't been looking for love.

She wanted her sisters to find love, though. They'd had little enough of it, raised by their tyrannical father; at one-and-twenty, it was past time for them to have some happiness. "Don't sell yourselves too cheaply," she warned. "There are good men in the ton if you are patient enough to find them."

The twins gave noncommittal nods, then wandered toward Sebastian as though they shared a single mind. Ellie sighed again. They were smart enough — and Sebastian elusive enough — that none of them were in any danger.

But she would rather see them make safe, happy matches than play the game she'd entered with Nick.

Madeleine gave up her bow with a laugh after hitting the

wainscoting a second time and joined Ellie by the wall. "If Ferguson ever upsets me, remind me not to shoot him," Madeleine said. "I'm more likely to injure myself than him."

"You should take lessons," Ellie said. "Your cousin seems eager to give them."

Madeleine wrinkled her nose in Sebastian's direction. "He's even more of a rogue than he was the last time he came home. I hope your sisters know he's not the marrying kind."

Ellie's reply was interrupted when Lucia slipped into the gallery. She held a small slip of paper and wore a grim expression. Ellie raised an eyebrow at her in silent question.

Lucia shook her head.

Damn. Ellie had tasked Lucia with adding up the original value of Ellie's collection from all the ledgers of her acquisitions. She took the paper and read the note like it was a prison sentence.

Nineteen thousand, two hundred and twenty three pounds, six shillings, and four pence.

Her stomach twisted. She might be able to sell most of it. But she couldn't sell everything. Some pieces would bring more than she had paid, but some were already out of fashion. Her Chinese collection, for example, was not entirely *en vogue.* If she sold every painting, every sculpture, every scrap of wall hanging, she couldn't possibly pay Nick in full. All she could do was shorten the length of their arrangement.

And unless she wanted to auction it all publicly — and humiliate herself in the process — it might take months to sell everything.

Ellie didn't have months. She wasn't even sure she had minutes. She had always thought she knew her own heart, but last night's passion and this morning's regret had surprised her.

Somehow, while she had worked so hard to reforge herself into a woman with no weaknesses, she had made a critical error. Her heart, guarded and locked and left unexamined in the dark, hadn't healed during its decade of solitude.

It had festered.

The face she showed the world was a dressing expertly applied over her wounds. Her heart, though, couldn't bear to be touched. Stripping away even a bit of the covering, as Nick had done the previous night — as he would likely do again that night, and every night after that until she repaid him or killed him — caused her unbearable pain.

She recognized the pain. She had sometimes let herself feel it on those rare occasions when her painting drew from the deep well of her heart. She could let the blood flow into her painting without thinking about where it came from or what monsters waited beneath it, then shut it off when she was done making art. But shutting it off wasn't the same as healing it.

The only way to heal a wound was to examine it, clean it, and keep treating it until no hint of infection remained. But Ellie, who was so good at examining others, couldn't do the same to herself.

She hated herself for her cowardice. But there weren't enough opiates or stimulants or lovers or parties in the world to make bearable the pain of really, truly *looking* at her feelings for Nick.

So she wouldn't look. The infection would kill her someday. But if she looked, and found that she really still loved him, and he wouldn't forgive her...

Ellie crumpled the paper and returned it to Lucia, who understood the dismissal implicit in the gesture. Her maid left as quietly as she'd entered. But Madeleine still stood next to her, and she wouldn't be put off so easily. "Is anything amiss?" she asked.

Ellie turned resolutely toward the archers. Percy Pickett was up next. "Merely some estate business. You should watch Sir Percival shoot. You wouldn't believe it from his attempts at poetry, but he's quite the archer."

Madeleine paused while Percy shot, but she used the stunned, raucous applause of the audience to cover her next words. "I hope you know that you're welcome to stay at Rothwell House as long as you like. I don't know what will happen between you and Lord Folkestone, but you will always have a home with us."

If Ellie moved to Rothwell House, Madeleine would be so sisterly, so smothering in her generosity. Ferguson would try to protect her, even from herself.

Ellie wouldn't last a fortnight without wanting to stab them both.

"Thank you, but there's no need for that," Ellie said. "I can manage quite well on my own."

Madeleine paused. There was a strange quality to her silence, as though she was taking aim with just as much solemn consideration as Percy did for his second shot. When he let his arrow fly, she spoke. "That's what I'm afraid of. You don't have to manage this alone, you know."

Ellie applauded Percy's shot, not looking at her sister-in-law. "Don't worry about me. I vow I'm not in trouble."

Why didn't Madeleine heed the warning in Ellie's voice? Why, when she heard Madeleine draw a breath, did Ellie feel some swift, ugly kick of rage — the rage of a caged, brutalized animal, ready to bite the first hand that might offer it rescue?

But Madeleine had never seen the beast lurking in Ellie's heart. "Ferguson and I saw you last night, quite late. I know it's indelicate to mention, but you seemed upset."

Upset was such a small word for what she'd felt. She hadn't gone directly to her room from her studio. She had wandered instead, through the disused rooms and darkened halls that she'd never wanted and yet now would miss tremendously. Only something like anger, or grief, or self-loathing, could have kept her from noticing her brother and his wife in whatever alcove they'd secreted themselves in.

Her lips curled over her teeth. "I thought I was clear that this isn't a bacchanal, Duchess. You should have been abed."

Madeleine's shrug would have been at home at Versailles. "If the marquess evicts you and you can never host us here again, we're keen to explore all its dark corners while we still have the chance. Was it Folkestone who made you so upset? Say the word and Ferguson will take care of it."

"Will he?" Ellie asked. Her voice dropped and her eyes narrowed as she turned on Madeleine. "The way he took care of himself by abandoning me years ago? Or the way Father took care of Nick? Ferguson will turn into our father, I'm sure — he may as well start by threatening anyone who comes near me. Or will he take care of it by compromising Nick as he compromised you? That would be deucedly awkward, not to mention illegal."

Through the dark, red-flecked tunnel that had become her vision, she saw Madeleine's face turn from confused to hurt to furious. Sweet, perfect Madeleine and her sweet, perfect vision of love. Ellie wanted to keep going, keep slicing, until Madeleine left her alone. And then she would burn the house, flee for the Continent, and seek oblivion among people who didn't know her and wouldn't pity her.

But it wasn't Madeleine's fault that she was happy where Ellie was not. And Ellie had never lost control of herself like that before.

Ellie drew a deep, shuddering breath, raw and rasping, glad her anger had been covered by the crowd congratulating Percy on two perfect shots. "I apologize, your grace," she said, when some of the red had faded to grey. "That was poorly done of me. I appreciate your offer, but I do not require help."

Madeleine looked like she wanted to argue, but Ellie's outburst had shattered her innocence. She sounded wary when she said, "Very well. Just...don't forget we exist if you need us."

That was like asking a soldier not to forget that other people were unharmed when he, in a moment of terrible luck, had lost a leg. Madeleine meant to be kind — *was* kind — but Ellie, in all her unfamiliar pain, couldn't accept it.

Still, there was no sense insulting her again. So Ellie put on her best smile, nodded, and shifted the conversation to a discussion of which amusements to pursue that evening.

And while they talked, she breathed. She let the pain go with every exhale. She used every inhale to rebuild her shields. If she couldn't heal her heart, she could at least ensure that no one — not her friends, not Nick, and certainly not herself — could touch it again.

CHAPTER SEVENTEEN

Half an hour later, it was Ellie's turn at the targets. Her guests would grow bored soon. She could read it in the way they had broken off into little groups, paying more attention to their own gossip than to those who chose to shoot. She could read the swirls and eddies in a social setting like an expert gamekeeper tracking his herds and flocks. And she was already prepared for the next phase of the afternoon. Even now, servants would be setting out a cold collation in the saloon downstairs — food and drink would keep her guests entertained, and not thinking of her, for another hour at least.

But as she picked up her bow, she sensed a different movement in the currents behind her. She didn't turn around, but she heard the whispers. She nocked the arrow, pulled back, stared down the shaft, and released the string.

It struck the heart of the target. Her father hadn't allowed hysterics, but it didn't matter — she had always found more satisfaction in a perfectly-placed arrow than a crying fit.

She could have shot again, trying to match Percy's record. But she heard a slow, loud clap add itself to the tumult of praise, and she wasn't sure her nerves allowed for another attempt. She handed her weapon to the footman, a slender blond with pretty, even features who looked like Eros as he held the bow.

154

This wasn't the time to think of painting her footmen. She turned back to her guests. But she only saw Nick. He stood slightly apart, near the door he had just entered, watching her with eyes that tracked over her skin like Greek fire. His hair was windblown and his cheeks were red with cold. But his voice was pure heat as he congratulated her.

"Tremendous shot, Lady Folkestone," he said, in a voice that silenced the masses. "Odysseus himself couldn't have done better."

She blushed. She never blushed. But she saw him, again, in the painting she'd made of him, with Ellie as Circe and Nick as the man who waited to do her bidding. "You're more of an Odysseus than I am, my lord — back from your wanderings and all that. Do you care to shoot? The rest of the party is just finished."

He didn't glance at any of them. "I'm no archer. It's not a popular pastime in the East End."

The silence turned uncomfortable. No one had mentioned his antecedents, at least not to her, but he wouldn't let them forget it. Ellie smoothed it over with a little laugh. "Of course. We can always try another diversion. Have you a scheme to entertain us?"

"I always have a scheme for you, my lady."

He sounded lightly flirtatious, in a way that made the women sigh. If he were always like this, the combination of his charm and his title would more than cover the sins of his background. He could melt all their hearts with little effort.

But there was nothing light or flirtatious about Nick's face. His eyes locked onto hers. His grin turned devastating, the grin of a man who was supremely confident that he could take what he wanted.

It was easy for him to be confident. For the next few months, at least, he owned her. But perhaps he, like her, had realized an unfortunate truth in the darkness of her studio the previous night: he could have had her without spending forty thousand bloody pounds to force her.

That thought brought her up short and cut the mutual seduction they'd woven. "What shall it be, Lord Folkestone? Piquet? Whist?"

Her cool voice didn't deter him. He held out his arm. "Take a turn in the garden with me, if your guests can spare you. There's a bit of outdoor business we need to discuss."

His tone, like hers, lost its flirtatious edge. She couldn't say no — his request was odd, but her refusal would be odder still. She nodded once. "I will need to change if I am to be outside," she said.

She had changed out of her comfortable morning dress for the archery and her white Grecian gown was no match for the snow. He nodded. "I shall await you in the entrance hall in half an hour."

He left without waiting to see if she followed. She sent her guests on their way to the saloon, knowing that they would spend the afternoon dissecting whether "a turn in the garden" was code for something more nefarious, but there was nothing she could do to stop it — particularly when she didn't know what Nick's intentions were.

By the time she reached the foyer, clad in a thick walking dress, flannel petticoats, sturdy boots, and a fur-lined cloak, she was brimming with curiosity.

"Did you find something during your conversation with the tenants?" Ellie asked as Nick put on his hat. "Or is this about… something else?"

He slanted her a look that said he'd rather this were about their bargain, but he shook his head. "The tenants had nothing of value to report, and there isn't time now for our…other activities. But there's something I wish for you to sketch."

He said nothing more as he led her down the hall to his study to retrieve a sketchpad, and then back past the dining room to the green baize door to the servants' hall. She had been in their domain less than half a dozen times in her entire tenure as marchioness, but Nick walked through like he was well acquainted with the rooms.

"Where are we going?" she asked.

"To one of the outbuildings," he said, steering her through the kitchen and around the massive spits where two boys turned the rods that roasted a score of pheasants over the fire. "We could have gone through the gardens, but it's too cold for my blood."

She didn't complain. Even for someone who had stayed in England all her life, the weather wasn't pleasant. But when they reached the servants' entrance and found Marcus cooling his heels on a bench near the door, she came up short.

"You shouldn't keep a traitor at your back when you're looking for a killer," she said to Nick. "Take care, or he may sell you out to someone else."

Marcus winced. "Ellie, I am sorry. Again."

She waved a hand. "Claibornes are always sorry. I should have known better than to trust you. You're cut from the same cloth as all the rest."

He had stood when she arrived, but rather than giving way, he leaned against the door and blocked their route. "Say what you will about me, but I did what I thought was best. You had more money and comfort these past ten years than your actual funds would have given you. Nick's money kept you free to pursue your own passions rather than marrying someone else. And it seemed that Nick might never come home. You were the only thing I thought would lure him back. As it turns out, we should have hired people to try to kill him in India — it might have brought him back years ago and saved all of us some heartache."

He grinned at her. The old Marcus was back — the one who had been her friend after he could see beyond the fact that she'd broken his brother's heart.

She sighed. "That doesn't make it right, you know. I don't think I can forgive you for this."

His smile died. "Seems that none of us can forgive each other."

Nick intervened. "Can we discuss this somewhere else? Half the servants are listening to us."

Ellie looked around to find more footmen, scullery maids, and chambermaids milling in the kitchens than were strictly necessary. She found her butler in the crowd and raised her brows. "Ashby, why aren't you attending my guests in the saloon?"

He had the grace to blush. "Just retrieving wine for them, my lady."

She knew the wine wasn't kept in the kitchen, but she let the remark pass. Ashby was a good butler, but she couldn't fault him for being concerned about Nick's arrival. She couldn't fault any of them. She had trained them to be loyal to her and her alone — she could guess that Nick's return, and what it meant for them, were all any of them were talking about.

Nick gestured her toward the door and they walked out into the snow. Several sets of footprints had already stamped paths to the main outbuildings. The coal, lamp oil, and foodstuffs were all stored in the cellars, but the staff still needed to feed the horses, milk the cows, and stoke fires in the orangery and other succession houses to keep the plants from freezing. One outbuilding, though, had fewer footprints leading to it — and a stout lock on the door that she hadn't noticed before.

Nick pulled a key from his pocket. But before he unlocked it, he turned to Ellie. "I should have prepared you better, but there was nothing I could say in front of the others. I brought the dead highwayman's body back with us yesterday..."

"He's in here?" Ellie interrupted. She'd successfully kept the vision of his bloodied face out of her mind that morning, but she wasn't sure she was prepared to see it again.

"I couldn't leave him in the ditch. There was no better place to put him. But unless we tell the magistrate to post notices, we have no way of discovering who he is."

"What do you want me to sketch? I remember his face — there isn't enough left to draw."

Nick dropped the key into his pocket and put his arm around her shoulder. "There's no need to see the face. I know you aren't accustomed to such things."

Ellie shook her head to clear it. She wasn't eager to see the man again, but if she had to, she wouldn't let herself vomit again. "I've seen wounds like that before. I can handle myself."

Nick's hand stopped in mid-caress. "Where would you have seen such a thing?

"Did you not hear?" She counted the months. Her father had died a year earlier, but it had taken a month or two for the rumors to spread. If Marcus had written the truth in a letter to Nick, he might not have received it before his ship left India. "I suppose you wouldn't have. Officially, Father and Richard died in a carriage accident. Sophronia pulled every string she could to sway the reports. But really, my brother shot Father in the head and then turned the gun on himself."

She said it as one repeated an oft-told bit of minor gossip — as though she didn't sometimes still dream of her father and wish he had survived. Her nonchalance was a lie, though. In the dreams where he survived, it was only to tell her that he loved her.

And that was as delusional as any other fantasy she could have.

Nick dropped his arm away from her. "Why didn't you tell me?"

"When?" she countered. "We've had more pressing issues to address. And anyway, it's all in the past. How he died doesn't matter, does it?"

But it did matter. There had been no time for deathbed conversions or last confessions. Just her father's voice from three weeks before his death — the last time she'd given in and taken dinner with him. He had told her to stop mourning and find some purpose other than redecorating "that peasant's house."

She'd never admit it, but he may have had a point.

Nick frowned. "Did he ever apologize for…"

"Charles?"

He nodded.

Ellie snorted. "Of course not. He'd have found another Charles for me if I hadn't become so disreputable and recalcitrant. But I understand him now, better than I did before."

"What do you understand?"

"He did what he thought was best. Do I hate him for it? Yes. But he wasn't evil. He just…wasn't very nice."

Before Nick responded, Marcus cleared his throat. "I'm sure this conversation is delightful, but may I suggest you continue it in the house? It's far too cold out here."

Nick unlocked the door and ushered them into the gloom of the windowless shed. Enough light came in through the door to make out an outline of the body; he added to it by lighting the lantern that sat on nearby stool. The corpse lay on the floor with a blanket covering it, and he knelt down to pull the blanket aside and reveal both arms, but not the head or chest.

"My batman discovered these tattoos when he checked for identifying marks. If you draw them, Trower can take them to the London or Southampton docks after the snows clear and possibly find which ships he sailed on."

Ellie looked over the corpse. Most of the tattoos were simple designs and short words dyed into his skin. They would be easy enough for a novice to create during his breaks in the ship's watches. Two or three were more intricate, created by a skilled artist — perhaps a tattooed warrior of the South Pacific?

She started sketching. The designs were small enough that she could fit them all on a single large page of her sketchbook. "Do you recognize any of them?" she finally asked after several minutes of drawing.

"No, but there is one he may have received when he crossed the Equator for the first time," he said. "Sailors who've never crossed it before are put through any number of ordeals — shaving, tarring, and other, mostly good-natured, humiliations. Passengers like myself just have to contribute the alcohol on our first voyage across. But I might have gotten a tattoo myself that night if I'd had another cup of rum."

She pictured him standing on the rail of a ship, the salt spray driving his hair back in the wind. It was enough to make her hand pause, wishing she could draw that instead of a dead man's tattoos.

"You must have seen such wonderful sights," she said, returning to her work.

He crouched beside her, examining her handiwork as she drew the last tattoo — a serpent wrapped around an anchor. "Sights beyond imagining. I wish you had been there to paint them. My words cannot do justice to them the way your colors can."

"Perhaps someday, with whatever funds I have left, I shall go abroad," Ellie said, shading in the serpent's head. "I should have done so years ago, but I wasn't quite ready to go alone."

He was silent at that, but she didn't notice until she'd finished the drawing — and realized, as she focused on their conversation rather than her pencil, how much she'd given away.

"No matter, though," she said brightly, shoving the sketchbook at him. "Now that you've returned, you can take the estate. Marcus, would you care to escort me to Greece now that you may take a holiday?"

Marcus raised his brows as she stood and dusted off her skirts. "Have your forgotten that you are angry with me?"

Nick laughed. It was genuine mirth, not the cutting disdain he so often gave her. "She can be remarkably inconsistent when she doesn't remember who she's claimed to love and hate."

"Claibornes," she muttered. "I shall go to the Continent myself, then. If you are very kind to me, Nick, perhaps I will send you a sketch occasionally while you moulder in the House of Lords."

"You *would* have me stuck in London for eternity, wouldn't you?"

She wouldn't. Nick belonged somewhere more primal, somewhere with a harsh purity to the sea and sky — not in Parliament or the ballrooms, where he didn't have the patience to even play those murky social games, let alone win them.

"I'd have you on an isle in the Mediterranean," she said. "Think of all I could paint there."

His eyes flashed. But he didn't respond. She was glad of it. She'd been too truthful, hadn't hidden that statement beneath a jaded, sultry tone. She wanted him, all to herself, with Homer's wine-dark sea and the flawless Mediterranean light serving as a backdrop for all the passion she'd always poured into her paintings of him.

That was a truth.

The worse truth, though, was that her heart — that poor, confused, angry beast — somehow had started painting a future with him again. A future with laughter, and love, and fire.

The future she had thought she'd finally, finally let go.

Stop mourning and find a purpose, her father's voice said.

Ellie turned abruptly for the door, wading through the awkward, heavy silence that followed her confession. "I hope I helped," she said, her voice too loud. "I shall see you both at dinner, yes?"

She didn't wait. They didn't follow. She heard Marcus's low whistle, heard Nick mutter something that made his brother laugh, but she didn't turn back. She knew her mythology — if she turned back, she would be lost.

She was already lost.

She dipped down, scooped up a palmful of untouched snow, and pressed it against her face. The cold shocked her and she sucked in a deep, cleansing breath. The crisp air burned as she inhaled, froze as she exhaled. It was enough to help her slow her steps, enough that by the time she returned to the house, her wet face felt composed.

But not enough to save her from herself. Which left the question — should she run as far from Folkestone as her funds and courage could carry her?

Or should she let her heart fight, grimly, hopelessly, incurably, for a future she was sure Nick would never give her?

CHAPTER EIGHTEEN

Hours later, after another of her chef's delectable but interminable dinners, Ellie wanted wine. Great, overflowing vats of wine, in such quantities that the fumes alone could cloud her judgment. She would drink to excess, flirt and laugh and dance until she could no longer stand, and confront reality in the morning. Or the afternoon, when her head stopped spinning. If she waited long enough, she could repeat the cycle again without confronting reality at all.

Could she spend the four months Nick demanded in a state of utter inebriation?

She suppressed a scowl and reached for her teapot, part of the Spode service that had been a wedding gift. Her father had commissioned it for her and Charles, and she had received it long after she'd already put off her mourning. "May I refresh your cup, Aunt Sophronia?" she asked.

Her aunt held up her cup with an irritated sigh. "I know you've found your respectability now that your sisters are with you, and I applaud you for it, but I had hoped for stronger stuff. Where are the perfectly matched footmen bearing chalices of wine?"

"Packed up and put away, your grace," Ellie said as she poured. "But the tea is excellent, don't you think?"

Sophronia sniffed. "I don't wish to waste my remaining years on tea. And from the way your fingers are drumming the pot, you don't wish it either."

Ellie deliberately set the teapot aside and folded her hands in her lap. "You are a terrible influence, aunt."

They were sitting slightly apart from the rest of the women in the company, who had spread themselves throughout the connected drawing rooms after dinner as they waited for the men to join them. But Sophronia was formidable enough to say anything she pleased, whether she had an audience or not. "I am above reproach," Sophronia declared. "And if I say we should have wine, then no one would think to question it."

"Very well, I shall summon the butler. You are not making it easier for me to reform myself."

Sophronia sniffed. "You never did invite me to one of your bacchanals. I refuse to allow you to reform before I attend one."

Ellie looked through the connecting doors to where Kate and Maria sat together, giggling and sharing secrets. Even if they had both set their caps for Sebastian, it was all innocent — not the kind of trouble they would have found themselves in at one of her earlier parties. She turned back to Sophronia with a small shrug. "You are too late for a bacchanal, aunt. And anyway, I couldn't play the jade forever. Everyone must change eventually."

Sophronia leaned in, suddenly serious. Ellie had seen the liver spots hidden under Sophronia's gloves, but her grip was still strong as she took Ellie's hand. "You can change however you wish, Elinor. I admit, I would rather see you become a patroness of Almack's than some dreadful, loose-moraled minx. But I thought you'd learned this lesson already — be who you want to be, not whatever someone else would make you."

"And if I don't want to host another infamous party?" Ellie asked.

Sophronia waved a magnanimous hand. "There are other hostesses who will take your place. But I'll still have wine tonight."

Ellie laughed. Sophronia was a force unto herself. Ellie was a force in some circles as well — and could be in others, at least as long as they didn't know of her sudden poverty and Nick's lascivious demands.

But did she want that kind of influence, the kind that gave her power without friendships and solitude without anyone to question her? Or should she take her aunt's advice and chart her own course?

Lady Salford joined them then, choosing to sit with Sophronia and Ellie rather than some of the younger ladies. "I must compliment your chef, Lady Folkestone," she said as Ellie poured her tea. "Your meals are as charming as I've always heard."

"Thank you, Lady Salford. I hope to persuade him to stay with me rather than Folkestone — I am sure his genius takes the credit for why people accept my invitations."

She couldn't afford her chef, or her parties, but Lady Salford couldn't know that. At least if Ellie turned respectable, she might live more cheaply. Far better to be thought a dull stick than a bankrupt one.

Lady Salford took the cup from Ellie's outstretched hand. The conversation stayed neutral, never dropping into unseen currents. Lady Salford was eminently proper — not boring, precisely, but not one to even tiptoe on the edge of scandal. How she'd raised her children to be such rebels was a mystery. Her daughter Amelia was a secret writer; her niece Madeleine, whom she had raised for decades, had acted on a public stage; and her son Sebastian was somewhat of an enigma, since he spent most of his time on his plantation in the

Caribbean. Only Alex, now Lord Salford, was proper — but perhaps he was just a late bloomer when it came to sin.

By the time the men entered the drawing room a quarter of an hour later, Ellie was itching for some sin herself. Propriety was all well and good. But the wine Sophronia had ordered and the restless prickling under her skin as she spoke of nothing and more nothing with Lady Salford combined to make her reckless.

If this were five years earlier, she might have taken a lover from one of her guests — a rake who wouldn't hurt her but also wouldn't press for the heart she couldn't give him. But she'd been done with lovers for ages.

Until Nick had walked into her ball and claimed her. He walked into the drawing room the same way tonight, part proprietor, part predator. He'd leashed his darkest elements, feigning some transparent bonhomie with Lord Norbury, who regarded him with the confused, suspicious air of a man who had been warned to expect a lion and was instead presented with a housecat.

Ellie would have laughed at the thought of Nick as a housecat, but she knew his claws weren't sheathed for her sake. Until tonight, he'd barely spoken to anyone in the party but her. His manners at the previous night's dinner had been cold and aloof. Tonight, though, he had mounted a charm offensive that would have left all the foreign diplomats in the Court of St. James in the shade.

"You must join me for the hunts next year, Norbury," Nick said as they entered. "My brother says we've a fine hunting lodge in some county or another, if I can find it."

Ellie raised an eyebrow at Marcus, who entered directly behind them. He shrugged slightly. Neither had ever heard Nick show the slightest interest in retiring to the country. Marcus walked over to where Ellie sat. She remembered an instant too late that she hadn't forgiven him.

"Your grace. Ladies," he said, bowing to them.

"Mr. Claiborne," she said. She kept her voice neutral. No one else could know of the rift that had sprung up between them. "I trust the gentlemen were comfortable with their brandy?"

His eyes flickered back to Nick, who had clapped Norbury on the back — odd, since Ellie was sure Nick would rather give up everything and become a lead miner in Derbyshire than become friends with the viscount. "Quite comfortable, Lady Folkestone, now that my dear brother has determined to play the host."

"How charming," she said.

Nick didn't approach her. He kept Norbury cornered instead, taking him through the connecting doors to the green saloon where they might have brandy instead of tea. Norbury glanced at Ellie on the way as though she might rescue him, but she shook her head.

"Poor Norbury looks like he's a Christian sacrifice in Rome, don't you think?" Sophronia observed.

"Norbury can hold his own," Ellie said. "And Lord Folkestone doesn't bite."

"Do you care to verify that personally?" Sophronia asked.

"Did you just *wink* at me?" Ellie asked.

"I would never be so vulgar."

Then she winked again.

Ellie sighed. She should turn Folkestone into a lunatic asylum and charge her family and friends for their upkeep. None of them were sane, and they were fast pulling her down with them.

She kept that uncharitable thought to herself. "Ladies, how shall we entertain ourselves tonight? Shall we have dancing? Or perhaps a game?"

"I would defer to you, Lady Folkestone — whatever the young

people prefer," Lady Salford said. "I am quite content to watch from beside the fire."

"If there are to be no professional dancers cavorting for us, I have no preference," Sophronia said.

"If you want to give a scandalous party for your own friends, I am sure I could help you arrange it," Ellie said. "But I will not be hiring any more opera dancers for this house."

"That is a shame," Marcus mused. "I quite like it when you hire opera dancers."

Sophronia tittered. Ellie almost rolled her eyes — she knew, even if no one else did, that his thoughts had turned to Lucia. But she caught herself in time. "If no one has a suggestion, I shall consult Lord Folkestone. Aunt Sophronia, please ensure that Mr. Claiborne behaves himself in my absence."

"I will if you promise to hire opera dancers for my party," Sophronia said. "And you must find a smuggler who will sell us real French champagne. Respectability is no excuse for drinking swill."

Most definitely insane. What did it say about her friends and family that Ellie was grateful to take her leave, even when Nick was her destination?

Or what did it say about herself? Even after the revenge he'd plotted for so long, she still felt his pull through the rooms like a tether. He'd hooked her, set the hook too deep to dislodge, and could pull her in without the slightest effort.

But a hooked fish still struggled. Ellie didn't fight the pull. If she was a fish, then she was a stupid fish, perhaps even a suicidal fish — willing to leap into the boat to lie, gasping, at his feet.

Perhaps everyone else was sane and she was the madwoman.

CHAPTER NINETEEN

Ellie knew Norbury held her in esteem. He loved his wife, but she was often sickly, and Ellie was a convenient partner at card games and dances when his wife could not attend. But when she reached his side, he looked more grateful than she had ever seen him. "Lady Folkestone," he said, bowing over her hand. "Have you come to rescue me?"

She hadn't, but she saw why he needed it. Nick alone was a force too strong to deny. But they had been joined by Sir Percival, whose poetic foolishness was of the same magnitude as Nick's intensity. Ellie stifled a laugh. "I cannot imagine why you want to be rescued."

Nick clapped him on the back again. Norbury winced and said nothing. Nick spoke instead, with a friendliness that would have done a charlatan proud. "I cannot imagine it either. We've had such an interesting conversation about India. Lost on Pickett, I'm afraid, but Norbury is quite knowledgeable."

Percy shrugged. "Can't see anything poetic about India. Too much heat, don't you know."

"And aren't we glad the heat didn't stop Dante from exploring hell?" Ellie asked.

Percy seemed struck. "Never thought of that, Lady Folkestone."

He retreated into a daydream. Ellie smiled and turned to

Norbury. "What's this about your knowledge of India? I trust you aren't planning to forsake these shores for hotter climes?"

"I'm sure I will see hell long before I see India," he replied.

Nick laughed, loudly, in a way that sounded forced to the point of mockery. "But you're a veritable saint, Norbury. With your influence in Parliament and no hint of family drama, you're surely bound for heaven. I never liked most of the investors in the East India Company, but you seem to be the exception."

Ellie saw the dislike in Norbury's eyes suddenly — a steeliness he never showed in her presence. But it was gone just as swiftly. "If you'll excuse me, Lady Folkestone, Folkestone, Pickett — I promised Salford I would partner him in whist."

He was gone an instant later. Ellie narrowed her eyes at Nick. "Do you care to explain why you abused that poor man?"

"No."

His tone was final. But then his eyes swept over her, turning finality into a promise of things to come. "I didn't expect you to seek me out so soon. May I help you, Lady Folkestone?"

She ignored the innuendo. "I came to see if there is an entertainment you prefer tonight, my lord."

"You would offer that in front of your guests? I am shocked, my lady."

Percy, forgotten beside them, snickered. "Our fair, cruel mistress is too discreet for that, Lord Folkestone. She is Artemis, not Aphrodite. She drives men before her in the hunt, but is never touched by them."

Percy was a poetic fool, but he was a perceptive one. If she wasn't mistaken, that comment almost sounded like a warning.

Nick didn't heed it. "Fair and cruel? You know her well, don't you, Pickett?"

Percy shrugged, losing interest fast. "The ton is small and Lady Folkestone is more intriguing than most. The poems I could write about her..."

Ellie cut him off. "Let us return to the topic. What would you like, Folkestone? Dancing? Some other amusement?"

"Not dancing," he said decisively. "Beyond that, I care not how we spend the next hour or two."

But he cared very much how they would spend the time after that. She saw it in the way his eyes turned dreamy, almost as dreamy as Percy's. But if Percy dreamed of poems, Nick dreamed of something far baser.

She just barely controlled her shiver. "I shall arrange charades for those who want it. If you don't wish to play, I'm sure you can find another game."

"I already have," he murmured.

She blushed. Then she stepped back, knowing she had already spent too much time with him. At a party where everyone longed for gossip and no one was creating any, she knew without looking that half her guests were watching their interaction.

"Very well," she said. "Be kind to my friends, though."

"When am I ever unkind?"

That begged for a setdown, but she raised her chin and gave him a sunny smile. "Enjoy your game, my lord. I know I shall enjoy mine."

She walked away before he responded. Now was not the time to spar with him. It was the time to make nice with her guests, make sure her sisters talked to the right men, make herself stay calm and collected...

Make herself stop wondering what Nick would demand from her that night.

*   *   *

Fifteen minutes to midnight. Nick had survived another day — not just without facing an assassination attempt, but without murdering any of Ellie's guests.

He had Ellie to thank for that. If she hadn't sought him out when she did, he might have continued talking to Norbury. And if he was honest, he knew he'd almost lost his carefully controlled, utterly false bonhomie. Nick didn't sense any rottenness in Norbury's soul, although the man was guarded enough that Nick couldn't be sure. But he still didn't understand why Ellie had befriended such a dull prig. To take it a step further, why had she befriended any of these people? From what he understood, this was a tamer circle than those she usually entertained — but still mostly shallow. When he had known her, she hadn't wanted an empty London life.

From his seat at the card table with Marcus, Nick surveyed the rooms. Most of the older generation had retired. The charades had ended, but Ellie made no sign that the party would ever dissolve. She had cornered the Earl of Salford in the main drawing room, but Nick couldn't get close enough to hear their conversation without his eavesdropping being apparent.

The twins were playing a duet for piano and harp, and Sebastian Staunton had been dragooned — quite willingly, it appeared — into turning pages for them. They were accomplished enough to flirt and play at the same time, and Sebastian wasn't stupid enough to miss that opportunity. Norbury read a book, ostensibly, although Nick hadn't seen him turn a page in the last quarter hour. Several other guests were playing cards or billiards, with enough wine around them to supply a ship of the line. And the Duke and Duchess of Rothwell were murmuring to each other on a settee in the drawing room — a welcome break from the way Rothwell had watched Nick throughout the evening with a disapproving scowl that would have done his father proud.

That left Miss Etchingham alone with her embroidery near the fire. He wondered at that, but it wasn't his place to comment. He tossed his final card on the table. "I'm sorry to keep stealing your money, brother."

"Where did you learn to play?" Marcus demanded, pushing another marker toward Nick. "You never won when we were younger."

Nick retrieved Marcus's marker and added it to the pile of notes in front of him. "Five months on a ship is enough time to learn any vice that involves drink or cards."

"It's not your skill that has changed," Marcus said, collecting the cards and tapping them together into a neat pile. "You just know better when to go in for the kill. Another hand, or do you think our hostess will let us go to our beds?"

Nick glanced at the clock. Twelve minutes. "She will let us go at midnight, I'd wager. Not enough time for you to win back what you lost to me."

"Tomorrow we shall try billiards. I would guess you didn't perfect that game aboard a ship."

"You don't lack a killing instinct either, do you?"

Marcus grinned. "My role models were woefully ruthless."

Nick surveyed the room again. He had spoken with all of the men in the party, both over brandy after dinner and in smaller groups as the evening's entertainments had unfolded. If his instincts were sound, it was unlikely that any of them were responsible for the highwayman's attack the previous day.

But he had ignored the women — not rudely, but only because it was so laughably bizarre to think that any of them might be plotting his demise. Still, he'd observed the party long enough to find Ellie's choice of friends odd. According to Marcus, Ellie had known the

Duchess of Rothwell and Miss Etchingham for less than a year. A newlywed bride and an impoverished spinster hardly fit the spectacle Ellie had created at her masquerade ball.

"Do you care to approach Miss Etchingham with me?" he asked his brother. "She looks like she might want company."

Marcus shook his head. "She's friendly enough, if a bit too much of a bluestocking for my tastes. With your charm, I'm sure you can draw her out better alone than with me interfering."

"Charm?" Nick asked.

Marcus grinned. "Did I sound too sarcastic when I said that? If charm doesn't work, give her the money you just won from me. She has more use for it than you do."

Nick laughed and left him to a game of patience. He walked over to the fire and bowed slightly as he greeted his target. "Miss Etchingham. May I join you?"

She smiled with what seemed like a genuine invitation. "I won't turn down an opportunity to abandon my embroidery hoop, my lord."

He took the chair beside her and stole another glance at the clock. Ten minutes. "Have you enjoyed your visit to Folkestone?" he asked.

"Very much, Lord Folkestone. How are you finding your home?"

There was no snide implication in her tone — just frank curiosity. "Well enough," he said. "But it will take ages to accustom myself to having so many lovely ladies in my house."

Miss Etchingham didn't preen or simper. She laughed in his face. "There's no need to play the flirt, my lord. I know my value, and it has never been described as decorative."

That statement puzzled him. Prudence didn't have Ellie's fire or the twins' classic blonde beauty, but her trim figure and sparkling brown eyes were still pleasing. "You'll forgive me if I say you must be mistaken."

She smiled, something wistful touching at the corners of her mouth. "I thank you for the kindness, my lord. But don't let's pretend that you've noticed any lady but our hostess since you've arrived."

Now Nick saw why Ellie liked the woman. Miss Etchingham missed very little, and her directness nearly matched Ellie's own. "Is that so?" he asked, trying to sound bored. "If I have given that impression, I apologize."

She laughed again. "I would guess that you only give impressions you wish to give, my lord. In that, you and Lady Folkestone are well matched. If you were whist partners, your control over your reactions would make you nigh on unbeatable."

"You are a direct one, aren't you?"

It wasn't meant to be a setdown, but he regretted the words when her eyes switched from vivacious to wary. "Please do forgive me, Lord Folkestone. I forgot myself."

He waved a hand, suddenly contrite. "No forgiveness necessary, Miss Etchingham. I'm sure I've heard worse."

"Not from ape-leaders who are taking advantage of your hospitality, I would think."

She glanced through the double doors to where Ellie and Lord Salford still talked in muted undertones. She was far more dependent on Salford's generosity than Nick's — and Nick wondered, then, whether that fact chafed her, despite the comfort of her position.

But he didn't know her well enough to ask. And ultimately, Miss Etchingham's future was not his responsibility. He pressed his other agenda instead. "Does our mutual friend bear any of the blame for your...unguarded tongue?"

Prudence turned her gaze back to Nick. "I do not hold Lady

Folkestone responsible for my personal failings, my lord."

He saw the spark in her eyes. Was it his imagination, or had she implied that he unfairly blamed Ellie for his mistakes? "Still, is it not detrimental for your reputation to associate with her?"

She frowned. "Ellie — excuse me, Lady Folkestone — has never gone beyond the pale."

"The rumors of her parties are legendary."

"'Legendary' is a key word, I believe. She has an eye for drama and an appetite for titillating people, but she herself is always perfectly composed. If she indulged in hysterics or public love affairs, perhaps she would no longer be received — but morality applies to titled, wealthy widows differently than it does to the rest of us. I believe she could walk stark naked into Almack's and still not be cut — it's hard to cut someone that self-contained. The ton knows they care more for her than she cares for them, after all."

No one could go to Almack's nude, not even Ellie, but he lost a few seconds considering it. Prudence's quick grin said she guessed his preoccupation. Nick cleared his throat. "Then is she always as she was at her masquerade? Aloof?"

"You won't catch me spreading tales about her," Prudence warned. "But I will say that, in all the time I've known her, I've never seen her display any emotion stronger than amusement or vague disapproval in public."

"And in private?"

"Did I not just say I won't spread tales?"

Nick shrugged. "I had to ask."

"Why did you have to ask?"

Her eyes were expectant, her posture even more so. She leaned forward as though she needed to be as close as possible to whatever words he might share. The answer mattered to her, for some reason he couldn't fathom — unless she really cared to know what Nick's intentions were toward Ellie?

He wasn't above playing on that sentiment. "I find Lady Folkestone most…intriguing. You'll forgive me for wanting to know more about her preferences."

Prudence looked at Ellie again, pausing as she collected her thoughts. "I cannot help you there, my lord. Whatever Lady Folkestone's preferences might be, she's remarkably skilled at not sharing them."

His Ellie, the one he had loved, had always shared her preferences. She had wanted to seize everything, so eager to go to London and see something beyond the small estate where her father kept her cloistered. She had never been able to hide her desires, or her fears, from him — which is why he had believed her when she said she preferred his cousin to him.

But when had she gotten so good at masking herself? And what did she really, truly want? The previous night had shown him that she was still capable of desire — if she unleashed that desire, where would she go and what might she choose?

Would she choose him? Or would she choose to escape him again?

The clock chimed the hour. Midnight. A footman entered the room, on the cue Nick had given him, and handed Ellie a note on a silver salver. Nick watched as she flipped the note open. Her eyes scanned the lines. If she felt anything when she had finished, her emotions didn't reach her face. She looked up, unerringly, to Nick, betraying only the briefest hint of a scowl as she folded the note again. Then she dismissed the footman and turned back to Salford as though nothing had happened — as though she hadn't just read the note Nick had arranged for her to receive, in which he said what he expected of her that night.

He turned back to Prudence. "I do believe you are correct, Miss Etchingham. Lady Folkestone is a puzzle."

But she hadn't always been. And tonight he would have another go at deciphering her — whether she wished it or not.

CHAPTER TWENTY

Ellie had fought hard to control her blush when she read the note that Nick had sent her. She must have succeeded — Salford had said nothing about it. He merely continued discussing her antiquities collection with her as though receiving a note at midnight didn't merit any curiosity whatsoever.

Or perhaps he was merely polite. Far more polite than Nick. Only a devil would make this arrangement, let alone send the note he had sent. Why couldn't she have fallen in love with someone like Salford? Someone kind, with a sharp mind, who might take care of her?

But Ellie didn't want a protector. Perhaps she didn't deserve one, either. Perhaps she deserved an inescapable adversary, a dark king to match the woman she had remade herself into.

Stop being dramatic. The party had dissolved five minutes after she received the note, when she had abruptly sent everyone off to bed. And now, after twenty minutes spent pacing in her room, she had come back downstairs to follow her orders. She took a breath and pushed open the door to the study. She closed it behind her and turned the key in the lock. Leaning against the door, she unfolded the note in her hand and read it again.

E. - The study, half past midnight. Lock the interior door. Unlock the door to the terrace but leave the curtains closed. Take down your hair for me and kneel in front of the desk. Wait there until I arrive. Don't move when I enter. Don't make a sound until I say you may. Tonight, goddess, we shall see whether you can worship me. - N.

Her father was wrong. There were times when one *had* to be dramatic. This was one of them. She strode across the room and tossed the note into the fire. She didn't wait to see the paper burn — the words were already seared into her memory.

She unlocked the terrace door. She shivered as she pulled the pins from her hair, placing them one by one on the lacquered white desk. Her sense of order was disturbed by having them there, so she slid open a drawer and tossed them inside — directly on top of Nick's copy of the agreement they had signed, the paper that bound her to him. She shut the drawer and shook her hair out until it fell in heavy waves down her back.

Then she moved around the desk to the open space in the center of the room. She eyed the floor dubiously. It was thickly carpeted, but she wasn't accustomed to kneeling. Ellie Claiborne knelt for no one and nothing.

But the saints of old had knelt until their knees bled — something Ellie would have done a decade ago, if she had thought her betrayal of Nick and their love was something she could do penance for. So she knelt. She felt ridiculous even as she sank to her knees, but there was nothing for it. Perhaps Nick would see how ridiculous it was and let her have a chair instead.

There was little hope of that. As soon as he walked through the French door a few minutes later, she knew he didn't find her ridiculous. The hunger in his eyes was so stark, the set of his jaw so determined, the slash of his lips so cruel, that she knew, then, how this night would go.

He would wring everything from her that he intended to wring. And her cursed, traitorous heart would give it to him — everything he asked for, everything he wanted.

Everything she wanted, if she were being honest. Because, stupid fool that she was, she would rather have this night, no matter where it led, than another lifetime without him.

* * *

She knelt for him. Nick had dreamed of her in that pose. He had dreamed of the words that would come from those lips. She would beg for his forgiveness. She would plead for him to come back to her. She would cry as he denied her. He would crush her heart so that she would feel the same roaring, angry emptiness that he felt. And then he would leave her with the knowledge that she would share his bed anyway, again, and again, until her debt was repaid.

But dreaming was so far away from doing. And now that Nick had her there, in exactly the pose he had imagined, he felt far more doubt than he'd ever expected.

She didn't greet him. So far, she had followed his instructions to the letter. Only her eyes moved to follow him, but she didn't tilt her head as he moved toward her — didn't turn as he walked behind her, although her spine stiffened with the tension of not knowing what he intended.

He wanted to touch her. But, more, he wanted to know her. He *needed* to know her, suddenly — needed to know why her image was so icy when her painting was so wild. Why she was so distant when her friends were so intimate. Why she, who seemed so jaded and fickle, had never professed love for anyone else.

He walked over to the decanter and poured himself a drink. It was still a hideous room — not the setting he'd imagined for this seduction, although using her in the room she'd decorated in a fit of pique against him was its own sort of poetry. Still, he would be damned before he sat on one of those lavender hassocks. He pulled the chair out from behind the desk and sat in it, directly in front of Ellie, his legs spread negligently in front of him. His erection pressed against his breeches, but he still had some control — there was still time for the questions he suddenly, urgently needed to ask.

"Tell me what your sins are."

Ellie sat back on her heels, startled. "I beg your pardon?"

"Your sins. I said I would learn them. And I want to learn them now."

"Now? You called me onto the carpet like a child, not a...?"

She couldn't complete the sentence. "A concubine?" he supplied.

She nodded.

"Funny, that doesn't seem to be a word you would hesitate over. But no, you're not a child. And we will get to the concubine part of the evening in good time."

She choked back a laugh, perhaps thinking that laughter wasn't allowed by the letter of his demands. She was so far from tears as to make his revenge, if he still wanted it, seem permanently unattainable. He frowned and tried to focus. "Your sins, Ellie. Now."

She met his gaze straight on. "You were the only sin that was deadly for me."

"Still regretting you gave your maidenhead to a peasant? My only regret is I can't take it again."

"Do you want me to say I regret that I have but one maidenhead to give for your lordship? I'm sorry, but you broke that toy — you'll have to take something else."

He sipped his whisky to hide his sudden grin and contemplated the lines of her face. In this mood, she wouldn't betray vulnerability. Her chin was too stubborn, her mouth too sultry, her eyes too guarded. She was the Virgin Queen again, cold and unattainable no matter what he said or what he forced her to do. But he knew how to break through the ice.

"Is there nothing else you wish to confess?" he asked.

If she lifted her chin any higher, she would snap her own neck. "Absolutely not."

He tossed back the rest of his whisky, wiped his mouth with his sleeve just to annoy her, and set the glass behind him on the desk. Then he leaned back in his chair and crossed his hands behind his head. "Then you may begin, goddess. Worship me."

CHAPTER TWENTY-ONE

Her mouth went dry. She was trying so hard to stay unaffected, but she was already wet for him — not visibly aroused like he was, but her secret need was a pressing, demanding, living thing that would eat through her resolve long before Nick would let her leave the room.

Why did she want him so badly? There was no warmth in his eyes. His mouth was grim. The words that came from it were even more so. There was a time, years ago, when she would have crawled across any room to have him again. Now she had no desire to crawl — but he had swept into this house and demanded it, as though no time at all had passed between her failure and his revenge.

Ellie wet her lips. His eyes followed the darting of her tongue. His arms tensed as though his hands were turning into fists. She narrowed her eyes at that — at the way he had arranged all of this, as though to remind both of them who was at fault for their doomed love.

Suddenly, she was angry. If one room of her heart held regret, and if another held guilt, there was a third room that held fury. Fury at him for letting her go so easily. Fury that he had left and never looked back. Fury that he had left her alone to destroy herself.

It was all her fault…but it was his fault, too.

She stayed on her knees like a penitent approaching an altar, shifting her skirts out from underneath her so that she could move forward without falling on her face. He didn't move at all, but his mouth fell open as though she'd finally, truly shocked him.

She didn't smile. If he wanted a goddess, he would get one — a vengeful, remorseless goddess, but a goddess nonetheless.

She nudged his knees apart, sliding into the gap he created for her. She unbuttoned his jacket, then his waistcoat, and slid her hands up his chest. His skin rippled and his muscles shuddered under her touch. She untied his cravat next, undoing the knot that made him look respectable, and tossed the cloth away. Then she undid the drawstring of his shirt, letting it gap a bit at the neck. With his jacket open and his neck bare, he looked dangerous in a way that appealed to some fantasy she hadn't realized she had.

But the sharper the need in his eyes, the more she was in control.

Her fingers trailed down to his waist and the bulge that waited for her. He sucked in a breath as she unbuttoned his breeches, working slowly to maximize the effect of her fingers brushing delicately over his confined erection. When she was done, she pulled the tails of his shirt out of his breeches and pushed them aside. And then, like she was unwrapping a priceless artifact, she freed his cock.

He grabbed her wrist. "What is your plan?" he asked, in a voice gone gruff with need.

She looked up, hoping he saw reverence instead of ruthlessness. "Worship, Nick. Isn't that what you want?"

He looked dazed. His blue eyes were dark. "This wasn't what I expected."

She tilted her head to the side. "Don't you want to debase me? Show me that I'm not a goddess? Throw me from the tower you've placed me in?"

He scrubbed a hand over his mouth.

She snorted, low and mirthless. "If you remember what you want, tell me. Meanwhile, this is what *I* want."

She licked her lips again, instinctively, and heard him groan as she lowered them to his cock. It strained toward her, not caring about whatever battle was raging in Nick's heart. She licked him first, swirling her tongue around the head, before opening her mouth and taking him inside of her.

For Ellie, this was a new experience — one she'd seen others do, in the darker alcoves of her darkest bacchanals, but never one she'd deigned to do herself. But her enjoyment of it, of how Nick felt in her mouth and how his fingers clutched in her hair, surprised her. She'd meant to tease him — but as her tempo sped up and the stroke of her tongue over his shaft became less tentative, it felt like real worship, striking a chord with how she wanted to care for him, how she wanted to please him. She wanted him to be happy when he was with her. She wanted to give him pure, selfless pleasure.

But there was nothing pure and selfless about their arrangement. She pulled back. His hand pressed against her head as though he wanted to force her to finish what she had started, but he dropped it before she started to panic.

"Bloody hell, Ellie. I know what I want now — finish me."

She laughed as she sat back on her heels and looked up at him. Somehow, his need now was lovely, not dangerous. "I will. But I want to finish us together. Will you let me do that?"

He nodded. She grabbed his hand and pulled him onto the floor, then stretched him out on his back. They hadn't kissed all day, but this wasn't a night for tenderness. She stayed away from his mouth, trailing kisses down his sternum instead, then pushing the sleeves of his jacket away. He had to sit up so that she could get his waistcoat, braces, and shirt off of him, and he tried to kiss her then, but she turned her head away. "No kisses, Nick," she whispered, pushing him back down to the carpet once his shirt was gone.

"You aren't good at worship, are you?" he observed, coming up on his elbows to watch her as she knelt at his feet to take off his shoes.

She tossed the first shoe away. "No one ever taught me how." Then she slid off his second shoe, letting her fingers linger on the arch of his foot. He jerked beneath her, and she smiled. "But I'm a fast learner. And I shall worship every inch of you, Nicholas Claiborne."

He exhaled, sharp and swift. "I have eight you could focus on first, if you want to speed up your lessons."

She grinned. "Patience, Nick."

In truth, she didn't worship every inch of him — by the time his breeches were gone and he was naked beneath her, she was too hungry for him to indulge in endless exploration. But her eyes missed nothing, even if her fingers couldn't move across him fast enough to keep her promise. Every bit of him was harder than it had been when he was twenty-two, as though the Nick she had painted then was an imperfect rendering of the god he would become. There were sinews and veins on his arms that she hadn't seen before. His shoulders and chest were broader, which made the taper toward his hips even more dramatic. He had more hair, too — not too much, but the smooth chest of a boy was gone, replaced by dark curls that started, lightly, at his throat and led her gaze down, inexorably, to the manhood that still strained for her.

Suddenly, she didn't want patience either. She pushed him flat and moved over him — something else they hadn't done when she was nineteen and too naïve to guess that she could find pleasure without being on her back. He was hard enough, and she was wet enough, that it was no test at all. She used her hand to guide him to her opening and slid down his shaft, feeling herself stretch as she took him to the hilt.

Nick burned for her. He had asked for worship, and he was getting it — but it felt more like an attack than a seduction. He put his hands on her hips, trying to get her to move faster, but she shook her head wickedly and pushed them away. "Patience," she whispered again, leaning forward so that her hair fell around them like a curtain. "Let me worship you."

He slid a hand up to her breast, and she accepted that easily enough — although it annoyed him that she had somehow stripped him naked without removing anything of her own. Even her shoes were still on, and he felt the heels grazing against his legs. He didn't care, though. He didn't care about anything except the feel of her stroking up and down on his shaft. He closed his eyes and dropped his hands, hoping that he could last long enough that she might find her pleasure too, but knowing it was a losing battle...

Until suddenly, shatteringly, she stopped. His hips surged up automatically to try to recapture the momentum, but she held fast. He opened his eyes just as she bent over to look him in the face. "Beg me, Nick," she whispered.

It was an echo of what he had done to her the night before. And it wasn't how their game was supposed to be played. But neither his heart nor his cock cared to put up a fight. "Please, Ellie," he grated out, mad at her, mad for her. "Finish."

She slid up, then down — and stayed down. She tilted her head. "That didn't sound like begging."

"What do you want me to say?"

She wiggled a bit, as though she were settling in for a story. He groaned. She wiggled again — she seemed to know just how much she needed to move to keep him on edge without letting him go over it.

Then she smiled. He didn't see any worship on her face. He didn't see any love, either. Despite the fact his cock was buried inside her, she was just as impenetrable as she had been an hour earlier. Her voice, when she spoke again, had all the condemnation of a priest calling an Inquisition. "Say you love me, Nick."

"Love you? *Love* you?" Something primal snapped, and even though he knew she'd pushed him into his anger, he couldn't stop. He reared up, flipped her on her back, and drove into her. "I hate you. I loathe you. I despise you. You *destroyed* me, Ellie. How could I ever love you?"

He couldn't speak anymore. He could only plunge into her, mindless, savage, needing the satisfaction of her body so he could stop his awful thoughts. She moaned, and he felt her tighten and shudder around him, but he was too far gone to care whether she'd found her pleasure. He buried himself within her and came, hard, before collapsing. He had just enough presence of mind to roll them onto their sides so he didn't crush her before his energy ran out.

When he could think again, he found Ellie leaning on one elbow, stroking his hair and gazing at his face. She didn't seem upset by anything he'd said — a little sad, perhaps, but the tears he'd planned to take from her that night were nowhere to be seen.

"You destroyed me, Nick," she whispered. "But if having you was a sin, I will never repent."

He'd thought she had smashed his heart a decade earlier. But some piece of it must have survived, because he felt it break again. He brushed his hand across her face and felt a track of moisture on her cheek — her tears weren't visible, but there had been at least a few in the time between the words he'd hurled at her and the moment he had awoken.

"I'm unrepentant myself," he said.

That drew a laugh from her. "How shocking, my lord." Then she dropped her hand to his chest, covering his heart. "I hate you, too. For destroying me then, and for coming back to do it again."

She sat up before he could grab her. It was only as she moved that he remembered that he had spent himself inside her — against every plan he had and all common sense. He reached for her hand, but she swatted it away. "We've hurt each other enough for tonight, don't you think?" she said briskly, pulling herself up to stand over his naked body.

He stood up to join her, not bothering with his breeches. "I am sorry that I did not remember the consequences. I will be more careful."

She looked confused for a moment. He dropped his eyes, pointedly, to her belly. She rolled hers. "Never fear. If I must, I'll take your bastard to the Continent when our arrangement is over."

He could see her, suddenly, heavy with his child. In that dream she was in his bed, in his home, laughing. She would imagine herself on an island, alone, where he could never touch her again.

He reached for her. She stepped back. "Let's cut bait, Nick. We hate each other, we've behaved abominably to each other for over a decade, and we wouldn't even be discussing a pregnancy if you hadn't arrived motivated only by revenge. I'll grant you, the physical pleasure is wonderful — you've gotten better, Claiborne," she said, in a condescending tone that made him wish he could throttle her. "But until you stop either worshiping me or dragging me through the mud, there is no future I see in which I would want to give a child over to you to be raised."

She wasn't even talking about marriage. She was talking about a bastard child — *their* bastard child — as though its bastardy would be inevitable. His anger rose. "I'll stop worshipping you and dragging you through the mud when you stop shutting yourself off and pretending you're the coldest bitch in Europe," he shot back.

She lifted her chin. "I *am* the coldest bitch in Europe."

Nick would have laughed, or strangled her, if he hadn't seen the flash of despair in her eyes. But he let her go rather than pressing her. She wouldn't crack tonight — in his effort to crack her, he had cracked himself instead.

So he bade her a stiff, kissless goodnight, pulled on his breeches, and poured himself another whisky. Ellie was a mystery — and he wanted to solve her.

But the bigger mystery, without hope for a clean outcome, was why he had told her he hated her — and why his heart still screamed the opposite.

CHAPTER TWENTY-TWO

The next morning, Nick wasn't in the mood to discuss his impending demise. To be fair, he wasn't in the mood for much of anything beyond finding Ellie and trying, again, to unearth whatever feelings she hid behind her mask.

But even though Nick had spent more time obsessing over Ellie than pursuing whoever wanted him dead, he could still force himself to consider that issue instead. It had taken a renewed urgency overnight. While he had lain in his chamber, mostly sleepless, his would-be assailant had struck a different target.

"Have there been any other fires in the area?" he asked Marcus.

Marcus had just joined him the breakfast room, and he speared a forkful of ham from the sideboard before replying. "No fires. I rode into the village after you dragged me out of bed this morning. No one has heard anything suspicious. The timing is good for someone wanting to escape notice, though. You're the most interesting bit of gossip around. It is easier for a stranger to pass through unremarked when everyone is more interested in what your return might mean for them."

Nick raked a hand through his hair. It was only eight a.m., and he had been in the breakfast room for half an hour waiting for Marcus's report, but his hair still smelled of smoke. His batman had awoken him at six with the news that the shed where they had kept the highwayman's body was on fire. The staff had contained the blaze, thanks to a stableboy who smelled the smoke before the fire spread to other outbuildings. But the shed, and the body it housed, were destroyed.

"I sent Trower to London to make enquiries about the tattoos," Nick said. "But the threat surely lies closer than that. The roads are better this morning than they were yesterday, but I find it unlikely that anyone in London ordered the fire."

Marcus placed his filled plate on the table and sat down next to Nick. One of the ubiquitous footmen poured his coffee and refreshed Nick's cup, then busied himself with tidying the sideboard. Nick didn't recognize the footman, but he could have passed him in the house a dozen times and not noticed him. Ellie's servants were innumerable, and they were meant to vanish into the background.

Marcus wasn't watching the footman, though. Nick couldn't fully trust a staff he didn't know, but Marcus had no qualms about speaking in front of them. He shoveled a bite of eggs into his mouth, pausing to chew before continuing his report. "No one is missing anything. Not horses, not clothes, not even foodstuffs. In the dead of winter, families would notice if preserves or seed were stolen. But the pub owner hasn't fed anyone he didn't know since you came through before the party."

Nick frowned. "Could someone lodge with a family nearby?"

"Possibly. Your tenants are mostly prosperous, but few would turn their noses up at extra income. But he would have to have a good reason for not staying at an inn and for keeping his identity secret — people might want his money, but they would be suspicious of perfect strangers."

"So it's likely someone who was already in the neighborhood?"

"Or with ties to it," Marcus said with a shrug. "Or he is staying farther afield — it would take days to investigate all the inns he could be at, particularly if he has stayed in London and only comes here to wreak havoc."

Nick leaned back in his chair. "Why was destroying the body so important? What could it have told us?"

Marcus cut into his ham. "The tattoos were the only evidence, unless he thought someone in the area might recognize the man himself. The assailant knew the body was there, but he must not have known that Ellie had drawn the tattoos already."

Nick swirled his coffee in his cup, losing even more heat into the chilled air of a country house in winter. "If it's tattoos, the connection between the dead man and the highwayman might have come at sea."

"That eliminates me and Ellie as suspects, if you follow that reasoning."

"And leaves Rupert."

Marcus winced. "It can't be Rupert. Even if he had ordered your death in India, he couldn't have heard yet that you've come home."

"Unless Sebastian Staunton is in his employ. He came from the Caribbean a few months ago."

They both considered that idea — and both snorted at the same time. "Staunton and Rupert are equally unlikely," Marcus said. "Can you picture Sebastian as a murderer?"

"No. He's so intent on seducing Ellie's sisters that he barely spares me a glance," Nick said. "And you are right. Even if Rupert does want me dead, he would be hard pressed to arrange it from so far afield."

Nick drained his coffee and rose to stand by the heater. Ellie had installed a standing porcelain stove of Swedish design when she had remodeled the breakfast room, and the green and gold painted enamel was a welcome change to the open fireplace in his bedchamber. He rubbed his hands together. She kept the house warm enough — on his money — that he wouldn't get chilblains like he had in the drafty, ancient expanses of Eton. But he still felt chilled — whether from the weather or from the risk he'd brought to all of them, he didn't know.

"I should return to London," he said. "No sense putting anyone here at risk of another attack gone awry."

He heard footsteps in the hall. Marcus must have heard them as well, because he held his response to Nick's remark. Nick turned as the footsteps stopped — just as Ellie entered the breakfast chamber.

Her eyes were cool and her red curls were perfectly contained atop her head, but even in a proper blue morning dress she had a sensuous, undeniable appeal. He wanted another chance at what they had done in the study the night before — a chance to see if the tenderness he'd denied her so far might break something that his anger had only fortified.

But this wasn't the right time to seduce her. "Good morning, Lady Folkestone," he said.

"Lord Folkestone. Mr. Claiborne," she said, greeting both Nick and Marcus even though she never turned away from Nick's gaze. "May I break my fast with you, or are you discussing business?"

She was formal, but he couldn't read whether it was a display for the footman or a crutch for her own resolve. Right now, though, he didn't want to push her. "We would be honored to join you," he said. "Our business can wait."

Ellie nodded. "Please, sit," she said, gesturing to Marcus, who had stood when she entered. "There's no need to stand while I fill my plate."

Marcus didn't protest. Nick stayed by the heater, though, and watched as she selected her breakfast from the array of dishes laid out before her. "I am surprised that we have the room to ourselves," he said. "Surely your other guests need to eat."

Ellie's hand paused over the meats, deciding between steak and kidneys. "Most of my guests won't be out of their beds before ten. We are still early, my lord — this may be the country, but I see no reason to keep country hours."

She had kept country hours when he first knew her, all alone in that small manor house where her father had left her to be schooled and then ignored. But her current life wasn't one of isolated contemplation. "Then I am surprised you are awake when everyone else is still abed," he said.

Left unspoken was that he had kept her awake later than her other guests, but not even a tremor of her hand betrayed any memory of the previous night. She settled in at the table and sent the footman for a cup of chocolate before saying, "Lucia told me about the fire. I could hardly stay sequestered in my room after learning of it."

So it wasn't a desire to see him that had lured her downstairs — or at least not a desire she would admit to.

"Your maid is well informed."

"That is what I pay her for. But she could not tell me what you plan to do about it."

"Find the responsible party, of course."

Ellie had taken a whole plate of foodstuffs. Her chef was French, but whoever was responsible for breakfast had an Englishman's taste. None of it seemed to her liking today, though. She ignored the meats and nibbled on a piece of toast as she considered Nick's words. "How do you propose to find him?" she finally asked.

Nick returned to the table and took his seat. "Marcus says no strangers have been seen in the immediate neighborhood, so the culprit may be based in London. It would be best if I went there to solve this rather than disturbing your party."

She paused in mid-bite, slowly looking up at him as her hand fell away from her mouth. "Running away, are you?"

"Not in the way you think." He paused, just long enough for his words to sink in, but not long enough to draw Marcus's attention before he continued. "But if my presence here poses a risk to your safety, it would be best if I left. My enemy, whoever he is, doesn't seem averse to risking others' lives to get to me."

"But won't it be harder for you to stay safe in London? With the crowds, it would be far easier to harm you there and come away clean — here, the villain must be much more careful, and can make fewer attempts as a result."

"Whoever the villain is, he can't be too effective in crowds. If he knew what he was doing, he would have succeeded in Madras," Nick said.

"But it sounds as though at least one of those attempts was hired done," Ellie protested. "What if the culprit has taken matters into his own hands? You may face a more motivated foe than you did in Madras."

The footman returned with Ellie's chocolate. Marcus filled the pause his entrance created. "I agree with Lady Folkestone, if she'll allow it."

Ellie sighed. Nick bit back a grin as he said, "I'm glad to see my safety has united you."

"That's going a bit far," she said.

Marcus raised his hands. "I'm not trying to forge an alliance. But I do think Nick is safer here than in London."

Nick looked at the footman again, gesturing to get his attention. "You may wait outside the room. Don't return until another guest joins us."

The footman bowed and left, betraying no curiosity at all over Nick's request. Nick waited until the door closed before he leaned in. "There is an army of servants here, many of whom aren't suited for service. Any one of them could join the enemy for the right price."

"Just because the staff happens to be younger than usual doesn't mean they are disloyal," Ellie protested. "This is a very good job, better than most of them could get outside the theatres — I doubt they would risk it. If anything, they have been more discreet than any of us could expect. Surely some of them have heard about the body in the shed, but if they have, they've kept it to themselves."

"How can you know that? Someone must have let it slip, or the shed wouldn't have been set on fire."

Ellie frowned. "It's possible, of course. Servants know everything we do, no matter how discreet we are — it's the price of having them. But they don't survive in my employ if I catch them passing secrets about me. And if any of them have said anything to our visitors' servants, you can be sure the subject of the highwayman would have been raised by now. Do you really suppose that my brother would have let it go unremarked if one of his servants had heard of it?"

"True. But how many servants are on the estate?"

Ellie looked at Marcus, who shrugged. "Folkestone usually has a butler, a housekeeper, an estate manager, Mrs. Grafton, my valet, the chef, his two assistants, six footmen, four upstairs maids, a laundress, and three downstairs maids. But with the party, there are double those numbers of footmen and maids, plus the guests' maids and valets. And their grooms and coachmen — and our grooms and gardeners."

"Don't forget the usual scullery maids, in addition to the extra help in the kitchens that we hired in from the village," Ellie said.

Nick had mentally counted as they spoke. The estimate stunned him. "If every guest has a servant, there are well over a hundred servants on the grounds. Can you really tell me that I can trust all of them with my life? Or, more importantly, your lives?"

Ellie nodded firmly. "My servants aren't prone to violence. If they were, I would have used them to throw you out of my ball that first night."

Nick laughed. "I shall hire some ugly brutes for you so that you may accomplish such tasks in the future."

She wrinkled her nose. "Thank you, but no. Still, you do have a point about the visitors. I shall see if Lucia has learned anything about them."

It shocked him, how adept Ellie was at considering these issues. His need for her raged ever hotter because of it. If she were nineteen, he would have shielded her from all of this. But Ellie no longer needed to be shielded. Protected, yes — he would certainly overrule her on the issue of her ornamental footmen. Shielded, though...

She caught him staring at her. She met his gaze without hesitation. His need to keep her safe stunned him. Imagining a world without her face, her voice, her paintings — it was impossible to imagine. Even if he gave in to what was prudent, let her go, and never saw her again, he would need to know that she lived and was safe.

The irony of wanting her safe when he was also bent on torturing her wasn't lost on him. But the question of what to do with her was one for when they were alone, not in the breakfast room. And certainly not with Marcus watching them as though he was appalled by what they were doing to each other. Nick cleared his throat.

"I will stay at least for a few days — until we have any evidence that proves whether the threat is based here or in London."

Ellie looked relieved. And then she looked aggrieved, as though remembering that keeping him safe at Folkestone also meant keeping him in her bed. "Do try not to be killed here. It will harm my reputation as a hostess."

"I appreciate your concern, Lady Folkestone," he said drily. "But I may harm it anyway. I intend to continue befriending your guests. If they are all like Sir Percival, I may save our assailant the trouble and burn the house myself."

Ellie protested even as she laughed. "Percy isn't that bad."

"His poems are awful," Marcus interjected.

"Yes, but he knows it, and he does it anyway because he likes it. If more people were like that, London would be a far better place. Even hardened industrialists like you may benefit from a few days of idle talk."

It wasn't the days of talk he looked forward to — it was her, at the end of every night, that made the days bearable. He didn't say it, though. He turned to Marcus instead. "It might be worth the effort if you returned to the village today, and perhaps the next town or two beyond that. As word of the fire spreads, someone may remember something."

Ellie finished her chocolate and pushed away her plate. "Is there anything you wish for me to do? Or should I merely keep the guests entertained until you are ready to bait them?"

He couldn't tell whether she wanted to help, whether she was just being polite, or whether she hoped to get him alone. He tried to read her, but her smile wasn't calculating or inviting and there were no clues in her eyes.

Perhaps he should stop trying to read her and start asking her. "Do you want to help?"

She blinked. The question surprised her, just as every choice she was offered by him surprised her. That blink was enough to reassure him, even though he tried to wait for her words rather than just listening to his gut.

"I want to help," she said. "I must take care of my responsibilities this morning, but I shall be free in two hours or so."

He looked at the clock. It was only half past eight, still too early to make a call. But he nodded in her direction. "Eat something else — you'll need your strength. And then you should change into something warmer. Meet me in the front hall in two hours. We are overdue for a visit to the dower house."

CHAPTER TWENTY-THREE

Nick's imagination had made the dowager marchioness into something of a dragon. She had raised one of the least pleasant men Nick had ever known — Charles's upbringing had to count for something. And the Claibornes' longstanding refusal to acknowledge Nick's family had continued even after all the other Claiborne men were dead, which meant the marchioness was just as stiff about class and blood as all the rest.

But when Nick and Ellie walked into the dower house, the elderly woman they found in the overheated, overstuffed drawing room matched her surroundings, not her station. She was so wrapped in shawls and scarves and lap blankets that her dress — black bombazine dripping with more jet beads than were strictly approved on a day gown — was nearly rendered an undergarment. She wore a ring on every finger and great drop earrings that emerged from foggy wisps of hair to bracket the pinched hollows of her cheeks.

"Lord Folkestone," she said faintly, sniffing as she extended a hand to him. "Welcome to my humble home."

She sniffed again as she said this. Nick didn't know whether she was more upset that he had her dead son's title or that she had been relegated to the dower house. Regardless, he bowed over her hand as though he were pleased to do so. "Lady Folkestone. Please accept my belated condolences on your loss."

The dowager's performance intrigued him. She let one of her shawls slip, and it fell away to reveal a braided bit of hair pinned to her dress. "My poor, dear Charles. In the prime of his youth, and yet he never experienced the marital happiness I had with his dear father. If only he had left an heir before he was taken from us."

She hadn't acknowledged Ellie — hadn't even looked at her — but he knew the direction of that barb.

Ellie knew it too. Nick turned in time to see Ellie shrug. "If there had been a babe, it likely would have been a girl. You had three daughters and only one son. My odds might have been just as bad."

The dowager glared at Ellie. "Impertinent as always, I see. If you can't mind your tongue, you may take your leave."

Ellie sat instead, choosing one of nearly a dozen chintz-covered armless chairs that had been squeezed into the room by some feat of organization that surpassed Nick's abilities. She bumped one elbow on a side table and the other on a pedestal displaying a mismatched assortment of knick-knacks. But when she spoke, her voice was kinder than before. "Shall we declare a truce, Lady Folkestone? It has been a decade — surely we can be in the same room without incident."

"With your reputation?" Lady Folkestone snorted, but her voice warmed to what seemed to be a familiar theme. "My only comfort is that Annabel and Clarabel found husbands that season and that Charles did not live to see the shame you brought to his name. My poor Christabel, though…no one will have her now."

Nick cleared his throat. The women, upon resumption of hostilities that had simmered for years, had promptly forgotten him, but he tried to bring them back to the present. "We did not come to distress you with talk of Charles, Lady Folkestone."

She squinted up at him, suddenly suspicious. "If you mean to turn Elinor out of the main house, she is not welcome here. My poor Christabel and I can hardly fit ourselves."

"I shan't come here," Ellie vowed. "The light is too atrocious. Of course, more people and fewer chairs might be a welcome change."

Nick saw the dowager take a breath. He rushed to fill the pause before she did. "I will not ask anyone to move. But I must ask you a delicate question."

"Is it Christabel you're after?" She eyed him appraisingly, then rang the very loud, very shrill bell that sat at her elbow. "Can't say I think much of the match given your antecedents. But having the title back in the family is a benefit."

Nick tried to interrupt as soon as she said the word "match," but the dowager was nearly uninterruptible. "I am not here for Christabel," Nick said forcefully. "I must ask you a question of a different nature."

Her forehead wrinkled in confusion under her equally-confused monstrosity of a cap. "What can you possibly want from me, if you won't have your cousin? You already have everything of value."

"It has nothing to do with money," Nick said.

Ellie coughed. "Everything has something to do with money, as much as we all like to pretend otherwise."

He shot her a scowl, but she smiled innocently at him. He turned back to the dowager. "Lady Folkestone, have you observed or hosted anyone new to the neighborhood in recent months?"

The dowager looked like she wanted to glower, if glowering were possible when one looked so frail. "Where do you propose I might have met anyone beyond my family? The local gentry are not suitable for Christabel to associate with, not while they still accept Elinor. And since Elinor barred me from the London townhouse and my other daughters are too busy to host me, I've no access to better society."

A woman strode into the room, preempting whatever Ellie might have said in response. "You rang, Mother?"

"Christabel," Lady Folkestone exclaimed. "I wanted to make you known to your cousin, the man who now holds the Folkestone title. He is just arrived from India."

"So I see," Christabel said neutrally. Her voice was forthright, almost husky — nothing like her mother's.

"Lord Folkestone, may I present my youngest daughter, Lady Christabel? She usually does not receive callers of Elinor's ilk, but in the interest of familial harmony I suppose I shall allow it."

Christabel curtsied to both Nick and Ellie. "Please forgive my mother. Too many years of us shut up here like a pair of pecking hens has turned her tongue to vinegar."

Lady Folkestone gasped, clutching the braided hair brooch at her breast. "Christabel! Have you learned nothing of manners from me?"

"Not everything you would teach me, I'll admit. But I trust our company will take pity on me, not hold me in judgment for it."

The girl — more a woman at twenty-five, but still fresh-faced and wearing an old lavender pinafore that would have been appropriate for someone years younger — smiled at Ellie. It was gone just as quickly, leaving her face as it had been when she had first walked in — a direct gaze, a sharp nose, and a chin that was too stubborn for prettiness.

But if she had spent the past ten years with only her mother for company, Nick found it amazing she still looked like a handsome girl rather than a raving lunatic. He bowed to her, kissed her hand, and noticed the strong odor of herbs where other ladies might have smelled of eau de toilette. "Lady Christabel, I find your manners exquisite," he said.

She grinned again, but he didn't know whether her pleasure came from his comment or her mother's scandalized gasp. "You are too kind, cousin," Christabel said. "Now, what has brought you to our sitting room? No one has bearded the lionesses here in an age."

"Christabel, if you cannot mind your tongue, you must return to the nursery at once," her mother said sharply.

Christabel sighed. It wasn't an exasperated sigh, though. There was too much pity in her eyes for exasperation. "Never mind, Mama," she said, taking a seat next to her mother and adjusting the blankets around the older woman's shoulders. "Let's hear what our visitors have to say, shall we?"

A cloud passed over Lady Folkestone's face, and her mouth crumpled in on itself. She blinked, twice, and when she refocused on Nick, she smiled. "Do you have any news from London, sir? Charles is so good about sharing the latest gossip, but with the snows his letters haven't reached us."

Christabel patted her mother's hand, shaking her head at Nick and Ellie as she said, "They can't have come from London recently, Mama, not with the roads the way they are."

Nick looked at Ellie. She was staring very hard at Lady Folkestone, as though trying to read the story of the intervening years in the lines on her face. They had been enemies for so long — how would Ellie react if her enemy was no longer the woman she had once been?

Nick turned back to Lady Folkestone and Christabel. "You are correct. I have been in the neighborhood for some days. Have you noticed any other newcomers to the area?"

The dowager looked to Christabel, who took the reins. "We do not entertain very often beyond the occasional relative, as I'm sure you understand," Christabel said. "I only leave the house to work in my gardens or run to the village. Mother frets if I leave for too long."

"As I should. You are too young to be calling unescorted," Lady Folkestone interjected.

Christabel ignored her. "Why are you asking about newcomers?"

"This may be a better conversation for later," Nick warned. "We wouldn't want to tire your mother."

She shook off the warning. "Mama likely won't bother herself over it above an hour. Please, do continue."

Nick finally sat down, as near to directly across from Christabel as he could be in the crush of furnishings. "We have reason to believe someone poses a threat to the neighborhood."

"What makes you believe that?"

Nick laid out the facts — the highwaymen's attack, the burned shed, and the attempts on his life that he had faced in India. "We thought you should be aware of the danger, living on the estate as you are."

Christabel frowned. "I've heard nothing of this from the servants. Surely a highwayman in the area would merit an investigation?"

"We were...delayed in reporting it to the magistrate. Snows, you know."

Christabel turned that statement over, and she didn't seem to like the conclusion she had reached. "Did you suspect my mother of being behind this?"

The question surprised him. "Of course not, my lady. This does not have a woman's touch."

Christabel leveled her gaze upon him. "A woman could do this, Lord Folkestone. We are not as weak as you men would rather believe."

"Is that a confession?" he asked.

"No. I would not have hired highwaymen — poison is far more

reliable than hired men."

This roused Lady Folkestone, who had been fiddling with the fringe of one of her shawls. "Christabel, enough." Her voice was sharp again, more lucid, and the distaste was back in her eyes as she swiveled her gaze between Nick and Ellie. "Do you have any other news to share that won't upset my poor daughter?"

"I am not upset, Mama," she said soothingly. Then she turned her gaze back to Nick — and this time, he saw a spark of humor there. "I am sure I am quite far down on the list of people who might have you murdered, my lord. An absentee landlord is better than a bad one."

"But then Marcus might inherit. If you approve of anything that has been done the last decade, you have him to thank for it."

"Not just him, I think." She shifted her attention to Ellie. "The housekeeper gave me a tour last summer — it was odd to see everything so changed from when I was a girl there, but you have a lovely touch, my lady."

"You are welcome to call anytime, Lady Christabel," Ellie said. Her speed was impulsive — not the deliberate, distancing tones he heard her use with most of her guests. "Perhaps dinner tomorrow night? Or at least the fireworks display in the village afterward? We are having a house party at Folkestone, and you might like to become acquainted with my sisters. I regret not having thought to invite you before, but in my mind you are still sixteen and not allowed to call on me."

Some stark yearning flooded Christabel's face, almost vicious in how swiftly it rose and how irrevocably reality took its place. She had no chance to respond before Lady Folkestone interrupted. "Christabel isn't out yet," she said, as firmly as her mind was lodged in another time. "And if she was, you're no fit company for a debutante, Elinor."

Ellie closed her eyes. "I would have been a good daughter to you, Lady Folkestone. And a good wife to your son. But it wasn't meant to be."

"My son never should have married you," Lady Folkestone spat out. Nick couldn't determine whether her words were a memory or a current opinion, but either way, her voice was pure venom. "If you were a good wife, he wouldn't have left your bed so soon. But you thought too highly of yourself to try to please him, didn't you? You're the reason he was cavorting with that...that woman when he died, instead of giving you an heir."

Ellie turned pale, suddenly, as though she might be sick. "You can blame me for anything you wish. But Charles's death was not my fault."

Christabel patted her mother's hand, but her focus was on Ellie. "I don't think Mama believes that it was, not truly. But perhaps it would be best if you left now. She's tired, and her...condition worsens when she is distressed. And really, there is nothing here that would help you with your search. I know everyone in the house at present, and none of them are murderers."

Nick stood up. But when he offered his arm to Ellie, she slid away from him. Instead, she pulled a slip of paper out of her reticule.

It was a copy of the drawing she had made of the highwayman. She handed it to Christabel. "Take this, if you please. It shows the tattoos we found on the highwayman's body. I know you wouldn't have seen his arms even if he was nearby, but perhaps your servants may have."

Christabel didn't even glance at it as she set it aside. "If I hear anything, I will tell you. Thank you for calling, though. It was good to see you again after all these years. And to meet you at last, my lord."

Ellie nodded back. "If you should change your mind about joining us, you are most welcome tomorrow night. No need to decide now — I will send a carriage at six, and you may take it or not as it suits you."

Christabel's face was expressionless. Her face was too strong to be expressionless — with no smile or frown, and no emotion in her eyes, she looked more like an ancient statue than a modern woman. But Nick didn't think he imagined the longing in her voice. "Perhaps. I thank you for the invitation regardless."

Ellie kissed her cheek and whispered something Nick couldn't hear. Christabel's face underwent the same transformation as before, as hope and excitement succumbed to the onslaught of reality. Then Ellie said goodbye to Lady Folkestone in a neutral voice that expected no answer.

She didn't receive an answer, either. Lady Folkestone fiddled with a shawl and didn't look up. So Nick took Ellie's arm and pulled her out of the room, not letting her dwell in the past.

But if they didn't dwell in the past, they would have to dwell in the present. And the present was nothing that Nick's revenge had prepared him for.

CHAPTER TWENTY-FOUR

"I never liked Lady Folkestone, but I did not enjoy seeing her as she is now," Ellie said as she settled back into their carriage. She and her mother-in-law had never liked each other, but she didn't relish the idea of the dowager falling into an irreversible decline. "I am sorry this trip was less helpful than you had hoped."

Nick took his place across from her. There was a stillness to him that matched the carriage — the pause in the instant before a rush of action. So she wasn't surprised when he dove into conversation as the carriage started to move. "I do not know what she was like before, but I still found our discussion quite informative."

"How so? She could be housing a whole host of assassins and not remember it."

"Any eliminated suspects are worthwhile. And even if her mind is no longer sharp, I trust Lady Christabel is sharp enough for both of them."

Ellie sighed. "I wish Christabel could live elsewhere. If I had known that her blasted sisters had left her to take care of Lady Folkestone alone in this state, I would have...but I could not have done anything. Charles's mother never did like me. It still seems we're no closer to learning the truth than we were before. And I would just as soon have not seen Lady Folkestone again."

"But you said you would have been a good daughter for her. Why?"

His question caught Ellie napping — but then, it wasn't a sentiment she had intended to share. She had said those words to Lady Folkestone because she knew that her confession wouldn't be remembered, but Ellie had momentarily forgotten her audience. She wanted to shrug off his question, but she forced herself to think over her response — not the one she wanted to give, but the one that might be a real explanation.

Nick waited, not rushing her. There was a solidity to him that she had never noticed before. Either he hadn't had it as a boy, or solidity wasn't something that had appealed to her younger view of romantic love. It was a solidity she could lean on, build on...not that she should be thinking of that, when his question was about the marriage she'd stupidly agreed to rather than the one she should have waited for.

"You know, I don't know why I said that," she said. "But Lady Folkestone was never bad, just difficult. And I don't think I had enough patience for her. I was so wrapped up in waiting for you to come home that my 'grief,' such as it was, wasn't enough for her. And then I needed to make myself ineligible so that Father wouldn't try to marry me off again — and I succeeded in making myself seem irredeemable. It's little wonder she came to hate me."

"So you were more devoted to my memory than his?"

Ellie rolled her eyes. "You know the answer to that. I won't puff you up by saying it again."

His grin was puffed up enough already. "Tell me that Charles knew you preferred me."

"I don't know what Charles knew. He knew that by winning me he had scotched your chances. He seemed pleased by that."

"Bounder," Nick muttered. "As though the title and estate weren't enough."

"They may not have been," Ellie said. "You should have seen these properties when I married him. Charles had the title, but I believe he would have preferred your wealth."

"You can't say he was jealous of me."

Ellie shrugged. "He never said it. But he pursued me like a collector, not a seducer. And while my dowry was respectable, there were bigger prizes than me that season if he would have taken a lower-born bride. Still, getting one over you was a cost he seemed oddly willing to bear. Folkestone would be a crumbling ruin by now if you hadn't inherited it. My dowry could only patch the damage, not reverse it — an odd choice to make, unless his jealousy overrode his prudence."

Nick didn't respond. But his amusement, such as it was, looked like the faint pleasure of recalling a bit of history that was long dead, rather than the visceral satisfaction of besting an enemy.

"Do you not care about Charles's role in our past anymore?" she asked.

It was another of those questions she shouldn't have asked. He leaned back in his seat. "If he were still alive, I would care. But we both know he married for spite and money, not love. The question I have is why you said you could have been a good wife to a man who would only use you."

"And other men wouldn't have used me? Isn't that what aristocratic marriages are? I *would* have been a good wife. It was what I was raised for. I would have given him children, hosted the right parties, behaved appropriately, and had a serene, if unsatisfying, life with him. But I couldn't be a good wife so fast, and Charles died before I accepted him. And his mother…"

Nick cut her off. "What do you mean, before you accepted him?"

She hadn't meant to say anything. Nick hadn't asked about her other lovers, just as she hadn't asked about his. But on this question, about the cousin he hated, she wanted him to know the truth. "We never consummated our marriage."

She didn't plan to explain further, but Nick didn't let it go. "How did you avoid it? Charles wasn't the type to leave an advantage unexploited."

Ellie frowned. "Charles wasn't evil, you know. He was hardly different from most peers — a little selfish, a little too convinced that it was talent and not an accident of birth that gave him everything. But he had a strong sense of duty and took his responsibilities seriously. If I hadn't had a dowry and the right bloodlines, he wouldn't have married me no matter how much he hated you. He may have had…unfair opinions about you, but he wasn't a monster. So when I pled my time of the month after the wedding and asked for a week, he didn't force me. Which I'm grateful for even more now — if he had died in my arms rather than with that opera dancer, I never would have forgiven him. I would rather deal with the scandal of where he died rather than having him die on top of me."

Nick exhaled, then closed his eyes. Ellie sighed and buried her hands even deeper in her fur muff. In the shadows, with his hair swept back under his hat and his shoulders tensing up under the capes of his greatcoat, Nick suddenly looked like a stranger — a dark traveler who heard her story with passing interest and would forget it before he reached the next town.

"The way you smiled at your wedding…" Nick said. "I thought you wanted him."

He opened his eyes — with the way they burned, how could she have ever imagined that he was disinterested? But his statement confused her. "How do you know how I smiled?"

"I was there, Ellie. Hiding in the back like a damn beggar, waiting for you to change your mind."

This time, she closed her eyes. She hadn't seen him at the wedding — but then, she hadn't seen much, since she was trying so hard to look calm and not retch during her vows. "I had to smile," she said. "It was either that or be sick. I didn't want to be known as the bride who cast up her accounts on the altar at St. Paul's."

When she looked up at Nick, the burn was gone. Cool contemplation took its place. He steepled his fingers in front of his face, resting his chin on his thumbs. His words, when they finally came, were quiet, as though they'd had to sneak past the bars of his hands. "And you thought you could be a good wife?"

"Yes. Not the best wife, perhaps, and I might never have felt anything stronger than affectionate concern for Charles. But I'd made my bed. And I would have settled into it eventually. Don't you see?" Her voice, like her heart, turned urgent. "When I knew I was bound to Charles, I could make a life around that, however bad it was. But add even the slimmest bit of hope that you might come back for me... it was the hope that made those first years unbearable. I could have borne a pleasant, passive marriage. I couldn't bear all those painful, useless dreams."

"Do you really think that? That you could have been happy if you'd fully lost me?"

"Not at first, perhaps. Not for ages. But perhaps I would settle for peace now. As you are so keen to remind me, I'm not the girl you loved. I've abandoned my childhood fantasies of happily ever after. As have you, I'd wager."

"Childhood fantasies? I never had them."

"Now *there's* a lie if I've ever heard one," Ellie said. "You may not have dreamed of princes and castles and large families, but you dreamed. And they've come true, haven't they? Enough money to buy the ton's regard and a title to secure it. Would that I had dreamed your dreams — I had all that ages ago."

He dropped his hands away from his face. "You seem to confuse goals and dreams. Goals are what I've accomplished. Dreams are something else entirely."

"Then what are your dreams?"

He frowned. "You are full of questions today."

"Would you rather I not care?"

"It would be easier if you didn't."

"What would be easier?"

He looked down at his hands. "Revenge. Atonement. Call it what you will."

She didn't know what to call it. She couldn't name any feeling between them, when hatred felt like love and revenge felt like a gift. "You said you hate me. Revenge is easy with hatred, isn't it?"

He didn't answer, just kept looking at his hands until she thought he would never acknowledge the question. Finally, he said, "I don't hate you. I hate what you did. But perhaps it had to happen that way."

"I would take it back if I could."

"I know. But if we had stayed together then, we wouldn't be who we are now. I find the woman you are preferable to the girl you were."

It wasn't forgiveness. And yet the sentiment moved her, far more dramatically than any meaningless words of rapprochement.

The carriage pulled to a stop in front of Folkestone. The spell broke before she could sift through her thoughts and find whatever truth she wanted to share with him. But as he started toward the door, she reached for his hand. "I am glad you are home, Nick. No matter what happens between us."

He squeezed her fingers but didn't respond. A groom opened the door and Nick jumped out to help her down. He didn't say anything more — just looked at her with an unfathomable expression, then offered his arm to escort her into the house.

So she went. Her hosting duties awaited; he no doubt wished to further harass her guests. But that look she couldn't read would haunt her — just as her own unreadable heart did. *Could* they reconcile, truly? Or would all his anger and all her regret conspire to keep them apart?

CHAPTER TWENTY-FIVE

Two hours later, Ellie was outside again. Her body might freeze to match the temperature Nick had accused her of being, but after being cooped up inside, her guests were eager for an outdoor diversion. One of her sisters had proposed ice skating — no doubt because Sebastian Staunton had mentioned how much he missed ice when he was in Bermuda. Ellie had raised an eyebrow at that, but once the idea was out, it had spread through the company like a contagion.

And so, they were skating. Her gardeners had cleared the snow off the pond nearest the house, and the ice was thick and wonderfully flat. She had plenty of skates to go around for anyone who had boots sturdy enough to attach the blades to. At one of her wilder bacchanals, there had been skating in the moonlight beneath a ring of torches around the pond, and the blades had stayed in some disused corner of the stables until today.

She knew her sisters' intentions weren't entirely innocent. She should try to provide a sobering influence for them — but Ellie had never been a sobering influence before, and she was grateful for the suggestion. Skating was far more fun than yet another conversation in her drawing room.

Especially when every conversation seemed to turn, inevitably, to Nick.

He was doing nothing at the moment, and yet even his idleness drew interest. He leaned against a tree near the edge of the pond and watched as she skated fast loops around the ice. She chose to indulge in her love for speed rather than playing the lady for her older guests. She had skated for hours and hours as a girl, when there was nothing better to do, and so she didn't have the halting, tentative strokes of some of her inexperienced friends.

But even with her speed, she saw how people looked at him. And she saw how he looked at no one but her. It was a conundrum, that — she knew some of her guests would befriend him, and genuinely, if he gave them the chance. But he was too closed for them to approach. And he saw their hesitation as a judgment on his origins.

She skated to the very edge of the pond, as close to his tree as she could get without taking off her skates. Picking her toe into the ice to maintain her balance, she held out her hand. "Won't you skate with us, Lord Folkestone?" she asked, staying formal for anyone who might hear her. "I know you had no ice in India, but surely you learned as a child."

She knew he had. They had skated together once, on thinning late-February ice on the Serpentine in Hyde Park. It had been her first week in the capital, and it was the only public place they could think to meet where her chaperone wouldn't overly care that she was talking to a man. Their skating was brief — only twenty minutes — but long enough for her to assure him that she hadn't forgotten him despite her father's attempts to dazzle her.

Perhaps it was that memory that made his mouth twist. He swept his eyes blatantly over her curves. She wore thick skirts and a beaver hat, but her military-inspired spencer nipped in provocatively at her waist. "I thank you, Lady Folkestone, but the view is better from here."

"I would have worn sackcloth if I'd known what you were after, but I can't afford it."

Nick smiled. "I will buy you as much sackcloth as you want. But it's uncomfortable stuff. You might prefer to take it off once you've dressed in it."

She thought she heard someone giggle behind her, but when she turned, whoever it was had already skated away. She lowered her voice. "If you won't skate, stop watching me. You are causing people to talk."

"People are going to talk about you no matter what I do. You are the most beautiful woman they've seen, and you don't care what their opinions are. Even if you were a nun, they would find that combination irresistible."

She didn't acknowledge the compliment — but she saved it, burying it in her heart so she might pull it out again later and cherish it. "Regardless, you aren't helping. Come skate with me. You might find the people on the ice more approachable if you deign to welcome their presence."

"You think I am the one who is unapproachable?"

She mimicked his cross-armed pose. "Who would approach one of the richest, most well-titled bachelors in the land when he won't even acknowledge their presence? I vow, you're stuffier than any prince I've met — and with the diplomats streaming through London, I've met dozens."

"I'm not stuffy," he protested.

"It is quite all right, Lord Folkestone," she said. "I like stuffy men. Take Norbury, as an example."

His mouth turned dangerous. "What about Norbury do you wish to discuss?"

She was warming to the task of teasing him, and it felt good —

the way it had always felt, back when he had been a sober young man on the verge of losing his mother and she had been so thrilled just to have someone to talk to. It felt like she could charm anything out of him, and that he could be dazzled by her...

Her repartee came to a sudden halt. "Never mind," she said. "I shouldn't have teased you. Forgive me?"

He stepped toward her, to the very edge of the bank, until they were only inches apart. "You seem to think that I'm standing over here by myself because I am afraid of playing with the ton. You seem to think me pitiable. But I don't give a damn about any of them."

His eyes dropped to her lips, and she thought he might kiss her. But he looked up again, and his eyes were fierce with the beast he kept leashed within. "I'm watching you because I enjoy watching you skate. Not because I don't know the others."

Then he grabbed her hand and brought it to his lips. "Enjoy the ice, Lady Folkestone," he murmured.

Ellie was dismissed. There was no use standing there any longer. If people hadn't noticed him staring at her, they certainly would notice how close they stood together, how long they talked when Nick never seemed eager to talk to anyone.

So she skated away, letting her muscles take over and supply the necessary grace that her nerves currently lacked. Her skating was smooth, but her heartbeat wasn't.

She had only been away for a minute — barely time to take a lap around the ice, let alone catch her breath — when Norbury caught up to her. "Do you have a moment, Lady Folkestone?" he asked.

She didn't want to talk, but Norbury had been her friend for half a decade — she couldn't snub him. "I always have a moment for you, Lord Norbury," she said, extending her hand. "Would you care to take a turn around the ice with me?"

She slowed her pace to match his. He was an athletic man, but he had grown up with a large family — it was unlikely he had spent as much time as she had skating fast, lonely circles as a youth. Being head of such a large family usually made him direct and impatient with rambling, but the Norbury on the ice was not the Norbury she had entertained so many times in the past. He asked about her health, the weather, the entertainments for the evening, and half a dozen other meaningless questions, until she was nearly mad with annoyance.

"Are you feeling well, my lord?" she asked obliquely, when he made an observation about the weather for a second time. "I rarely see you this preoccupied."

He sucked in a breath, then let it out in a gust before looking over to her. "This is lamentably forward of me — but is Folkestone a good man?"

She slowed her skating, so much that he was ten feet ahead of her before he realized it and turned around to rejoin her. When he reached her, she said, "You are correct. That is a lamentably forward question."

He sighed. "I know. But we have known each other for ages. Will you indulge my curiosity?"

His brown eyes were concerned. His forehead furrowed over them. His mouth was tight, too. He had never seemed to care about her beyond mere friendship — surely this wasn't jealousy?

But they had been friends, and he had been a pleasant companion at all the events where his wife was not well enough to attend. She gave him the courtesy of an answer even though she didn't understand his questioning. "I believe Folkestone is a good man. One of the best, in fact."

He looked over to where Nick still watched them. Nick didn't look like a good man at the moment — he looked like he wanted to skate over and interrupt them. Or perhaps he looked like he wanted to beat Norbury with a skate rather than using it to reach them.

Ellie winced. "He may look brooding, but he really can be charming."

"I don't doubt your judgment of his character," Norbury said. "I just wish that he had not come home."

"Why would you wish that? He should have come home years ago."

"Of course, of course. But this party would be so much more at ease if he had stayed away."

Norbury had a point, but Ellie didn't acknowledge it. "No one has left in protest, have they? I'm sure we will finish out the week with just as much pleasure as we might otherwise have."

He still hadn't looked away from Nick. When he finally did, his face was serious. "Please take care, Lady Folkestone. You may be an excellent judge of character, but I worry for you with him. Promise me you won't find yourself in danger with him."

She couldn't promise that, of course — she was already in far too deep. "I trust I'm in no danger from Folkestone. But I thank you for your concern."

He seemed to want to say more, but perhaps she misread him — perhaps it was just a cloud passing over the sun that made her see more concern than she thought he should have for her. In a moment, he smiled and bowed. "I only wish you happy, Lady Folkestone. Whatever that happiness may be."

*　　*　　*

Nick wished he had taken Ellie's offer of skates, if only so he could go onto the ice and drag her away from Norbury. From the way they looked at him, he knew they were discussing him — and while Norbury had been civil when Nick had cornered him after dinner the previous night, Nick didn't think Norbury was using these moments to convince Ellie that she should be happy about Nick's return.

But he had chosen not to skate. If he didn't want to embarrass Ellie publicly, he couldn't chase after her now. She could handle herself, no matter what Norbury was saying.

He settled back against his tree. It gave him a prime view of the pond and a safe shield behind him — something he hadn't known he needed, until he realized how much safer he felt with something to lean against. But even the strongest tree couldn't save him from the next person to approach him.

"Folkestone," Ferguson said as he came to the edge of the ice, knelt down, and removed his skating blades. "A word, if you please."

Nick didn't please, but the Duke of Rothwell wasn't asking — he was telling. "Of course, your grace. Do you know, I believe the last duke I saw was your father? We were mercifully short of dukes in Madras."

Ferguson stepped out of his skates and joined Nick by the tree, standing perpendicular to Nick so that he could see both Nick's face and the people still on the ice. "Sounds charming. I never was much for dukes myself. But when you come into a title you didn't plan for, you sometimes discover it's not as bad as you thought."

Ferguson never should have inherited the duchy. He had two older half-brothers who would have inherited before him, but their premature deaths made Ferguson the next heir. In that respect, he wasn't so different from Nick — he, too, had grown up somewhat left out, believing others would carry on the family line.

But Nick still remembered Ferguson from Eton, where he had been quick enough to join the others in poking fun at Nick's background. So it was with an edge to his voice that he said, "Have you come to give me pointers on how to be a gentleman? I warn you, I'm a slow study."

Ferguson snorted. "I doubt that. My connections tell me you have a solid head for numbers, an uncanny ability to drive the best bargains, and adequate concern for your employees and dependents."

"What connections have told you that?"

Ferguson pulled a snuffbox out of his greatcoat and offered it to Nick. Nick refused.

"Abominable stuff, isn't it?" Ferguson said, tossing the box back into his pocket unopened. "But if you want a career as a rake now that you've returned, it is one of the best affectations you could choose. That, or a quizzing glass."

He had evaded Nick's first question, but that statement raised even more. Nick stayed focused, though. "Have you been looking into my affairs?"

The duke's sidelong glance was deadly serious. "I will protect my sister, Folkestone. Depend upon it. If my connections found anything suspicious, you would have already heard about it from me."

Nick raised an eyebrow. "The apple doesn't fall far from the tree, does it?"

Ferguson brushed a piece of lint off his greatcoat. "I do hope that wasn't a comparison to my father. Ellie will be displeased if I kill you on the dueling ground."

"Then if your men have found nothing, and you don't wish to fight me, why are we having this conversation?"

"I didn't intend for a conversation. I planned for a monologue. They're becoming my forte — as I said, titles have their uses, and one is that most people don't interrupt."

He paused. Nick said nothing. Ferguson had changed since Eton — perhaps for the better, despite the path this meeting had taken. There was certainly something appealing about his humor, odd as it was. If they had met again in some other way, without Ellie between them, perhaps they would have become friends, or at least gambling partners.

But Ellie *was* between them, just as she was between him and everything else. Ellie was the central sun in his solar system. He was a satellite that revolved around her, just as everyone at this party did. She would always be between him and the world — but her brilliance made up for the inconvenience.

He didn't say any of that to Ferguson. Finally, perhaps convinced that Nick would stay quiet during his monologue, Ferguson spoke again. "Let us cover what I already know. Ellie told me last year that she had loved you, but that our unlamented father encouraged her to marry your cousin. She also said she waited for you, but you had never come back. This can only mean you were furious with her. You can understand why that would not make me sanguine about the possibility of a civil, cordial reunion between you."

He paused again. Eventually, Nick sighed. "Do you want an acknowledgement, or is that considered interrupting your monologue?"

Ferguson grinned. "You may refrain from applause until the end. I like you, Folkestone. The people I've interviewed who knew you in Madras liked you. Your brother likes you, even though your return diminishes his responsibilities. But liking you doesn't mean I won't find a way to destroy you if you harm Ellie in any significant way."

"You've been interviewing people about me?"

Ferguson looked around. "Quiet, if you please. It wouldn't do if Ellie or my wife overheard you. But don't be so surprised. If you had a female relative and someone in her past could one day turn up to cause her problems, you would have done exactly what I did. I needed to prepare for the day you might come back, even if Ellie hadn't."

"Still, spying on me is beneath you."

"Not for Ellie's sake. I'd do it all again to protect her. It's the least I can do, since I wasn't here when the two of you had your first falling out."

Then he leaned in, and even though he was shorter than Nick, he somehow managed to look utterly threatening. "I'm watching you, Folkestone. If you hurt her in any way, I will personally beat you within an inch of your life. Then I will ruin your business interests so completely that you will lose every scrap of clothing that isn't entailed."

Nick didn't flinch. "What is between Ellie and me will stay between Ellie and me."

"You really are a slow learner, aren't you?"

Nick looked out onto the ice again. Ellie had parted ways with Norbury, but her skating was slower — sadder, perhaps. Her head was bowed, and she seemed to evade anyone who might want to talk to her with just enough grace to not cause offense.

He turned back to her brother. "I may never learn with Ellie. But for the rest — I vow I will keep her unharmed."

Ferguson scanned his face. Then he nodded. "Don't fail, Folkestone. I want to see her happy. If you are the one who can do that, I will fête you. But if you aren't..."

He left the consequence unvoiced. Nick acknowledged it with a curt nod. "She will be fine. She's made of sterner stuff than any woman I know — she will probably survive us all."

Ferguson laughed. "True. Then I'll leave you to it."

"Is this where I am expected to applaud your monologue?"

The duke laughed again. "I can see why my father hated you. Unlike him, I think you are exactly what Ellie deserves."

He left before Nick responded. Then he called for his wife. She skated over to him, and he swung her off the ice and into his arms. Madeleine laughed and put her hands onto his shoulders as he bent to remove her skates, then leaned down to whisper in his ear. From the way she looked at Nick, he knew they were talking about him.

Everyone liked to talk about him, it seemed. But he was too struck by Ferguson's parting shot to care. It almost sounded like Nick would have Ferguson's blessing if he pursued Ellie in earnest. Not that he needed it. She could legally marry whomever she liked. But Ferguson's comment was the opposite of what Nick had expected.

And he hadn't realized that her family's approval mattered to him until he had it.

He cursed and left the pond, walking back to the house with a ground-eating stride. He told himself he didn't love her. He told himself he didn't want to make her his bride. He told himself he would be happier with any other woman at his breakfast table for the next thirty years.

But he was a liar. And he was also a coward. Because, in his secret heart, he knew that he would rather never ask her than risk her turning him down again.

CHAPTER TWENTY-SIX

Hours later, after everyone had retired for the night, Ellie shivered as she pulled a voluminous golden veil over her flowing hair. "If Nick wanted me to catch my death of pneumonia, he needn't have spent forty thousand pounds," she muttered. "It's little wonder there are no seraglios in London. We would all freeze to death."

Lucia sniffed, her temper still high. Ellie had returned to her chamber ten minutes after midnight and found her maid cursing, with fervor and fluency, over the blackened morals of the Claiborne men. "He doesn't give a fig for your comfort, my lady. But you do look splendid. I'll allow that he has taste."

Ellie tugged down the bottom hem of her bodice, but it ended in the middle of her ribcage. She couldn't cover her belly unless she wrapped a blanket around herself. "I look like a prime fool. Is this how my guests feel when wearing the costumes I prescribe for them?'

"At least the costumes you demand cover everything," Lucia said loyally.

Ellie noticed that Lucia didn't answer the question, but it didn't matter. The dress Nick had sent wasn't a dress — it was a fitted bodice and a floor-length skirt as seductive as anything she had seen in paintings of the East. The skirt fastened with a drawstring, the bodice with little hooks down the front — but she wore nothing under either piece. It would be quick work to remove them again.

In another mood she would have loved this ensemble. It was gold, worked throughout with gold thread and thousands of amber-colored beads. Lucia had taken her hair down, per the instructions Nick had sent, and rimmed her eyes with kohl. And she'd reapplied Ellie's jasmine perfume before handing her the veil. The veil didn't cover her eyes. It covered her hair instead, with two inches of heavy trim that weighed the veil down over her forehead. Without pins to hold it in place, it would be easy enough to drop for him.

Ellie's hands fisted in her skirts. She forced herself to relax. Lucia frowned unhappily, but she didn't say anything — what was there to say?

Ellie nodded briskly, feeling like a colonel trying to calm a frightened recruit. "Go to bed, Lucia. Despite his theatrics, I am quite sure the marquess won't harm me."

"Why do I feel like I've prepared you for a sacrifice?"

Ellie didn't answer. She loved Lucia as much as any friend she'd had, but at this moment, familiarity was unhelpful.

She turned to the connecting door. She hadn't used it as a bride. Charles had died before they had ever ventured beyond London. Later, she had dreamed of using it as Nick's bride instead. As those chances had dwindled to nothing, she had had nightmares of some other woman walking through that door — of him taking a meek, quiet girl who was too stupid to think of what she wanted from life and, in her amiability, unable to make a choice that might betray him.

She was thinking too much. She couldn't think if she wanted to survive this. She marched to the door, but the heavy sensuality of her golden skirt and the feel of her bare feet sinking into the carpets slowed her stride.

His note had said not to knock. She turned the key in the lock and opened the door before she changed her mind. It was only later — much later — that she wondered why she had obeyed him. He wouldn't beat her or humiliate her in public. Theirs was a private game, so what could he possibly do to her if she stopped playing? Impoverish her, yes, but he wouldn't truly force her into his bed.

But at that moment, her choice was made — whether it was by him or by her own heart didn't particularly matter. She pushed the door open.

Nick sprawled in an armchair by the fire. She wouldn't be cold, not with the blaze he'd created for her. She hoped the crackle of burning wood would cover the way her breath hitched. He still wore his evening dress, although he'd tossed his cravat aside and unbuttoned his jacket. Somehow, it only made him more dangerous.

His eyes met hers. "Close the door."

She pushed it shut behind her.

"Come to me."

She didn't break eye contact as she walked toward him — she couldn't waste any opportunity to read his intentions. But as she reached him, she found his eyes weren't purely lustful. Yes, she saw lust there — saw how his eyes flickered to her hips, then to where her navel peeked above the waistband of her skirt. It wasn't all there was to him, though. If all he wanted was to take her, he wouldn't have wasted time waiting for her to change her dress.

When she reached him, he held out a hand for her. But the flat of his palm ordered her to stay rather than beckoning her closer. She shook her head. "What is your plan, Nick? Why am I here?"

"You can guess. Stay still."

She sighed. "You are much more cooperative in my paintings."

He leaned back and clasped his hands behind his head. "If you paint yourself looking exactly as you do now, I'll give you a hundred pounds."

She resisted the urge to hug her arms around her bare torso. "Never. This dress is obscene."

"Do you not like it? Only the highest class of woman could afford such attire. I would have brought you a sari instead, but you would probably spend a week trying to deduce how to wrap it."

"Why the fixation on clothing? Your note indicated I wouldn't be wearing anything for long."

"Always so impatient," he murmured. "I have dreamed of you like this for a very long time. And if I want to spend all night looking at you, I will."

He seemed good for it. He examined every inch of her, blatantly, heatedly, with a gaze that tracked across her curves as closely as any hands could. In this garb, she was all curves — her breasts molded by the tight bodice, her hips flaring under the heavy contours of her skirt. It was a dress made for dancing, for pleasure — for a sensuality born in heat and sunlight, not a lurid seduction in a cool English bedchamber.

It was also a dress made for her. He claimed to hate her — but his fantasies told another story.

"You are beautiful, Ellie," he said, after an eternity. "More beautiful than I remembered. I thought surely my dreams had gilded you more than you warranted. They were gross distortions compared to this."

She shifted uncomfortably. "Spare the compliments, my lord. You can have me without murmuring sweet nothings in my ear."

His eyes narrowed. "That's what you want, isn't it? For me to fuck you while you stay aloof and untouched by the whole sordid affair?"

It was hard to keep from breaking when she didn't *know* what she wanted, but when her mind couldn't work, ten years of habit took over. She shrugged. "It's your affair, not mine. But I've guests to see to in the morning, so I hope you don't take long."

His restraint was admirable — so calm she almost hated him for it. "I have changed my mind about my revenge."

Her stomach dropped. Her jaw dropped with it. "Are you letting me go?"

His smile was just as grim as anything she'd seen from him. "Never. But I thought the idea of sharing a bed with me would upset you. It only seems to excite you."

Ellie still gaped. "I'm not excited. I'm pragmatic. You bought your way into my bed. I may as well enjoy it."

"That takes the shine off my revenge, doesn't it?"

"What is your plan, then? Make it so bad I don't enjoy it?"

He smirked. "It is impossible for me to be that bad."

"Insufferable," she muttered.

"Call me any name you like. But every time I take you, you are going to feel something. Pleasure, hatred, ecstasy, regret, joy — feel whatever you want. But you *will* feel. And in my bed, you won't be the icy queen you play for everyone else."

She did hate him then. "That wasn't part of our agreement."

"I believe it falls under 'you will do anything I ask in bed or outside it.' Or was that not comprehensive enough?"

She suddenly wanted to run. She had thought their first two nights had been an anomaly, with a depth of feeling that was inevitable on their first couplings. Surely by now she should be able to stay disengaged.

But if he saw that her behavior was an anomaly — if he recognized that she never shared herself like that — he was determined to make it a habit.

"You cannot control my feelings, Nick."

"I won't tell you what to feel — but you *will* feel. Now come here."

CHAPTER TWENTY-SEVEN

She wanted to run. He saw it in the way she came up on the balls of her feet — in the way her eyes widened, then narrowed, shock followed by the need to act.

He was the worst sort of cad. But he had dreamed of her like this for so long, spent so many nights wishing for her. Now that he had her...

He wasn't a hero. And he wouldn't let her go.

But he didn't want a pliant, thoughtless thing in his arms. He wanted her alive — as awakened by the possibilities between them as he was. He held out his hand. "Come to me, Ellie." His voice was softer than it had been. He couldn't seem to keep an edge to it when her kohl-rimmed eyes were so stark. "I vow I won't hurt you."

"No one can keep such a promise."

But she reached out her hand and let him pull her into his lap. Her veil fell away, revealing her hair — the same red waves he'd dreamed of any number of times.

He couldn't resist her — couldn't help himself when her lips were so close to his and the blood rushing from his head to his cock made it so damned hard to remember what he had planned for her. He kissed her. He swore she kissed him back. Her hands roved over his shoulders. Her lips opened for him, and he heard her approving moan

236

as he claimed her.

Suddenly he didn't want what he had planned for her. He didn't want a slow, devastating seduction; didn't want to play the patient lover until she finally admitted that she wanted him as much as he wanted her. He still wanted to hear her need for him, but at this point, he would take what he could get.

He knew, somehow, in a dim corner of his mind that hadn't quite flickered out, that these were the ravings of an addict. One more card, one more glass, one more pipe — one more time sinking into her, and surely he could save them both. It was madness — but it was no madness he wanted rescued from.

He stopped kissing her long enough to stand up. She didn't say a word as he pulled her up with him. He pushed her hair back on both sides of her face, brushing her temples with his thumbs. He kissed the top of her head and breathed in her scent. It fired his pulse — gave him the final spur to overwhelm his control and give in to his fantasies.

He kissed her again, hard, using her hair to tilt her up toward his mouth. She moaned as their lips met — moaned again as he bit her, lightly, tugging at her lower lip before plunging into her with his tongue. But a kiss wasn't enough anymore. He needed to see her, now.

He broke away and dropped his hands to her bodice. He'd planned to make her strip for him. But now he wanted to strip her himself — not reverently, as he always had before, but forcefully, irrevocably.

The bodice opened down the front, with hooks made of stiffened thread catching into fragile loops on the other side. He wrenched it open, fraying threads and scattering beads as he shoved the bodice down her arms — letting her breasts out of their cage to fit perfectly in his hands.

For Nick, seeing her breasts for the first time in a decade was its own reward. For Ellie, his gaze was a new kind of torture. He looked so hungry for her, so damned reverent even though he shouldn't be — so in love with her, even though she knew he'd never admit it.

Just as in love as she was — and just as unable to forget the past.

She couldn't bear the way his blue eyes lit up, the way he concentrated on her as though he had to memorize every color, every smooth contour and every pebbled surface between the ridge of her collarbones and the stiffened peaks of her nipples. But she kept her eyes open. It was torture to watch him — but not as bad as the torture of letting him go.

His hands grazed across her breasts — then turned rougher, as though he remembered, at great personal cost, that her breasts weren't an altar. He squeezed her nipples between his thumbs and forefingers, with just enough force that it almost felt like a bite.

"You don't know how I've dreamed of this," he murmured.

She knew. She'd dreamed of it too — dreamed of him loving her again, touching her again, taking her again. But he kissed her again before she could confess, and his mouth swallowed whatever she might have said while one hand still caressed her and the other skimmed lower, down the curve of her bare torso to the waistband of her skirt.

A quick tug on the drawstring was enough to make the skirt collapse around her legs. It was so stiff with embroidery and beading that it was almost a shell — almost like she was Venus coming out of the waves for him.

He stopped kissing her and stepped back. She regretted the candles then — every inch of her was illuminated. But it wasn't her nudity that made her self-conscious. With her painting, she'd stopped being precious about the human body long ago. It was that he was still clothed where she was not — and she wanted to see him, all of him, the way he currently devoured her.

"Won't you undress?" she asked.

"I undressed you. You can return the favor."

She stepped forward and pushed off his coat. His waistcoat came next, then his braces, and then his shirt, which he had to pull over his head himself. He bent to take off his shoes as well, but she stopped him. "Allow me, my lord," she murmured.

She knelt. Her hair fell around her as she pulled his shoes off his feet. As she rolled his stockings down, she caressed the arch of each foot. Then she kissed the bridges, right on the top where the shoe buckles would have been. She heard him inhale — heard pain in the sound, as though it rasped over broken glass.

She came to her feet and met his gaze. There was a world of feeling there she'd never seen before — a world of feeling she could experience herself, if she could only find the key to unlock her own heart.

She stroked her hand against his chest, resting her palm over his heart. "I dreamed you would come home for this — even though I can't feel what you want me to feel."

She didn't know why she had confessed that. His hand closed over hers, trapping it against his heart. "You aren't the woman I loved, are you?"

She jerked her hand away from him, but he held it trapped against his chest. "You know it's true. You aren't the girl I loved when I was a boy. You don't see the world as a parade of beauty. You don't trust, you don't confide, you don't laugh, you don't let yourself hope…"

His hand tightened over hers. She was too shocked by his litany of bitterness to respond. "But I'm not the boy you loved, either," he continued. "I don't give a damn what you've done these past ten years, or how many lovers you've taken, or why none of your friends can tell me anything of substance about you. All I know is that I want the woman you are, not the girl you were."

He was wrong. She *did* hope — a hope he awakened again, sharp and painful, as he looked at her with a gaze that held dreams of the future rather than nightmares of the past.

She pulled her hand away. This time he let her go. "I can't, Nick. Don't make me hope again. Ravish me, ruin me, do whatever it is you came here to do. But don't raise my hopes."

He put both hands on her cheeks, holding her so she couldn't look away. "Stay with me, Ellie. Here, in this moment, where nothing else matters. The past doesn't have to consume us forever."

She wrenched her face out of his hands. "You can't forgive me. I can't forgive myself. We're lying to ourselves when we say we can do this without the past coming between us — *it's all there is*. Don't you see that? All we are, all we've been for the past ten years, is obsession and hatred and regret. I don't know a single fact about your life beyond that — not what you traded, or where you lived, or who you spent your time with, or even whether you enjoyed it. And you don't know any facts about me. So don't you *dare* think to make me love you again. You're in love with an illusion — just as you always were."

She'd fought to stay calm even though she couldn't keep her voice from rising. But she could only sound rational by sounding cold — and by sounding cold, she had taken them back to her father's drawing room, where she had lied to Nick and told him she couldn't love him. His jaw tightened and his teeth ground together. His effort to control himself was etched in the lines around his eyes as they narrowed. All the love she'd seen there turned to ice.

"I'm not the boy you spurned, but I'm no illusion. Tell me now you don't want me to take you to bed — or stop talking altogether."

CHAPTER TWENTY-EIGHT

If he had asked her eight years ago, she would have said yes — would have done anything to atone, to please him, to show him that she loved him.

If he had asked her five years ago, she would have said yes, because she was lonely and had already disrobed.

If he had asked her a week ago, she would have said yes, because she had missed him for so long and would take whatever pleasure he offered.

She *had* said yes the previous night.

"No," she said. "If this is really a choice, I choose no."

"*What?*"

His voice was harsh, but his eyes were more confused than angry. She suppressed the urge to stroke his cheek and instead crossed her arms over her bare chest. "I said I can't, Nick. Or rather, I could, and it would be wonderful, and I would never want to stop. That's why I cannot."

He clasped his fingers behind his head. His eyes flickered over her face, trying to read her emotions instead of shamelessly scanning her naked body. She didn't know whether she would have painted him in that pose as a prisoner awaiting punishment or a devil inviting her to take the last step toward her own destruction.

242

"I could take you anyway," he said, almost to himself. "I should have when you broke our engagement. I should have dragged you to Gretna Green and married you, not let you go."

"Why didn't you?"

The question slipped out before she thought about it. He dropped his hands and the shutters fell over his eyes. He picked up his shirt and thrust it at her. "Put this on before I forget that I gave you a choice."

She pulled the shirt over her head. It reached the middle of her thighs and the neck gaped open over her bosom, but it was better than nothing.

"You should go to your chamber," he said.

Ellie took a deep breath. Then she took another. And another. There were so many words she wanted to give him — so many feelings she hadn't let herself give names to, and now they overwhelmed her. Everything turned hot, until even the tips of her ears burned from the friction between the identity she'd chosen and the feelings she'd buried.

Nick had been deadly serious, but as she started to gasp like a flopping fish, his voice softened. "Ellie...it will come out all right in the end. We've survived this long — we will survive tonight as well."

"What if I don't want to survive?"

"Don't say that," he said, suddenly grim. "I won't allow you to not survive."

"I don't mean I want to die — but were the last ten years living? Was it living when my whole life was an endless masquerade? Was it living when I cannot remember feeling anything other than remorse? Was it living to spend ten years running from a ghost?"

Tears pricked against her eyes, as hot and furious as the sound roaring in her ears. Nick wrapped his arms around her, pulling her toward his chest without saying a word in either agreement or dispute. He simply tucked her into his embrace. He stroked her back, then kissed the top of her head.

"Feel, Ellie," he whispered. "You are not a ghost if you can feel."

She felt. God, she felt — all the sharp pain of fresh love, not the weak throb of memory. She couldn't bear to have it sharp again, couldn't bear how Nick's return and his revenge were the whetstone that had given a new, knife-sharp edge to the love buried in her heart.

She also couldn't bear how her memories had become a crypt. The past ten years had been an exercise in burying everything beneath a hundred protective layers of cynicism and solitude. But her crypt was *safe*. All her pain had faded and chilled there, until it had turned to stone instead of fire.

She inhaled. Her perfume mingled with his scent. The faded bergamot of his soap was overlaid with his sweat. His chest was still bare, and she felt both more hair and more muscle than he'd had when she first knew him.

Nick had changed. Aged. The changes were slow, like flowers growing over a grave — and yet fast, like snow melting in spring. He was a mass of contradictions, but only two mattered to her: he was the boy who hated her enough to spend a decade plotting her ruin. And he was the man who loved who she really was, not the image she portrayed.

Even though there was nothing she could offer him that he didn't already have. He didn't need her dowry like Charles had. He didn't need her to maintain her reputation and bloodlines like her father had. He either needed her love, or he needed his revenge — but those were for *her*, not for her bloody pedigree.

She escaped his embrace. "I should go to my chamber."

"Running from ghosts again?"

"Better than going to bed with them, isn't it?"

Nick sighed. "Perhaps. Can't say I am happy with your choice, though."

Her choice. She didn't know many men who wouldn't try to force her when she was in their chamber, late at night, wearing only their shirt. He'd always let her have her choice, when no one else had.

"Why didn't you elope with me?" she asked again.

His eyes narrowed. "No wonder you're plagued with ghosts if you won't let them rest."

"Very well. Goodnight, Nick."

Her hand was on the doorknob before he responded. His voice made her turn around even though she wasn't sure she wanted his answer. "I thought you didn't want me," he said, his back still to her. "You never should have wanted me in the first place. I thought you had finally come to your senses."

"I didn't want to elope," she said. "But if you don't deserve me, it's in the opposite sense of your meaning. You don't deserve someone who would forsake you for her father's approval. If I had defied my father and eloped with you...I am still sure he would have harmed you. The only way he could have made good on such a *mesalliance* was by making me a widow so I could marry someone else."

Nick's head had been bowed, but he straightened as she spoke. His back rippled with dangerous energy. But he still didn't turn around. "You thought I would be harmed if we married?"

"It's not an excuse — or at least not a good one. I really was convinced that the proper choice for a girl in my position was to marry well. And I so wanted Father to be pleased with me. It was something I'd wanted long before I knew you, and it was so hard to say no to him."

"But you thought I'd be harmed?"

"Do you remember the first day I tried to break our engagement?"

He nodded. He wasn't still anymore, though — he walked over to one of the chests in the corner and threw it open. His belongings had been delivered from London earlier in the week, but he hadn't unpacked — did he intend to leave again?

She took a breath. "After that first attempt, I almost changed my mind. I loved you, I was sure of it. And I knew, finally, that Charles had offered for me mostly to stick a knife in your side. I tried to tell Father that I wouldn't marry Charles, although I would still marry whomever he chose. If I had to be pragmatic and make Father happy, I could still do it in a way that wasn't quite so awful to you."

Nick finally emerged from his chest with a cloudy glass bottle. He grabbed a penknife from the top tray of the chest and started digging into the wax seal, but he looked up when her words trailed off. "I'm still listening."

"There's not much left to share. Father was proud enough to make jilting Charles unthinkable, and vengeful enough that he thought you'd gotten your just deserts for making the mistake of aspiring so far above your station. And then, almost as though he were offering it as a boon to me, he said he could arrange for you to leave London. Something about his connections in Parliament and the business your company did for the Navy, and how simple it would be to find some malfeasance to pin on you as treason..."

She trailed off again. He'd given up on extracting the cork beneath the seal and pushed it into the bottle. He held the bottle up in mock toast. "All this talk of your father has killed whatever erection I still had, so I thank you for that."

He drank straight from the bottle. Then he grimaced — whatever he drank was harsh stuff.

"I didn't mention him to make you sleep better," she said. "And I'm not using him as an excuse. I regret it now, but I was so young then. I would have been swayed by him *or* you, whoever was more persuasive. The thought of your life being ruined for being in love with me...well, my father won."

He took another pull from the bottle. "So I just have to be the most persuasive man around to win you?"

"I'm not a prize anymore. And I like to think I can't be persuaded by anybody."

"But that's another lie, isn't it?" He walked toward her. Her stomach flipped. With his lowslung trousers and his loose grip on the bottle dangling from his fingers, he looked like a marauder in mid-pillage. "I can persuade you, just like he did, because you're so bloody scared of feeling anything that you'll do the first thing that offers you an escape. If I told you to drink this and then let me fuck you against that door, you'd do it just so I'd shut my mouth and not make you think about what you're feeling."

"I'm going to bed," she said.

"Or that." He tipped the bottle into his mouth again. From this distance, the fumes alone could intoxicate her. Her wide eyes met his as he pulled the bottle away from his lips. He wiped his mouth with his other hand. "Run, Ellie. Run like you did then. Run like you do every day. Don't make a choice. Don't do the hard thing. Don't try to be anything more than a ghost of what you could have been."

She was furious, suddenly, and she hit in him the chest, right over his heart. "As though I'm the only one who ran. Where will you go this time? China? Canada? I would hope that cannibals in the

South Pacific might eat you, but whatever you are drinking has surely pickled your insides. You may be *present*, but you're not *here*, not if you must drink something every time we argue. So don't pretend you are better at feeling than I am. I will remember this tomorrow — all you'll have is a headache."

His mouth tightened. His eyes were unbearably sad. "I never found you in a bottle of this stuff. But I never forgot you there, either."

Stop. She took a breath. They'd danced around the same fight ever since he had returned, two players in a game no one else could see and not even they knew the score of.

But she didn't want a game.

She took the bottle from his hand. "Stop. What I'm about to say — you don't have to respond tonight. But we can't keep doing this. Not for another hour, let alone four months. Either we try — really try — to be real for each other, not ghosts. Or we let each other go. But this…this is self-torture, not revenge. For both of us."

It was disjointed, discombobulated, perhaps not even what she wanted to say at all. There were voices beneath it that she suppressed, like hope scrabbling at the inside of Pandora's box. But it was the best she could do.

After an age, he nodded. "Go to bed. We will talk tomorrow."

She left, taking the bottle with her. Neither of them said anything else as she slipped through the door and closed it between them.

She didn't lock it, though. She leaned her head against it instead. With his scent and shirt enveloping her, she could pretend she still leaned against his chest.

She didn't want a game. But could she listen to her heart long enough to know what was real?

CHAPTER TWENTY-NINE

She had taken his bottle of arrack. It was the first thing he thought when she left. The cheap, rum-like liquor that he had drunk in India was no match for the smooth Scottish whisky he preferred, but it was better than nothing. He didn't really want to taste it ever again. But wanting a drink was better than considering her parting shot.

Nick shoved a hand through his hair as he stared at the door she had closed between them. Did she stand on the other side, staring at the door as he did?

Ellie was right. This was self-torture. He left, unable to stand the torment of wondering what she was doing in the chamber that mirrored his. He met no one in the passage; it was nearly one in the morning, still early for people accustomed to London life, but late for those who preferred country hours. He strode down the hall, and the carpet running down the center dampened his steps even though he didn't care who heard him.

Perhaps he should have cared. As he passed a bedchamber near the stairs, someone opened it from the inside. "I thought it must be you," Marcus said in a low voice. "How does your revenge progress?"

Nick stopped, scowling before he turned around. "It progresses. Were you waiting to waylay me?"

"No. I've already waylaid the person I intended to waylay. But the intelligence from that interview made it impossible for me to sleep."

"First Ferguson, now you. Is everyone in this house spying on me?"

Marcus shrugged. "It wouldn't surprise me."

Nick looked down the hall. No one stirred — but that didn't mean no one was listening. "If you wish to say something, come to the study. No one will disturb us there."

Marcus nodded and shrugged into his jacket before accompanying Nick down the stairs. There were no servants about, but a handful of guests still chattered in the drawing room. Nick turned toward his study silently, avoiding any interactions that would prolong the night. Even Marcus was an imposition he resented. If he couldn't be with Ellie, after the way his aching need for her had been denied, he didn't want to play the host.

The study was dark and the embers were banked. They spent a few moments lighting lamps and stoking the fire before Nick took his seat behind the desk. Marcus sighed as he eyed one of the hassocks. "You should redecorate sooner rather than later if you intend to stay. You would have liked how Ellie initially decorated this room for you. I think the furniture is still in the attics someplace if you care to drag it out."

"I'm not here to talk about Ellie," Nick said flatly. "Who did you stop before you saw me in the hall?"

Marcus walked over to the decanter, almost as though he hadn't heard the question. He offered Nick a glass, but Nick refused — Ellie's condemnation of his drinking still rang in his ears, and he was stubborn enough to pretend that she was wrong. Pouring his own glass, Marcus leaned against the fireplace mantel rather than sitting on one of the hassocks. Finally, he broke the silence. "Lucia. Mrs.

Grafton, I should say."

"And?" Nick prompted.

"And I won't betray the lady's confidences by sharing with you."

"The lady? She's a maid. A maid I'm paying for, if I'm not mistaken."

Marcus narrowed his eyes. "You don't know the first thing about her. If you had, you wouldn't have involved her in your revenge with Ellie. She told me how you're dressing Ellie up like some sort of high-priced plaything. She won't forgive you for what you're doing. She won't forgive any of us."

Nick held up his hands in a gesture of surrender. "I won't apologize for Ellie. But I didn't know you had interests toward her maid."

"There are many things you don't know. As much as I prefer England, perhaps I should have been the one to go to India."

He swirled the whisky in his glass. Nick recognized the weight of memory — he had labored under his own long enough that it was easy to see the signs of torment in others. "Be glad you stayed here, brother," he said. "I am. You couldn't have done more for the company or the family anywhere else."

Marcus looked up. "I know. But for myself? I think Sebastian Staunton had the right idea. He moved to another continent to start something of his own. As long as his brother is alive, Sebastian is just an idle gentleman here. Your absence gave me an illusion of responsibility. But illusions aren't enough to build a future on."

Nick didn't respond. His own illusions were too fresh to offer any comfort to his brother.

The silence amplified the crackling fire. Somewhere in the distance, someone laughed. There was still pleasure around them, even if Nick didn't feel it. He only felt the chill — of the weather, or of regret, he didn't know.

Finally, he sighed. "You have to find a way past the illusion, Marcus. Now that I'm back, you'll have time for it."

"Are you staying?"

Nick shrugged. "For now."

Marcus eyed him over his glass. "And what will your answer be in June?"

Nick didn't understand for a moment. When he did, he realized that he'd forgotten the terms of his agreement with Ellie. He was thinking about forever, or never, not a span of mere months.

"I liked India, but it never felt like a true home. If…"

He trailed off. Marcus smiled sympathetically. "Trouble with your revenge?"

"I won't betray the lady's confidences by sharing with you," Nick said, imitating Marcus's former annoyance over Lucia.

"Can't say I'm surprised. I've known Ellie long enough to always put my money on her."

"Traitor. Are you sure the two of you aren't plotting to kill me?"

Marcus drained the rest of his whisky. "Again, if we were, my money would be on her. But if you had seen how she obsessed over these rooms, choosing things you would like, making homes for you — no one puts that much love into someone she intends to destroy."

"Thank you," Nick said abruptly.

Marcus frowned. "For what?"

"For watching over her while I was gone. Even if Lucia gave you an ulterior motive."

Marcus was smart enough to catch the gratitude beneath the teasing, but he still played along. "Don't worry yourself. Invitations to Ellie's bacchanals over the past ten years were all the payment I needed. The first one she gave after Charles died, when two dozen half-clothed opera dancers performed for the audience — if Charles died in the arms of one of those Cyprians, he died a happy man. I hope you won't reform her too much."

"We both know reforming Ellie is a lost cause."

"I'm glad you know that."

Marcus sounded more serious then, but he didn't press. Instead, he set aside his glass and looked at his watch. "I should return to my bed. My money is on her, but I trust you'll come out all right. If you can't forge through the path you're on — I know you well enough to know you'll find a different path."

Marcus left before Nick responded. Or perhaps he knew Nick wouldn't respond.

The problem with the killer would resolve itself eventually — either with Nick's death or the killer's. The problem with Ellie, though, wasn't so black and white. Did he want his revenge? Or did he want her happiness?

And were those two things mutually exclusive?

He had thought they were. When he had believed that she had refused him all those years ago because she didn't love him, he had assumed that his revenge would destroy her. But if he were honest with himself, if he let his eyes and ears and hands tell him a new story that refuted the mantra his heart had chanted endlessly, he knew she had loved him before, truly and honestly.

Her voice had admitted it in her studio, breaking as she begged him not to leave her again. Her eyes had admitted it, the moment she realized that he had returned. When she had told him, years ago, that she would marry his cousin, she had done it coldly and implacably, leaving no room in the air around her for him or his love — snuffing out whatever she'd felt for him so comprehensively that it was as though she'd never felt at all.

But in her paintings — the fierce, wild ones that stood unframed, not the pretty, predictable efforts that hung from the walls — he had seen glorious, focused, fiery passion. Not the icy Virgin Queen she played for her guests; not the jaded, indolent widow she feigned for him.

Those paintings, like the Ellie who always came apart for him when she gave in and forgot the past, were the Ellie who might have been.

Could Nick resurrect her? Could that Ellie unlock who *he* might have been — make him a better man than the one who looked forward, with shameless hunger, to having her again? Or did he still hate her too much? Did he hate her enough to leave that would-be Ellie locked away in the darkest pits of her own heart, a goddess condemned to gnaw at her own flesh for all eternity?

Did he hate himself enough to refuse what they could have? Or could he give up on the plans of the past ten years and choose a different path?

CHAPTER THIRTY

Ellie spent most of the night wide awake. She almost drank from the bottle she'd taken from Nick, but the fumes put her off the stuff. In the morning, she didn't feel tired — just restless and unhappy, wondering what Nick's response to her demands would be.

She had to stop thinking of him. She rang for Lucia early, dressed in a comfortable morning gown, and went to her salon. Her books would distract her until she had to mix with her guests. But her salon wasn't empty. Prudence sat there alone, scribbling something on a piece of paper as she perused the book propped open on her writing desk. Most mornings, Ellie was glad to see her. But her greeting, when it left her lips, sounded annoyed rather than pleased.

Prudence was too perceptive by half. "Are you feeling unwell?" Prudence asked, laying aside her pen. "You seem...piqued."

Ellie must have sounded worse than that to make Prudence stop writing. "Is that what you would call it? To tell the truth, I don't know what I feel."

"Shall I ring for tea?"

Ellie noticed that Prudence did not offer to leave. She tried to ignore her flaring annoyance. "No need — I sent for a tray. But I believe I shall take my chocolate and my thoughts elsewhere."

Prudence eyed her thoughtfully. "I know how tempting it is to

255

think you might find it easier to be alone. But you are a reasonable woman. You may find that company may help if solitude has yet to do the trick."

"You are the first to ever call me a reasonable woman."

"Intelligent, then," Prudence said with a grin. "Reason is given too much adulation anyway."

Ellie sat down across from Prudence, lounging on the same chaise where she had received Nick — was it only four nights earlier? It felt like four months. The broken glass had all been swept up, but it seemed that Nick's scent still hung in the air, an invisible web that held her down and wouldn't let her forget.

"Do you smell bergamot?" she asked Prudence.

Prudence sniffed the air tentatively. "No?"

Then it was on her skin, not in the air. She had slept in his shirt, with his scent wrapped around her. A proper woman might have blushed, but Ellie shrugged it off.

Further questions were forestalled by a footman bearing Ellie's chocolate. "Would you care for a cup?" Ellie asked as she poured.

Prudence shook her head. Ellie waited until the footman was gone before she picked up the conversation again. "What did you mean, earlier? About finding that solitude isn't doing the trick?"

"I won't claim to understand you, Ellie. We've both lost brothers and had our share of difficulties with our parents, but we aren't the same. Witness how you've been your own mistress all these years, while I escaped my mother only by taking refuge with Lady Salford."

"I think you give yourself too little credit," Ellie interjected.

Prudence held up a hand. "I know my failings. Solitude does that, you know — gives us a chance to chew endlessly over what we might have said or done or been."

"It's not so bad as that," Ellie said. "And you can't accuse me of solitude. When is my social calendar ever empty?"

"But you only host lavish crushes. When was the last time you had an intimate *tête-à-tête*?" Prudence pressed on despite the way Ellie's mouth compressed. "Your calendar is full, but what do you get from those engagements? Something that enriches you? Or merely peace from the voices in your head?"

Peace. It was what she had told Nick she wanted. But Prudence made it sound so bleak — and Ellie wasn't ready to give her the point. "When have you ever known me to have doubts?" Ellie asked.

Prudence saw through the diversion. Still, her voice softened. "I only guess, Ellie. Perhaps…perhaps I need to understand you so I can see what I would have to do to secure my own independence. But my current guess is that you haven't enjoyed being the merry marchioness — you've survived it."

"Leave me," Ellie ordered suddenly, with the same abrupt, frosty tone she used when Lucia, or Marcus, or anyone else stepped out of line with her. "If you're going to prattle on about things you know nothing of, then leave."

Prudence didn't even flinch. "That tactic may find success with Madeleine. She is so shocked when you don't pour your heart out that she stops asking. But I *know*, Ellie. I feign amiability just as you feign cynicism."

"You believe my cynicism to be an act? I assure you, it's not. People *will* use you for their own ends, Prudence. And you *will* do things that are unforgivable. With your family history — even with what Amelia did to you in Scotland — I thought you would understand that."

Their friend Amelia had spent the previous summer trying to "save" Prudence from an arranged marriage she desperately needed —

only to be compromised by, and later married to, Prudence's would-be fiancée. But Prudence just sighed. "If all you let yourself do is lament the past in your studio, it's little wonder you think you believe what you just said."

"I don't think it — I know it."

"And yet you save people. What would have happened to Lucia, do you think, if you had believed her transgressions to be unforgivable? Or to Madeleine — she and Ferguson never could have married without your help. Why do you help people if you think betrayal or your own failings are the inevitable outcome?"

Ellie couldn't respond. Her blocked response was an almost physical experience. Her mind drained of words, just as her breath was knocked out and her throat closed against her. Prudence, the friend Ellie had thought to take to Europe with her, the woman Ellie pitied for having less freedom and money and prospects and all the rest...

"I'm not kind, Prudence," she said. Her voice was low, and she couldn't look Prudence in the eyes. "You are remaking me in your own image, not the one I deserve. It's not altruism or genteel goodwill that drives me. Just the regret that I didn't stand for myself when I should have, and the desire to stop others from making the same mistake."

She sipped her chocolate, but the bitter concoction brought her no joy. When she finally dared to look at Prudence, there was no shock there — only consideration.

Finally, Prudence spoke. "I am sure a vicar would tell you to be more selfless. But in the face of great personal disappointment, you chose to help those who needed your help and found what enjoyment you could in the rest of your life. Your decision to give others the chance you didn't have, rather than trying to take it away from them... that says all I need to know about your character."

Ellie believed her. It was the belief that struck her, even more than Prudence's words. The woman Prudence described — it was how Ellie wished she saw herself on the days when everything was dark.

It wasn't much — not a proclamation that Ellie was a hero, or a saint, or any other superlative. But if she believed it, if that assessment of her character was correct, then she was *human* — not the goddess Nick had made her into, not the fallen soul she'd believed herself to be, not the perfectly cool aristocrat the ton applauded.

And in that small, still moment, with the fire blazing and Nick's bergamot scent whispering around her like an old friend, she knew what she wanted.

"Prudence," she said, "how did you know what to say?"

"I didn't," Prudence said, shifting in her chair. "But perhaps... perhaps I wish someone would say something similar to me."

Regret flickered over Prudence's face. Ellie wondered, not for the first time, when Prudence would do something about it. "Do you love Lord Salford?" she asked abruptly.

Prudence blinked, then pressed two fingers to her temple as though she'd been coshed over the head. "I beg your pardon?"

"Alex. Do you love him?"

Prudence turned back to her writing desk. "I haven't the faintest idea why you would even suggest such a thing."

"Take a bit of unsolicited advice, then, as repayment for giving it — whatever it is you regret, do something about it. If it's Salford, say something. If it's your circumstances, run away and have an adventure. You are a rational woman. If what you are doing doesn't bring you joy, change it."

Prudence snorted. "Felled by my own logic. That is why I study history, not philosophy."

But there was amusement in her voice, enough to make Ellie laugh. She left Prudence to her books — not because she wanted solitude, but because she felt like painting something, anything, for the first time in weeks. She went up to her studio, ready to pour her heart onto the canvas.

Perhaps she and Nick couldn't be real for each other. There was a chance that too much had happened to them, that there were too many words they couldn't take back and too many wounds they couldn't heal. But she was willing to try. Either he would see her heart and believe in it — or he wouldn't be able to forgive her, no matter what she said.

Either way, she would have peace. She just had to hope that Nick could make the choice they both deserved.

CHAPTER THIRTY-ONE

Ellie painted all day. A maid brought a tray for her sometime in the afternoon, after she had shamelessly ignored her guests — she would rather give them reason to gossip than waste a precious hour of daylight.

But while it was likely easier that she had not seen Nick, she couldn't help but wonder what he would say when they were alone again. When she finally descended to the drawing room at six o'clock, after dressing in a lush green evening gown, Nick still hadn't appeared.

Most of her guests were present, though. They were eating an hour earlier than usual to make way for the larger entertainment Ellie had planned. She always included the villagers and tenants in an event during her house parties, and the neighborhood would be celebrating in the village that night with ale and other refreshments. Her aristocratic guests would proceed to the village for fireworks at nine — late for the farmers and shopkeepers, but early enough that her chef was likely still cursing her plans.

After scanning the drawing room in search of Nick, her eyes found Christabel instead. Her former sister-in-law stood apart from the group, looking handsome but slightly stunned in a pale blue muslin gown that gave her figure a softer, more feminine look than the outgrown pinafore she'd worn at home. Ellie joined her immediately.

"I am delighted you decided to come, Lady Christabel," she said, kissing her cheek.

Christabel didn't look delighted. She looked equal parts determined and terrified. "Thank you, Lady Folkestone. And thank you for the loan of a dress. I haven't seen this many people from the ton since your wedding — I hadn't realized how out of step with fashion I had become."

Ellie had whispered the offer of a dress at the dower house in an attempt to win her over into coming. She was glad it had worked — but she hadn't realized just how isolated Christabel had been. "Did your sisters never bring you to London for a season? I admit, my circle didn't include debutantes often enough for me to notice, but I assumed they would see you settled properly."

Christabel's lips compressed. "They grew too busy with their own lives, and all too happy that I was in the country watching over Mother."

Ellie could fix this. She could take Christabel under her wing. She was little different from all the other people Ellie had rescued — and her vague sense of guilt over Christabel's abandonment added to her determination. She opened her mouth, ready to offer it...

But then Nick walked through the door.

He looked disheveled, somehow, despite his perfectly tied cravat and impeccable evening suit. But even the best valet couldn't prevent a man from shoving his hand through his hair too many times. He looked like he hadn't slept at all. The corners of his mouth turned down with the weight of the thoughts he carried.

Did he want her? Or was he considering how to say goodbye to her?

* * *

He was a coward. He should have sought her out. He should have told her what he felt. But how could he tell her when even he didn't know for sure?

So he'd avoided her during the day — not a difficult task, as it turned out, since he heard from one of the footmen that she was in her studio throughout the daylight hours. And at dinner, they were seated at opposite ends of the vast table, with forty or so people and more than that number of dishes spread between them.

But there was something different about her. He could barely see her through the candelabras and epergnes and other interfering decorations, but when he did catch a glimpse of her, she seemed to glow. It couldn't be with happiness. She was too distracted for happiness. But her occasional smile seemed meant for herself, not for either of the guests next to her.

It was a mystery he wanted the answer to. The answer had to wait. Dinner ended. The company dispersed to gather cloaks and hats for the ride into the village. He thought about avoiding the festivities, but Norbury was the only guest who had declined, after claiming he'd caught a chill. Nick would rather keep Ellie in his sights than spend an hour with his least favorite houseguest.

But Ellie slipped away from him, choosing to share a carriage with Lady Christabel and Percy Pickett. Perhaps it was for the best. Whatever he decided to confess to her, he didn't want an audience for it.

They reached the village just in time for the fireworks. The Folkestone village was a trim, neat little cluster of shops and houses with an open green in the middle. A church flanked one side of it, but he was more familiar with the pub on the other side of the rectangle. If he planned to stay in England, Nick would need to learn more about the town, the tenants, and everyone else in the neighborhood. He would have to put down roots in soil that he'd always assumed would reject him.

But the villagers who bowed and curtseyed to him seemed genuinely pleased that he was there. And for the first time, Nick thought that perhaps spending parts of his year here, rather than in a warehouse or counting room, might be a worthwhile endeavor.

He found Ellie as the first firework shot up into the sky. She was buried deep in the heart of the group, but she stood out for him under the sparkling shower of light. She still had that glow, the one that made him want to learn her secrets.

She had looked almost the same at Vauxhall a decade ago — lit up under fireworks, not knowing that he watched her from the shadows. But on that night, she had been astonished and delighted by everything around her. Now, fireworks were something she could have whenever she wished. She yawned slightly, stifling it with a gloved hand, and looked out over the crowd rather than up at the sky.

He was sad, suddenly, that neither of them seemed to enjoy such simple things as fireworks, or dancing, or a perfect bit of moonlight. But if some fairy came and gave him a choice, he would stay in this moment, not return to that one. She'd been more easily delighted in that life — but she was more certain in this one.

He was old enough now to see the value in certainty. And it didn't hurt that her father was dead in this life and couldn't run Nick off like he had at Vauxhall. Nick strolled up to her, but she didn't tense when he greeted her — if anything, she relaxed.

"So you're not avoiding me after all?" she murmured.

He could barely hear her voice under the excited chatter around them. He leaned in to her ear. "No more than you are avoiding me."

She looked up at him. Another firework lit the sky, and her blue eyes were eerie under the sparks. "You said we would talk today.

Should I expect a note tonight, or have you changed your mind?"

He scanned her face, but he couldn't read what she wanted of the conversation. Did she want a farewell? Or a future?

Before he could respond, he heard a crack of exploding gunpowder. There should have been a firework immediately after it, but the expected display never came.

His hackles rose. Gunpowder without a firework could only mean a gunshot, unless someone had brought firecrackers or one of the fireworks had malfunctioned. He looked out over the crowd. No one else had noticed. Their faces were all turned up to the sky, waiting for the next display. He heard laughter, happy conversation, easy jests — both the villagers and the aristocrats were enjoying themselves, despite the cold.

No one screamed. There was no indication that anything was amiss. He tried to relax and pretend nothing was wrong — that he hadn't heard anything strange, and that he wasn't a coward in the face of her questions.

She must have seen something of his conflict flicker across his face. "Is something wrong?"

"Perhaps we should rest tonight," he said, pitching his voice low so no one would overhear him. "I'd wager neither of us have slept since I came home, and I at least am too old for all-hours revelry. There's time to talk tomorrow."

Her eyes narrowed. "If you're too old for revelry, I'm too old to wait."

He would have grinned, but a child ran up to them, weaving through the crowd and skidding to a stop just short of Ellie's skirts. "Mr. Claiborne needs you, milady," he said, his high-pitched voice creaking with excitement. "He said you must find Lord Folkestone and come to the church."

Ellie frowned. "Was he alone?"

"He had a lady with him. He said to find you, then the surgeon. And not to tell anyone else."

His eyes were wide and his shoulders were thrown back with importance, like a little lieutenant given his first command. Nick gave him a shilling and sent him running off through the crowd on the second half of his errand.

But when Ellie started toward the church, he grabbed her arm. "This could be a trap."

She shook her head impatiently as another firework shot up into the sky. "The child belongs to the pub owner. He knows what Marcus looks like. Something's wrong, Nick. And unless Marcus is the one setting the trap, we need to join him. Will you let me go? Or shall I start screaming until someone else takes me there?"

Her eyes flashed in a way that underscored her threat. Nick turned her loose. But he caught up with her as soon as she escaped the crowd and beat her to the church door.

"At least let me go in first," he said.

She gestured him ahead of her. He tried the door and found it unlocked. The church was almost entirely dark. Only a single lamp illuminated the scene, enough to be visible through the windows but not enough to draw too much attention. Marcus knelt, facing a woman who sat in the pew closest to the door. With her dark bonnet and cloak, Nick couldn't recognize her — but the concern and fury mingled on Marcus's face gave him a guess.

"Close the door before Lucia catches a chill," Marcus ordered.

Nick stepped aside, letting Ellie in to the church. But before he could close the door, a walking stick tapped against it. "Lovely night for a bit of worship, isn't it?" Ferguson asked, strolling in before Nick could stop him.

Ellie had already rushed to Lucia's side. "What happened?" she asked, dropping into the pew next to her maid. "Did you feel faint?"

Nick knew the answer even before Lucia shook her head. "Your service is even more dangerous than I thought," she said shakily.

The maid pressed her hand tightly against her left arm. Marcus tore a strip of fabric from what appeared to be her petticoat and handed it to her. She winced as she added it to the bloodstained cloth she already held against her skin.

"Did you see who shot you?" Nick asked.

"How did you know she was shot?" Marcus interjected. "No one else seemed to notice. We came here rather than the pub to keep it quiet."

"I heard the shot. The others must have thought it was a firecracker."

"I heard it as well," Ferguson added. He moved into the room, away from the door, as though he didn't want to be the first man hit in a siege. "My question is, why hide here? Why not tell everyone else to take cover?"

Nick ignored him and knelt with Marcus in front of the ladies. Lucia was as calm as ever, but her breaths were shallow and her mouth was tight. "How badly are you hurt?" he asked gently.

"It's a flesh wound — it will heal," she said in a clipped voice.

Ferguson wasn't accustomed to being dismissed. "My wife, my sisters, and everyone else seem to be in peril," he said, as disinterestedly as he said most things. "I find myself quite perturbed."

Ellie glared at him. "I am the only person likely to shoot you. Go back outside and watch over them, if you're so concerned."

"I believe I'm more concerned about you at the moment," he said, leaning against the pew on the other side of the aisle, where he could watch both Ellie and the door. "Why did someone shoot your maid?"

"He was aiming for me," Marcus said grimly.

"And your first thought was to hide? Why not gather men and search for him?"

Marcus ripped another strip from Lucia's petticoat. He moved to sit beside her, taking over the task of keeping pressure on her wound. "I'd rather she not bleed to death while I go off into the woods looking for a madman."

Nick stood, leaning against the back of the pew in front of Lucia. The duke had a point, unwelcome though it was. "Care to join the search with me, your grace?" he asked.

Ferguson laughed. "Not until I have an heir more suitable than my cousin. Unless you know who the madman is?"

"I have my suspicions," Nick said briefly. "And I doubt you're in any danger. It seems confined solely to me and Marcus."

"Or, more accurately, me and Lucia," Ellie said.

Lucia sighed. "I should have shot both the highwaymen on the road. And here I thought I didn't need another lesson in misplaced mercy."

Her tone was surprisingly light. Nick didn't know many men who would handle being shot so calmly, but Lucia acted like she had been shot every day of her life.

The surgeon arrived then, accompanied by Lady Christabel and a slight whiff of ale. "What seems to be the matter?" he asked, walking toward them. "I heard a maid wasn't feeling well?"

He gasped when Marcus lifted his hand briefly to show him the blood. "She accidentally gouged herself on a nail," Marcus said, lying smoothly. "She needs stitches."

The surgeon turned to Christabel. "Perhaps you should wait..."

"Nonsense," Christabel said briskly, striding over to Lucia. Nick slid out of the way, joining Ferguson across the aisle to make room in front of Lucia. "If I had my bag of herbs, we could make better progress, but let's get you comfortable, shall we?"

She pulled away the cloth and tsked in sympathy when she saw the wound. "That's a nasty scrape. Is it bleeding as much as before, or has it slowed?"

She kept asking questions with a gentle voice that Nick hadn't expected to hear from her. The surgeon seemed content to let her take over, swigging furtively from the flask in his pocket when he thought no one was looking.

Finally, she wrapped another strip of petticoat around Lucia's arm. "Mr. Claiborne, if you will escort the lady to a private room in the pub, I shall meet you there. I keep a bag with the publican and can do the stitches there. Ask for some laudanum if the lady wants it..."

"No opium," Lucia interrupted forcefully.

Christabel shrugged. "Then a glass of whisky wouldn't be amiss. I'll join you in a moment."

The surgeon followed them out. If his destination was the pub, it was for his own glass of whisky. As soon as they were gone, Christabel looked Nick square in the eye. "That wasn't a scrape. What really happened?"

He thought about lying. But Christabel already knew about the highwayman — with this attempt, the neighborhood was in even more danger. "She was shot. Someone used the fireworks as a diversion to make an attempt on Marcus."

Christabel paled. She hadn't reacted at all to the sight of Lucia's blood, but she suddenly looked like she might be sick. "How terrible," she said faintly.

Ferguson, ignored until now, offered her his flask. To everyone's surprise, she took it — and drank from it with nearly as little reaction as Ellie would have. "Thank you, your grace," she said, still sounding dazed. "I knew you were concerned about a highwayman, but I didn't expect this."

"A highwayman, did you say?" Ferguson asked, his hand pausing as he replaced the cap. "You're the second woman tonight to mention a highwayman."

Christabel nodded. "The story just seemed so…unlikely."

"Doesn't it, though?" Ferguson said, slanting a glance at Nick.

Nick gestured toward the door. "The fireworks seem to be done. We should return to the group before we are missed."

Ferguson looked ready to argue, but Ellie nodded. "I will go with you to the pub, Lady Christabel. I don't want to leave Mrs. Grafton alone during her ordeal."

"I shall come with you," Nick and Ferguson both said simultaneously.

She shook her head. "What do either of you know about nursing patients? Ferguson, escort your wife and the twins home. And Nick, I'm sure your talents would be better spent interrogating my guests."

She was right. He already had a suspicion. Norbury's absence from the fireworks had turned from enviable to damning. Waiting to confirm it might make the trail go cold.

But the thought of Ellie injured — or worse — instead of Lucia had Nick on edge. "Very well," he said. "But find me when you return to Folkestone. We must talk."

She paled at that, as pale as Christabel had been when discussing murder. Was she really that scared of what he might say to her?

"Of course, my lord," she said. He told himself her voice was cool for the benefit of their audience, not as a genuine reflection of her feelings.

Then she swept out with Christabel at her side — two women who seemed ready to battle any foe.

Ferguson twirled his walking stick. "Shall we go hunting now, or after I've beaten you for hiding a bloody highwayman from me?"

Nick pulled on his gloves. "I meant to tell you, I'm sure, but I didn't want to interrupt your monologues."

"My father must have *detested* you," Ferguson said, clapping him on the back. "Hunting it is."

CHAPTER THIRTY-TWO

When Ellie returned to Folkestone shortly before midnight, she didn't have to search for Nick. The door between his room and hers was ajar.

She shrugged out of her pelisse, hat, and gloves and tossed everything onto her bed. Then, before her courage failed her, she walked through the door. She had managed not to think of him at the pub, although brooding might have been preferable to the grisly sight of Lucia's many stitches. She had left her maid in Marcus's capable hands — and, surprisingly, Lucia hadn't protested his involvement in her affairs. But Ellie's stomach suddenly felt full of stones.

Did Nick want her as much as she wanted him? Or was his love a phantom that no amount of desire could resurrect?

When she entered, she heard the echo of the previous night. He sat in the same chair, next to an equally large fire, and his eyes were hooded and unreadable.

"Will you join me?" he asked.

Asked. Not told. She shut the door and walked to him. When his hand extended, it wasn't to stop her — it was to invite her to take the other chair.

Part of her wanted to stay on her feet, keep him off balance, gain the upper hand. But if she wanted him to be real for her, she was honor-bound to be real for him.

She sat. "Did you learn anything from the guests?" she asked.

It wasn't the question she wanted an answer to. He shrugged it aside. "My batman returned from London — the tattoos were too common to learn anything from. Your brother and I made a bit of progress here, though. But all that will keep until tomorrow. Is Lucia feeling well?"

"She will live, although she'd feel better if she allowed Christabel to dose her with laudanum."

They fell silent. Neither seemed quite able to make eye contact, not with the ghosts of the previous night's conversation chilling the air between them. Then, abruptly, Nick stood up. "Stay there a moment," he said. "I have something for you."

He disappeared into his dressing room and returned a moment later with a small box and a leather pouch. "What do you want, Ellie?" he asked, his voice taut, as though he'd had to force the words out. "Pleasure? Or freedom?"

On "pleasure," he raised the box. On "freedom," he offered the pouch. As he waited for her response, his hands seemed perfectly balanced — a choice between two fates, with nothing to tip the scales.

Nothing but him. "Why must I choose?" she asked.

He sat down again, balancing the pouch on one knee and the box on the other. "Because I can't think about any future beyond tonight if you're here only because I coerced you."

She laughed incredulously. "But you *did* coerce me."

He nodded. "But if you had the choice, right now, to walk away with all your debts forgiven — would you take it?"

"I'd be a fool not to."

Nick closed his eyes. For a moment, he was twenty-two again, reacting to that first, unbelievable moment of betrayal. But Ellie saw a difference in the tightness of his jaw, in the way he sighed but didn't grimace.

He had expected that answer, in a way he hadn't expected her to leave him the first time.

"I'd be a fool not to," she said again. "But perhaps I'd rather be a fool than a pragmatist."

"Would you rather be a fool than a free woman?" he asked, opening his eyes. "What about all your vows to be your own mistress?"

"I can still be my own mistress. But I would enjoy it more if you were with me."

Her heart caught in her throat. It was as close to a declaration as she could get.

It seemed to be enough for him. In an instant, he'd set aside the objects in his lap, stood up, and pulled her into his arms. Her cheeks were still cold from her carriage ride home. His hands burned against them. He looked dead into her eyes, as though he could read her soul.

"I believe you," he said.

He kissed her before she could think. Her body responded for her. She was ravenous for him, as ravenous as he was for her, and she wasn't satisfied with the firm, hard, vow-sealing kiss he gave her. She wanted that, wanted to feel like they'd branded each other — but at this point, brands were superfluous compared to the marks they'd left on each other's souls.

She opened her mouth and he took her offering. It was like they were young again, kissing with all the fuel of their dreams behind them — enough fuel to burn away their regrets. She dug her fingers into his shoulders, urging him on as she felt him start to unfasten the buttons down the back of her dress. He had a long job ahead of them

— but then, they had all night.

Their kisses turned shorter, more like sips of pleasure compared to the long, thirst-quenching draught of their first one. He finished with her dress. She slid his jacket from his shoulders. The rest of their clothing followed in the same pattern — hurried, but smooth, and with no concern for worship or winning.

"Why wasn't it like this before?" she murmured against his lips before kissing him again.

He pulled her chemise up over her head, tossing it to join his trousers on the floor. "Don't know. But if we're fools for this, we were even bigger fools to avoid it."

He picked her up and laid her out on his bed — their bed. No matter what happened after, she would always consider it theirs.

"Do you know, this is the first time I've ever taken a lover to bed?" she said.

His hand had found her thatch of curls, but he paused and looked at her eyes rather than her breasts. "Truly?"

She leaned up on her elbows and stroked her hand over his heart. "You and I never had a bed — all those pesky chaperones. So it didn't seem…right, with the others."

"And here I thought I wouldn't have to work to make this good enough."

He grinned as he dropped his lips to her breast. She fell back into the mattress, her own grin matching his. "Wouldn't want you to get too complacent, my lord."

"Never complacent, Ellie my love."

His mouth closed over her breast, sucking lightly just as his fingers found the most sensitive place beneath her curls. She arched up, putting a hand on his head, sifting through his hair as though pillaging for treasure.

But the treasure she sought was already there, wrapped around her like a net of spun sugar, fragile and almost unbearable sweet. The Nick in her arms was the one she'd caught glimpses of the past few days, the witty, sardonic man who would laugh just for her. If she could keep his laughter, let it soak into her skin until, together, they lit up every last bit of darkness...

His fingers took on more urgency, and suddenly there was no room for thought. "I need you, Ellie." He brushed a kiss across her lips. "I'll need you until I die, in this life and every other."

He moved against her as he said this, and there was no pause — no waiting for her to beg, no time for her to answer. He sank into her, slowly, but irresistibly, and she spread her legs, wishing madly that there was more she could give, more he could take.

"This life and every other," she whispered.

She pulled his head down and kissed him, hard and thorough, wanting the taste of those words to mingle on their lips. When he moved in her again, she felt the craving and the completion, twin gifts they gave each other with every stroke. And when she finally came apart, he joined her there — not a conqueror, not a captive, but a missing piece of her heart that had finally found its way home.

*   *   *

When they could breathe again, she turned onto her side, stroking her fingers across his chest. "If I'd known how good a bed could be, I'd have risked my chaperones finding us, ruin be damned."

He laughed. The sound rumbled through her fingers. "Best that you didn't know. I'm sure I only survived tonight because of your advanced age."

She poked him in the side. "Careful, Claiborne. I'm still younger than you."

Nick caught her fingers and brought them to his mouth, kissing each one before dropping his head back on the pillow. "Perhaps Charles had the right idea after all. If I died here, with you as my last thought, I'd die a happy man."

"Don't say that," she said.

He looked up at her, his blue eyes serious. "I'm sorry. But chances are you'll be my last thought no matter when it happens." He paused, just long enough that she thought he was done, and then added, "You, or kippers. I'm quite fond of them."

She giggled. "You are so adept at wooing ladies, aren't you?"

"There's only one lady I care to woo tonight."

She remembered, then, the choice he had given her. "What were those objects you had for me?"

"Does it matter? I like the choice you made."

She scowled. "You know I'm too curious for that."

"Very well," he said with an exaggerated sigh. He rolled out of bed, still naked, and strode to the chair he'd sat in. He picked up the pouch first, untied the leather thong that bound it, and unfurled it.

"These are the receipts for what you owe me — ten years' worth," he said, holding up a sheaf of papers.

Then he tossed them into the fire.

Ellie gasped. "Why did you do that?"

"As I've said, you weren't the woman I wanted revenge against." He didn't even look at the notes as they burned — as though forty thousand pounds, and all the years he'd waited, were nothing compared to the next moment.

Instead, he came back to the bed with the mysterious box. "You said the other night that you don't know what I did in India. And, frankly, it's not worth sharing, at least not now. I mostly drank too much, fought every fever a man can have, made an obscene amount of money…and dreamed of you."

He flicked open the clasp on the box. Inside lay a pile of delicate gold chains, threaded through dozens, perhaps hundreds, of tiny bells. He lifted a strand from the box. The bells chimed softly, whispering foreign dreams in the air — dreams Ellie had never had and yet, suddenly, longed for.

He leaned over her body, grazing his hands down her leg, and fastened the chain around her ankle. "I thought I would have you dance for me in these," he said. "I dreamed of you serving me like a harem girl, wearing only bells and your glorious hair."

He fastened another set of bells around her other ankle. She shivered, but he wasn't done.

"If you saw what's in my trunks, you'd know what I did in India. Jewels, fabrics, artwork, more jewels — every bazaar, it seemed, had something you might like. I think I have a flacon of perfume from every man who ever tried to bottle jasmine under glass. I said it was for my revenge, that I'd taunt you with it…"

He clasped another set of bells around her wrist. When she shifted to catch his hand, her body turned to music — but he evaded her grasp. "I lied to myself, Ellie," he said. "Easier to say I hated you. Easier to plan for a guaranteed revenge than to risk not winning you back. Easier to hope you'd marry someone else, so I'd never have to bring these dreams back to face you…"

She cut him off as he fastened the last bracelet around her other wrist. The mingling of music and regret was discordant. These bells called for joy, not penance.

"Shut up, Nick," she said fiercely. "Stop talking and kiss me."

Nick heard the certainty in her voice. He reveled in it — he'd rather let her feel his heart than try to say the words he somehow couldn't get out.

He was already hard for her again, his heart pounding so fast that surely the beat alone would make her bells ring for him. This time, though, he was slower, more patient, more thorough — the way he'd wanted to be the first time, before his cock had overruled him.

The peak, when it came, was briefer than before, but no less intense. He spent himself inside her again — and, again, pretended it was an accident rather than a choice.

Not that Ellie seemed to mind. When he could think again — after a longer interval than the previous time — he tipped his head toward her. She held her wrist above her, staring up at the bells as she turned them this way and that to catch the firelight. Her smile, as dark and mysterious as any goddess's, was supremely satisfied.

She must have sensed his movement, because she dropped her wrist and turned her head. They were inches apart, and her smile, when directed at him, was bright enough to overwhelm him.

"You were more than worth the wait," she said.

He wanted her again — but another time would kill him. Despite his earlier words, he wasn't ready to die, not when he had this moment to savor. So he contented himself with pulling her into his arms and learning how she felt as she fell asleep against him, the little sounds she made as she dreamed. The fire slowly died, and the crackling embers mingled with her bells to lure him closer to sleep.

In the morning, he would settle with Norbury. And then....

And then he didn't know, exactly, what would happen. But

winning wasn't good enough anymore.

All he wanted was Ellie. And he would do whatever it took to stay by her side.

CHAPTER THIRTY-THREE

Ellie awoke to the smell of ham and the sound of a beverage being poured. She was sprawled on her stomach and had slept more deeply than she had in days — but food never failed to awaken her.

"How late is it, Lucia?" she mumbled into her pillow, not turning over.

"It's just after nine."

Nick. She flipped herself upright, pushed her hair out of her face — and heard the soft chime of bells all around her as she realized she was still in his bed. "What are you doing?"

"Do you care for toast? I will toast it for you."

He was sitting in his armchair, fully dressed, in a suit that was a better match for a London rake than a sleepy country lord. But there was nothing sleepy about him today. His eyes were sharp, and they missed nothing as they looked her over. She winced. Her hair would look like a nest of brambles. She pulled the sheets up around herself, covering everything she should cover — but still, she felt suddenly shy.

Nick had never seen her wake up in the morning. No one had, save Lucia and her other maids.

She tried to contain her hair, but she couldn't without dropping the sheets. Nick coughed. "Toast?" he asked again.

He held a toasting fork. It was so odd to see him doing something

281

domestic that she laughed. "Trying to keep me well-fed, my lord?"

He grinned. "Unless you prefer to be put through your paces first."

She did, but she was too curious about why he was there to distract him. "Toast first, if you please."

He nodded. But before he put the bread on the toasting fork, he stood and brought her a cup. "I thought this would awaken you."

He had brought her chocolate. She took it from his hand, letting her fingers graze on his as she reached for the handle. "Is Lucia feeling better? You don't have...bad news about her, do you?"

"She will be fine, but Marcus ordered her to take at least a fortnight off. You can ring for another maid later. We need to talk, Ellie."

She didn't like the tone of his voice. It was too serious, as though he dreaded whatever he needed to say. She sipped her chocolate, pretending she'd heard nothing to warn her. When she thought she could sound innocent, she said, "What do we need to talk about?"

He jammed a slice of bread onto the toasting fork, thrust it toward the fire, and scowled. Then, he said, "You're not going to like it. I thought I would do this without telling you, but you deserve better than that. And anyway, I need your help."

She frowned. "Can you be more direct, please?"

He snorted. "My little field marshal. I'm sorry to interrupt your morning like this, but I believe I know who wants to kill me."

She nearly shrieked. "You are wasting time with my toast when you know something that important?"

"I thought you liked toast," he said.

He wasn't teasing. He looked down at the toasting fork as though it had betrayed him. Ellie sighed. "I adore toast, and I thank you for it.

But isn't the killer slightly more important?"

Nick turned the toasting fork over the fire. "Of course. But if your guests stay true to their usual schedules, I have an hour before I must begin my efforts to eliminate him. There is time enough to make you toast."

"'Eliminate' sounds dire."

"Not as dire as what I would have done if he had harmed you," Nick said. "But you aren't going to like the person I am about to name."

She thought back over the past four days. And she knew, suddenly, that she was about to be disappointed, not shocked. But she put a hand to her chest in mock surprise. "It's not me, is it?"

Nick laughed. "Would that it was. I'm sure I could find a satisfying way to punish you."

"Shall I confess, then?"

He shook his head. "I know it's not you. But I believe your friend Norbury is involved."

"Norbury." Ellie sighed. "Are you sure?"

"You don't sound as upset as I expected."

She sipped her chocolate again, considering. "I'm more sad than upset, I think. Norbury is a decent man. He's never been anything but kind to his wife, despite her ailments, and he is generally well-liked."

"Then why are you not more surprised?"

"He was very odd about your return — he even warned me about you yesterday. I didn't think much of it since I knew he wasn't the highwayman. I would have recognized his voice if he had been the one who waylaid us. But perhaps he's involved in a way I didn't expect."

Nick slid her toast off the fork and brought her a tray with the toast, ham, and a soft-boiled egg. She sat up higher, crossing her legs under her like a child and tucking the sheets around her so that they wouldn't fall. "I haven't had breakfast in bed in an age," she said as she pulled the tray closer. "Your revenge shall spoil me."

"I hope so." He sat on the edge of her bed, reaching out to steady the tray so that it didn't tilt toward him as he settled into the mattress. "I think you could do with a bit of spoiling."

No one had ever spoiled her — no lovers, no family members, and certainly not her father. But she wouldn't waste a bright morning, fresh toast, and the man at her side on dead memories. She smiled at Nick. "If you thought toast would buy my loyalty, you have succeeded. Whatever happens with Norbury, you have my blessing."

"As easy as that? I will hire a servant just to make you toast if that's all I must do to win you."

She laughed. But as she knocked the top off her egg, she suddenly realized her eyes were filling with tears. There was something welling up within her that she didn't recognize and couldn't identify. How could toast make her so maudlin?

She reached up to wipe her eyes, but Nick caught her hand. "Look at me," he said softly.

She didn't want to, but he reached out to touch her cheek and tip her toward him. The tears spilled over her lashes and down her cheeks. "I don't know what has happened to me," she said, picking up her napkin. "Toast has never made me cry before."

He released her. She turned away and dabbed at her eyes. But then he edged closer to her and put his arm around her shoulders. "You can be upset with Norbury, you know. You can even be upset with me. I didn't want to ruin your morning, but you deserve the truth."

She turned her head into his chest. She didn't sob, but it was a close thing — her breath hitched in, and she felt something that could have been a scream inside her throat if she hadn't swallowed it again. When she could trust her voice, she whispered, "I trusted him. Why is it always the ones I trust who betray me?"

Nick kissed her head. "Norbury could be innocent of all of this. My evidence is mostly circumstantial — all related to his investments, and his friendship with you."

She hoped Norbury was innocent. But she understood Nick's suspicions. "He asked whether you were a good man yesterday — almost like he needed to know. He must know something."

"I will find out," Nick said, squeezing her shoulders. "Now, eat your breakfast."

She pulled away from him. "What are you going to do to Norbury?"

"Wait for him in the breakfast room. I don't want to arouse his suspicions by summoning him. But once he's in the breakfast room, I'll make sure he answers my questions."

"You said you needed my help. What do you want me to do?"

He nodded at her tray. "I want you to eat, and then enjoy a leisurely morning as far from the breakfast room as possible. I've asked my batman to loiter in this wing of the house to make sure you're safe."

Ellie frowned. "But I know Norbury better than anyone. Surely he will talk to me."

"I thought of that. But then I thought of him injuring you, or taking you as a hostage, and it made me so angry that I nearly cut my own throat while shaving."

"If only I'd known I could make you angry enough to do that — I could have escaped days ago."

He stroked her thigh through the coverlet. "No escape, my love. Just promise you will stay safely upstairs until I tell you we are done."

She could escape — Nick had made that possible the previous night, even though she hadn't wanted him to. But she nodded. "I will stay away. But you will tell me every detail of what happens. And if you aren't forthcoming, I shall 'worship' you again until you break."

His lips quirked, giving the lie to his attempt at severity. "You won't break me, but you are welcome to try. Now, my lady, if you will excuse me, I must go set my trap."

He sounded formal. But the way he pulled her toward him, the way he claimed her mouth, was more feudal than civilized. His lips seared against hers. He pulled away too soon, but she tugged him back and kissed him again, slower, melting for him. When she finally let him go, her lips were swollen and his eyes were fierce.

"I'm not going to die, Ellie," he said.

She hadn't allowed herself to think of that possibility, but she recognized the way it hummed nervously beneath her other thoughts. She tried, transparently, to lighten the mood. "If you do die, I hope Marcus knows I'm clear of my debt to you."

Nick grinned. "I will tell Marcus. If he tries to collect from you the same way I did, you have my permission to gut him."

"Two Claibornes dead on the same day? Dreams do come true, don't they?"

He tweaked her nose. "Do not worry. I order you not to."

She made a show of turning back to her breakfast as though he was already dismissed. When he didn't move off the bed, she turned back to him. "Is there anything else, my lord?"

He focused on her face as though memorizing it. Then he pushed a piece of hair behind her ear and stood up. "Enjoy your toast. Perhaps, when this is all done, we can see whether we can be real for each other."

He was gone before she could speak again.

CHAPTER THIRTY-FOUR

When Nick left Ellie, he laid his plans. He started with a few terse orders to the servants, followed by a long discussion with Marcus. His brother was still angry about Lucia's injury — if it wasn't for Nick's desire to keep everything quiet for Ellie's sake, Marcus might have already shot Norbury in retaliation. Instead, he went off to verify Norbury's whereabouts while Nick went to the breakfast room to put their plan into motion.

He would resolve this today, no matter the outcome. In a perfect world, Norbury would confess. In a less-perfect world, Nick might need to force it out of him.

But at least Nick had a plan and allies for this confrontation. What came after, when the business that had brought him back to England was finished and all that remained was the future...

He couldn't consider it until he could guarantee Ellie's safety. When he reached the breakfast room, a footman stationed outside confirmed that Nick's preferred guests were waiting for him. All others, in the unlikely event that they descended early after the previous evening's display, would be steered toward the saloon instead.

He opened the door. Ferguson and Salford looked up from their papers. "What is your scheme, Folkestone?" Ferguson asked without preamble. "Shall we bait a trap? Perhaps dress Salford up as one of your maids and see whether the culprit accidentally shoots him instead of you?"

Salford sighed as he set aside his paper. "I wager you're more suitable than I am for that. Your features are more delicate than mine."

Ferguson inclined his head as though "delicate" was a compliment rather than a barb. "Thank you, Salford. I hadn't thought you had noticed."

Salford rolled his eyes and appealed to Nick for intervention. "Why have you called us here, Folkestone? And is the duke's august presence necessary?"

Nick already regretted involving them. But Ferguson wouldn't be put off. They hadn't made enough progress the night before to satisfy either of them. Norbury had supposedly retired before they had returned from the fireworks, and they couldn't drag him out of bed without alerting the rest of the house party. Instead, they had spent a profitable hour questioning some of the servants about Norbury's movements. Everything the servants said had damned him further.

Still, even though Nick would rather take care of Norbury alone, Ferguson wouldn't settle for Nick conducting the investigation himself. And if Nick was stuck with Ferguson, then the Earl of Salford's sobering influence was one Nick thought he might need during the upcoming confrontation.

"I would gladly let his grace cry off, but it seems we're stuck with him," Nick said to Alex. "What has he told you?"

"The usual nonsense. Ferguson is rarely capable of serious conversation."

"I am always serious," Ferguson protested. "Particularly when mayhem is involved."

"Mayhem?" Alex turned to Nick. "So the discussion of traps wasn't entirely nonsense. What trouble have you gotten yourself into?"

Before retiring the previous night, he had asked Alex to join them in the breakfast room — with a vague warning to be prepared for a matter of some delicacy, since he couldn't tell Alex the entire story in front of their other guests. Now, Nick laid it all out for both of them — the attempts on his life in Madras, the highwaymen who had attacked Ellie's carriage, the fire that had destroyed the dead villain's body, and the injury Lucia had suffered during the fireworks display.

Salford seemed calm, as though he heard such calamitous tales every day. When Nick finished, the earl stood and went to the sideboard. "I never took you for such a fool," he said over his shoulder as he began to fill a plate with shirred eggs. "Ruthless, and rich as Croesus, but not a fool."

"Don't say we agree about something, Salford," Ferguson said, joining him at the sideboard.

"Stranger things have happened," Salford responded.

Nick took a breath and tried not to sound irritated. "I'm not a fool. If you won't help, you may leave."

"Touchy, isn't he?" Ferguson observed.

Salford selected a few sausages from one of the chafing dishes. "I suppose I would be equally touchy if I had been fool enough to risk the lives of forty guests, not to mention scores of servants, just for the chance to bed Lady Folkestone."

"Leave Lady Folkestone out of this," Nick said through gritted teeth. "She's no concern of yours."

Alex returned to the table with his plate. "Is she a concern of yours?" he asked slyly.

Ferguson tsked as he rejoined them. "Stop gossiping like a meddlesome spinster, Salford. I agree with Folkestone on this one. My esteemed sister is no concern of yours."

Salford shrugged and dug a fork into his eggs. "It's not a judgment on her character. I think she is one of the finest women in England. But why tell me all this now? I'm not the highwayman, if that's what you think."

Nick barely suppressed a snort. Salford had a refreshing streak of humor that Nick hadn't expected, but Nick couldn't imagine the earl indulging in any sort of adventure beyond overbidding for an ancient vase. "You're not the highwayman. But I believe I know who hired him."

Ferguson stole the moment. "He thinks it's Norbury. What do you think, Salford?"

Alex frowned. "Norbury? I've never met a more strait-laced peer."

"More strait-laced than you?" Nick asked.

"Assuredly so. He absolutely dotes on his wife. No hint of scandal there."

Nick ignored the buffet and poured himself a cup of coffee from the pot in front of his place at the table. "Still, he has investments in India that would be far more profitable if my company retired from the field. Like most peers, his estates aren't thriving — he could be desperate for money. I found a groom last night who swears he went riding alone for several hours on the same day that the highwayman attacked Ellie. And he didn't attend the fireworks display. It would have been trivially easy to sneak over to the village, shoot someone, and leave again."

Alex still frowned. "You said he shot Mrs. Grafton while aiming for Marcus. Why try to kill your brother if all he cares about is removing you from India?"

Nick shrugged. "Madmen make mad decisions. That's a question only he knows the answer to."

"Do madmen have the patience to plot death from half a world away? He must have set this into motion over a year ago, given how long it takes to sail between England and the subcontinent."

Damn the earl for sounding so reasonable. "It's unlikely, I know. But no one else fits the facts. And I want this business settled today, before anyone else hears about it."

"You must want it settled badly enough," Alex observed. "Rather bold of you to say you've kept me in the dark when Miss Etchingham or my mother could have been harmed because of your silence, then ask for my help to resolve it."

The earl cut into one of his sausages. The force behind the gesture was the only hint that he was more perturbed than he seemed. Despite the accusation in his words, his voice was still utterly calm.

Even Ferguson frowned. "Never thought you'd take this so well, Salford. When Folkestone invited you to join us this morning, I expected the bloodbath to come now, not when Norbury arrived."

Salford smiled. "I like Folkestone, despite his faults. At least it's not my sister he's trying to seduce."

Ferguson's face darkened. Nick held up his hands and appealed for calm. He didn't know what had happened when Ferguson had married Alex's cousin Madeleine, but even though the men were friendly with each other, there were still undercurrents between them that Nick couldn't navigate.

And, frankly, he didn't care. "Enough. I apologize for not warning either of you about the highwayman. I am not accustomed to taking other people into my plans, and I didn't believe you to be in danger. Now, either say you'll help me confront Norbury, or leave the room before he comes down."

Ferguson reached for the coffee pot. "You know I'll help. Acting as a second is one of my favorite pastimes."

"Salford?" Nick asked.

Alex leaned back in his chair. "Very well. But you owe me, Folkestone."

Nick nodded. Marcus slipped into the room then, winded but pleased. "I checked the stables — Norbury did not leave overnight, at least not on horse. And the housekeeper confirmed he did not order a tray for breakfast. Since he retired early last night, he should be down at his usual time."

Nick looked at the clock as Marcus drained the last bit of coffee from the pot. It was already a quarter past ten — Norbury should arrive soon.

With four men assembled against him, including three high-ranking peers, Norbury couldn't do anything too rash. He might even decide that confessing, and accepting a quiet offer of transportation to a far-off colony, was better than risking his own neck.

It was unlikely at best. No peer would go to Australia willingly, and Nick couldn't trust that he wouldn't come back. Nick didn't want to shoot him, or anyone else. But he would do what needed to be done — if not for his sake, then for Ellie and whatever future she might want.

By the time Norbury entered ten minutes later, Nick was deathly calm. Norbury didn't seem concerned to see any of them. He gave a general greeting to the room and moved immediately to the sideboard. It wasn't until Nick nodded and Marcus locked the door that Norbury made any gesture of discomfort.

He stiffened as the sound of the bolt being thrown in the lock echoed through the room. His hand froze over the kippers, the tongs dangling from fingers that had suddenly gone stiff. He set them down, slowly, and brought his half-filled plate to the table. "Is there a meaning to this of which I am unaware?" he asked.

"I thought we could have a friendly conversation among peers," Nick said.

Then he pulled a pistol from his coat and set it on the table.

Norbury's eyes darted to the pistol, then back to Nick's face. "What do you wish to converse about, Folkestone?" he asked. His display of calm was admirable, but his voice was higher than it had been.

"To be clear, we all wish to converse with you," Ferguson interjected, pulling his own pistol from his coat.

Nick rolled his eyes. "There's no need for theatrics, your grace."

"This isn't theatrics. I just don't want to be left out of the fun. And if Norbury won't talk to you, perhaps he will talk to me."

Alex narrowed his eyes. "No one told me to bring a weapon."

"Ah, Salford. You never get invited to participate in nefarious deeds, do you?" Ferguson said with mock sympathy.

Salford responded by pulling a gun from his coat. "It never hurts to be prepared, though."

Nick hadn't stopped watching Norbury during this display. The viscount seemed very close to apoplexy. He edged his chair back as though thinking, vainly, that he might be able to run — or perhaps risk serious injury by tossing himself out the closed window.

"There's nothing to fear, Norbury," he said in a soothing voice. "Just tell us what we need to know."

"I don't know what you need to know," Norbury said.

"Do you really have no idea?" Nick asked. "Or are you just telling yourself that?"

Norbury took a deep breath, which led directly into a coughing fit. When he could finally speak, his voice turned into a wheeze. "No idea, Folkestone."

"I suppose we could shoot you," Nick mused, "but it would make it hard for me to live in England going forward. I will do it without remorse, though, if it means that Lady Folkestone and our guests are out of danger."

Norbury's eyes still watered from his coughing, but they widened as he dabbed at them with a handkerchief. "What danger do you believe Lady Folkestone to be in?"

Nick leaned forward. "If you were better at this, I wouldn't be concerned. But you and your minions can't seem to kill me, and eventually she's going to pay the price for it. They already came close once."

Norbury blanched. "Whatever has happened to you, you can't lay it at my doorstep."

He stood, unexpectedly, and all three of them leveled their guns at him. Marcus leaned against the door and crossed his arms over his chest. Norbury's eyes darted between them. "Do you really mean to shoot me?" he asked incredulously.

"I would rather not," Nick said. He set aside his gun and gestured for Norbury to sit. "We confronted you here, rather than in public, because I want to give you an opportunity to save face. I know your friendship with Lady Folkestone is of long duration, and there is no need to ruin your family for your misdeeds. We can settle this quietly. I have a ship that will take you anywhere in the world, as long as you never return. But if you don't tell us what you know, I'm not averse to beating it out of you."

Nick didn't want to beat him any more than he wanted to shoot him — although the longer Norbury delayed, the more he was tempted.

Norbury squeaked. Then he coughed again.

Salford put aside his pistol. "You know, Folkestone, I believe the man really is ill."

"Did you think I lied about that?" Norbury asked. "What are you accusing me of?"

Nick's temper broke. "We know you have been trying to kill me. It all makes sense — your India investments, your friendship with Lady Folkestone, your absence from last night's fireworks. Now, would you rather be transported to Australia quietly, or stand trial for attempted murder?"

CHAPTER THIRTY-FIVE

If Norbury didn't kill Nick, she was going to do it herself.

It took her an hour to reach that decision, but she didn't make it lightly. She mulled over it as she finished her breakfast. She pondered it as a maid dressed her in a simple lavender day gown with a purple sash — something that would be appropriately mournful for marshaling the servants to dispose of a body from her house party. She considered sending someone to make room in the ice house, but the weather was still cold enough that a body would keep in an outbuilding — provided people didn't continue burning the outbuildings to destroy the bodies within them.

She was losing her mind. She let it happen, though. Making a plan for how to store a dead Norbury was better than imagining Nick's body in his place. But she didn't fully decide to murder Nick until, as she and Prudence sat quietly in her salon an hour after Nick had left her, Madeleine marched in and demanded to know what Nick had gotten Ferguson into.

"I didn't know Ferguson was involved in anything with Nick," Ellie said, laying aside her newspaper and sitting up from her lounging position on the chaise. "I thought they hated each other."

Madeleine shook her head. "I think they came to some sort of understanding while ice skating. Or, at least, Ferguson says they did.

296

You know how he is. Folkestone probably thinks my husband still hates him, but I think Ferguson was quite charmed."

Ellie rolled her eyes. "Trust Ferguson to give up on protecting me the moment someone charms him."

"I thought you didn't want to be protected," Madeleine said pointedly.

"Would you care for some tea, Madeleine?" Prudence interjected. "I shall pour."

"What I would care for is an explanation," Madeleine said, sitting down in the armchair next to Prudence's. "Ferguson left before I was even half awake, saying he had a pressing errand with Folkestone. But I haven't seen him this excited about someone other than me since that stupid duel he was in last autumn. If Folkestone leads my husband to an early grave…"

She trailed off. Prudence pushed a cup into Madeleine's hand, then looked at Ellie. "Do you know anything about this?"

Ellie drummed her fingers on her teacup. "It doesn't concern us, not truly. And it's not my story to share."

"Tell me something," Madeleine said. "Please."

She was going to kill him. This wasn't the conversation she wanted to have with Madeleine and Prudence — not now, when she was worried for him and couldn't control her inflection as she shared the story with the other women.

But if Ferguson had been coerced into helping Nick, Madeleine deserved the truth.

"Did Ferguson tell you what happened during last night's fireworks display?"

"No. He just said he needed to discuss something with you."

Ellie added her brother to the short — but growing — list of bodies she might need to dispose of. "Then you will like this even less than I thought. Folkestone is convinced that Norbury is behind several attempts on his life. Since Ferguson became aware of this when my maid was accidentally shot last night, I'm sure Folkestone asked him to help apprehend Norbury."

Madeleine's mouth dropped open.

"Surely Ferguson took you into his confidence?" Ellie asked innocently.

Madeleine glared at her. "He did not. Your gloating is unbecoming. I'm sure he merely thought to protect me."

"I'm sure he did," Ellie said, trying to sound reassuring. "He was most annoyed with Nick for hiding all of this from him when you and our sisters were in residence."

"I am going to kill him," Madeleine muttered.

Prudence held up a hand as though to negotiate a truce. "No need to plan a murder until we know whether they have been successful. Ellie, do you know if Folkestone asked Lord Salford to assist him as well?"

Ellie shot her a look. "I do not. Is there a reason for your question?"

"No," she said tartly. "If Salford dies today, I'm sure Sebastian will give me just as much of an allowance for caring for his mother as Salford does."

Ellie laughed, but Madeleine couldn't be distracted. "Why didn't you tell us all of this already? I would have told you immediately if a potential murderer came within twenty leagues of us. You're as close to a sister as I've got, or nearly so…"

She stopped talking abruptly. Ellie bit the inside of her own cheek, tamping down on the swell of guilt. "Nick asked me not to say anything. He thought it would be easier to catch the culprit if the party stayed intact."

Madeleine looked down into her cup. "You could have trusted me, you know."

There was an awful silence.

Ellie's guilt grew. And she knew that it wasn't just Nick's request that had kept her from speaking to Madeleine and Prudence.

For a moment, she was nineteen again. What if that moment when she had told Charles's sisters about her love for Nick — that awful fork in the road of her life — had never happened?

She had always thought it was her fault — that if she had kept her own counsel, Charles never would have noticed her and she never would have been coerced into marrying him.

But should she regret what she had told them? Or should she simply regret that they were human, and likely well-meaning, and had never known the consequences of what they had done? All her silence in the years since then, all the secrets and all the moments when she had refrained from sharing anything with anyone — that hadn't punished anyone else.

She had only punished herself.

Ellie leaned forward, over the table between them, to touch Madeleine's knee. "I trust you. I just…it didn't occur to me to ask for your help. I didn't want to worry you."

"But that's what friends do. That's what sisters do — worry over each other. I've seen you worry over all of us. Can you allow us to worry over you?"

Ellie pulled back. "You don't need to worry over me. Everything will come out all right, and we can finish our party as though nothing happened."

Madeleine scowled. "This isn't just about the murderer. I am worried about you and Nick."

"I am, too," Prudence chimed in.

Ellie sighed. "Two against one isn't fair."

"Fair or not, you're stuck with it," Prudence said. "Unless you'd rather not be."

Would she rather not be stuck with them? Life had been so easy without them wanting an intimacy she didn't know how to share.

But perhaps easy wasn't what she wanted. What did she deserve — endless punishment for a secret someone else had accidentally betrayed? Or a chance to begin again?

She drew in a breath, exhaled, and then drew in another. "Very well. You may worry about me."

Prudence grinned. "Thank you for the decree, your highness."

Ellie's laugh broke some of the tension. "You are welcome."

Madeleine looked at the clock. She didn't seem to notice how momentous this was for Ellie — but then, she wouldn't find it momentous for one friend to worry about another. "Did Folkestone say when he expected to be done with Norbury? Should we go and make sure they're not all murdering each other?"

"No. I promised Nick I would stay away. Whatever his plan is, I don't want to ruin it by interrupting at the wrong time."

Prudence tried to turn their attention to the latest news from London, but none of them cared to discuss anything else. They weren't silent for long, though. When someone tapped on the door, Ellie leapt up. "Nick?" she asked.

The door opened. It wasn't Nick.

It was Christabel. She still wore her cloak, a dark, sturdy wool without any of the trimmings that someone of her age and class should have had. A dark blue bonnet framed her pale face. The shadows under her eyes seemed dark enough to be permanent, not a mere trick of the light. Trower, Nick's batman, hovered slightly behind her, frowning as though he wanted to bar her from the room.

Ellie stood to greet her and she accepted the embrace, but Christabel barely returned it. "I apologize for disturbing you, Lady Folkestone. May I have a word, if you have a moment?"

Her voice was urgent. Ellie glanced back at Madeleine and Prudence. They both stood at the same time, too gracious to mention that Christabel's visit was unfashionably early. "We will leave you to your talk," Madeleine said. "But if either of you should need anything — or learn anything — please don't hesitate to call."

"Thank you, your grace," Christabel said, dipping into a slight curtsey. "I am sorry I cannot be more sociable this morning."

Prudence laughed. "I never feel sociable in the morning myself. But it was lovely to see you again, Lady Christabel. I do hope to meet you in London if you come for a visit."

She nodded as though her life still held every possibility she deserved. "I shall send a card if I come to the capital."

Madeleine and Prudence left. Ellie gestured at Trower to stay outside — an order that he didn't seem to like, but he closed the door between them.

"Do you want tea?" Ellie asked her visitor. "Or something stronger?"

Christabel's laugh was shaky. She untied her bonnet, but she left her gloves on. From the way she twisted her fingers in front of her, perhaps the gloves gave her comfort. "I'd prefer something stronger, but it won't help. And there's little time for it, in any event. Perhaps I should have gone directly to Lord Folkestone with this…but I can't."

Ellie nearly pushed her into a chair before returning to her chaise. "What is the matter? I can help you with anything if you tell me what it is."

Christabel didn't speak for a moment. Her breath rasped in the silence. Her eyes, when she finally looked up, were clouded by a concerning mixture of fear and hope. "Do you ever think something awful may not come true as long as you don't say it aloud?"

Ellie nodded. "The things I've refrained from saying could fill volumes. But that doesn't mean you should stay silent."

"Very well." Christabel squared her shoulders and lifted her chin. The transformation — from tentative girl to confident lady — was shockingly sudden. "I have been the worst kind of fool. But when I stopped being a fool, I realized that I know who your highwayman is."

CHAPTER THIRTY-SIX

"What? How?" Ellie asked, stunned to the point of incoherency.

"Yes, I know it's unlikely," Christabel said. "When would I have ever met someone new, let alone someone who might be a highwayman? I should have known from the very first that he was after something other than me..."

Ellie cut her off. "Don't tell me Norbury was pursuing you?"

Christabel's mouth dropped open. "Who? Norbury? That dull prig you've somehow become friends with? Of course not."

In another conversation, Ellie might have taken umbrage at Christabel's characterization of him — but now was not the time. "Then who? Because Nick is downstairs preparing to accuse Norbury of attempted murder."

"Norbury?" Christabel asked again. She bit the side of her lip, considering. "If that were true, I would certainly be happy to know it."

But before Ellie could respond, Christabel squared her shoulders again. "It's not Norbury. I believe it is a man named Stephen Edgewood."

"Who?" Ellie asked.

Christabel sighed. "This conversation is going to take long enough that Folkestone might shoot Norbury long before we've finished it. He knows who Edgewood is, I think. I searched Edgewood's papers and found letters about Corwyn, Claiborne and Sons. He must have been a former employee. The papers indicate that Folkestone fired him in India eight or nine months ago."

"Where did you find his papers?"

"In my house." Christabel twisted her fingers again. "He came six weeks ago, after having sent a letter to Mother asking if he might visit. He claimed that he was her third cousin. I was suspicious at first. There was no reference to him in Debrett's description of the family, and I couldn't find him in the family Bible. But Mother — well, you could tell her that Prinny was her second son and she would agree with you, just to avoid admitting that she had forgotten it. She was more than happy to welcome a visitor who claimed to be her cousin. And once I met him…"

She trailed off. Her pale face suddenly turned to fire.

Ellie's heart broke for her. "Has he been there all this time?" she asked gently.

Christabel nodded. "Fool that I was, I thought he was staying for me. He certainly made it seem that way."

"He could be, you know. Just because he happened to arrive before these suspicious events doesn't mean he has anything to do with them."

"It was a dream," Christabel said. Her self-deprecating shrug made Ellie want to kill the man herself. "After the shooting last night, I went home. Edgewood had begged off the fireworks, but he was nowhere to be found when I returned. But I must have known all along that something was wrong, because I took the opportunity to search his papers. It was easy enough to do. His valet has run off, so no one was there to guard his things. And the combination of those letters, and the fact that his valet had always seemed more like a sailor than a polished gentleman's man, made me wonder if the valet was your dead highwayman."

"Did you ask him about this?" Ellie asked.

Christabel's look said that Ellie's question was one of the stupidest ideas she had ever heard. "I was besotted, not idiotic. Who do you think would save me if Edgewood decided to kill me for meddling?"

Ellie grimaced. "Of course. We must tell Folkestone before he kills Norbury. He will apprehend Edgewood, if Edgewood is indeed the killer."

Christabel stood and started to retie her bonnet, as though her visit had been a mere exchange of pleasantries. "I'll leave you to it, then. Thank you for your help."

"Come with me," Ellie said. "Folkestone will need a description of Edgewood to decide whether he might be the killer."

Christabel frowned. "I want nothing more than to be left out of this and forget he ever existed."

"I know. You don't have to say a word about how you know Edgewood. Pin the blame on your mother for letting him stay with you. She won't be able to refute it."

Christabel's grin was almost wicked. "Mother was right. You are a detriment to my character."

Ellie smiled as she escorted her out of the room. But when Christabel couldn't see her face, Ellie's smile died. She didn't understand how Christabel could be so composed — as though it had been inevitable that any man who loved her must have had another goal in mind. If Ellie had discovered that Nick was merely using her in his attempts to kill someone else, she wouldn't have taken it well at all.

When this was over, she would find a way to help Christabel. But uncovering the truth — and keeping Nick from accusing the wrong man — was more urgent than that.

*   *   *

It was almost farcical, how quickly Nick's control of the situation vanished. He had been so sure that Norbury was the killer. He was ready to hustle him onto the first ship to the penal colonies, all Norbury's denials be damned. No one would be injured, Ellie wouldn't be in danger, and nothing unforeseen would happen...

And then, suddenly, sickeningly, the quarry had changed. Instead of the safe, warm breakfast room, he now stood fifty yards from the dower house, under the cover of a small orchard near the footpath that ran from Folkestone to the dowager's abode. Ellie shivered next to him in her thin morning dress and thick pelisse, cold but undaunted.

"Shall we knock on the front door or sneak in through the kitchens?" she asked in a low voice.

Beyond her, Christabel frowned. "If you send me in first, I can determine where he is and signal to the rest of you."

None of the men liked that idea. "I'd sooner burn the house down and shoot whoever comes out than send you in alone," Marcus said. "The man has no qualms about injuring a woman. He could kill you without a second thought."

Christabel didn't deny it, but Nick saw something in the corners of her mouth that hinted at why she hadn't told anyone about Edgewood before. She hadn't admitted to anything when she and Ellie had come to the breakfast room and stopped the inquisition against Norbury.

Nick could guess, though. Edgewood had always been charming. It was his charm that had made him so effective in India. *Too* effective, as it had turned out. While he'd been striking bargains for Corwyn,

Claiborne and Sons, he had also embezzled a significant sum for himself. Nick had never seen a crack in the man's façade until the day he had fired him. Edgewood had turned ugly, but only for a moment — just long enough for Nick to be glad the man was leaving India, but not long enough to suspect that he would plot such an extensive revenge.

"I should have guessed it was him," Nick said, for the second time since Christabel had saved Norbury's hide. "And Marcus is correct. Edgewood is charming, but I don't trust him within ten leagues of you."

Christabel sighed. "Still, let me go in first. I would like to keep this quiet, after all. If we can remove him from the premises without killing him, I would be much obliged."

Salford and Ferguson had been muttering behind them ever since leaving Folkestone. The walk from the main house to the dower house was short enough that it was better to sneak over on foot rather than risk warning Edgewood by coming in carriages. But the earl and duke weren't pleased.

"You aren't luring me into pulling a gun on another innocent man, are you?" Salford asked acerbically. "Norbury is likely still puking over the close call he had."

Nick winced. Norbury had nearly fainted when Christabel's information had saved him — but the man had every reason to be angry with all of them. Nick knew that wasn't a mistake he could easily atone for. "I am sorry about that. But Lady Christabel's suggestion is sound. Edgewood has even more motive than Norbury did. And there's no reason for him to have come to this neighborhood unless he was lying in wait for us. I know he isn't related to the dowager, whether she remembers it or not."

"I agree," Marcus said, checking the pistol he had pulled from his pocket. "He had motive to kill me as well. When he came back from India, he approached me for a job. I told him that since he had returned without a character from Nick, I would make sure none of the India firms hired him. He must have thought it would be easier for me to die in a shooting accident in the country than in London. If he came to the neighborhood and heard about the dowager's illness, he must have seen her house as a prime place to stage his attack — and live in comfort in the meantime."

Ferguson brushed a piece of lint off his greatcoat. "Can we get on with it before I die of boredom? I didn't expect such a prolonged affair."

Nick tried to pull the group back together. He wasn't happy that Christabel and Ellie were present. But he couldn't keep Christabel from returning to her own house. Ellie wouldn't let her go without another woman for company. And Ferguson and Salford were still impossible to manage, but they were better for this task than Ellie's milquetoast footmen.

With Trower as a silent but lethal addition to their party, they outnumbered Edgewood seven to one. With the added benefit of surprise, surely they could capture him without incident.

Nick laid out the plan. "Lady Folkestone, Lady Christabel — you will stay outside with Trower and cover the front door. If Edgewood comes running, shoot him."

Christabel had refused to take a rifle, and Nick didn't expect her to need it — Trower would take care of them without either woman needing to fire a shot. But Ellie nodded intently. She held up the bow she had insisted on bringing and pulled an arrow out of the small quiver strapped to her back. He couldn't help but laugh. Trust Ellie to look both deadly and gorgeous at the same time.

She scowled at him. "Laugh now, but I can fire three arrows before you can reload a pistol."

He made a bow of apology and turned to Salford and Ferguson. "Can I trust the two of you to cover the back of the house without shooting each other?"

Salford's mouth twitched. "Send Edgewood our way. If Ferguson accidentally dies today, I'd like to pin it on your highwayman."

Nick ignored him and turned to Marcus. "Shall we, brother?"

Marcus adjusted his gloves. "Let me go in first. I'd rather die than inherit your bloody title."

"No one is going to die, bar Edgewood."

"Still, it's your turn to run the estate. If you leave it to me, I will be very much annoyed."

Beside them, Ellie sniffed. "Not as annoyed as I shall be. Don't do anything stupid, Folkestone."

Nick turned to her. Her eyes were bright, and she seemed entirely focused on the task at hand. He only caught tiny hints of her nerves. Her gloved hand tightened on her bow. She squinted at him, as though memorizing the way he looked in this moment. Would she paint him like this? Not as her slave, not as a youth besotted with her, but as the man who would do anything to protect her?

She smiled as though she knew what he was thinking. "Be safe, Nick," she said. "And come back to me."

He would have given anything to hear those words a decade ago. But he much preferred hearing them now, from a woman who could truly love him rather than a girl who only thought she did.

He nodded. "Be safe, Ellie."

He couldn't say more, not with their audience. He heard Salford murmur something to Ferguson. The duke muttered a response that made Salford laugh. They trooped away from the group and disappeared around the back of the house to guard against Edgewood's escape.

Ellie ignored them. She turned to Marcus instead. "You be safe as well," she said. It sounded like an order, not a plea. "I still vow that if anyone kills you, it should be me."

Marcus grinned. "If I inherit the marquessate, I'll let you shoot me, and gladly."

She wrinkled her nose. "And leave me with Rupert as the marquess? He would drive me mad within the month. Imagine my reputation if I killed every Claiborne male of your generation."

The group laughed, but then fell into a sudden, awkward silence. They needed to wait to make sure Ferguson and Salford were in position, but waiting gave them too many moments to worry. They had done an admirable job of feigning comfort on the walk over. All that calm bled away in the final moments before their assault on the house.

They would be fine. Edgewood didn't expect them and wouldn't be armed. It would all happen quickly and without incident.

But Nick knew that even the best plans couldn't account for everything. He checked his pistol a final time. The sky was slate grey, leaden and heavy with the threat of another snowstorm. His breath misted in the air, and he caught Ellie stamping her boots — either from nerves or an attempt to warm herself up, he didn't know.

He wanted to kiss her. But he needed to focus. A kiss now, in this moment, would feel too much like a permanent goodbye. So he nodded instead. "If he comes out that door, aim for his heart."

Her lips quirked. "I always aim for the heart."

He smiled at her. Then he made eye contact with his batman. The man didn't have to say a word to communicate his intent. If Edgewood came through the front door, Trower would shoot him before anything could happen to Ellie.

Nick and Marcus left them and walked to the house. They held their pistols openly; this wasn't the time for subtlety. "Shoot first, or ask questions first?" Marcus asked in a low voice.

"Ask questions. I was ready to kill Norbury. It doesn't seem right to kill Edgewood without a conversation, since we could be mistaken again. But if he sees both of us, with guns, I doubt we'll have to ask anything before he shows his hand."

Marcus nodded. Nick knocked on the door. When a manservant answered, he took one look at their guns and held up his hands.

"Where is Edgewood?" Nick asked in a low voice.

"In the dining room, my lord," he stammered. He pointed through the drawing room toward another set of doors. The house was small enough, and old enough, that the main rooms were all interconnected.

Damn. Nick gestured to Marcus. "Wait in the drawing room. I'll go around to the door that leads to the kitchens. As soon as you hear my voice, come in through the drawing room door."

He left before Marcus could argue. The footman led him to the back of the house. "Keep the servants away," Nick ordered quietly. "And make sure the dowager stays upstairs."

The footman nodded and backed away from him. Nick eyed the closed door to the dining room. He felt a rush of nerves, followed by a deadly sort of calm. The world seemed to slow down, just for a moment. Everything became focused on that door knob and the moment that lay beyond it.

He opened the door. Edgewood sat at the table, just as Nick had remembered him — impeccably dressed, oozing charm, seeming at ease with the world. He looked up from his plate. His blue eyes were shocked. Nick saw a swift, instinctive rush of hate before Edgewood regained control.

"Lord Folkestone. How pleasant to see you here," he said.

Marcus rushed through the other door as soon as Edgewood spoke. Edgewood turned toward him, raising his hands as though he were the only sane one in the room. "And Mr. Claiborne. Another pleasant surprise. Is there some service you require from me?"

He was utterly calm. Too calm. Norbury, who was innocent, had been petrified. Edgewood seemed amused, as though two men with guns drawn were just a game to him.

"You know why we're here, Edgewood," Nick said. "You have two choices. A one-way trip to Van Diemen's Land, leaving tonight. Or a public hanging at Newgate and a box in potter's field. What's your preference?"

Edgewood leaned back in his chair. "You already fired me. Am I really so irksome to you that you must further ruin my life?"

Nick leaned against the door frame, pretending to be as calm as Edgewood. "You deserved to be let go. But if I had known that you would continue to plague me, I would have had you arrested instead — you should have been grateful that all I did was fire you."

"As though anyone there would have cared," Edgewood said with a laugh. "Half the men in the East India Company were doing something illicit — skimming profits, taking bribes, or exploiting villages. If I had worked for them instead of you, I could have been rich by now."

"You were more than comfortable."

"Comfortable? In India?" Edgewood scoffed. "There isn't enough money in the world to make that hellish place bearable. No white women, little entertainment, a fever every fortnight. In some ways I was relieved when you sent me home. Perhaps you would have hated it, too, if you had grown up with the higher classes as I did."

Nick knew when he was being baited. He didn't rise to it. "It's a shame that all your class made you such a bad shot. All those times you missed me in India, and then you come here and shoot a maid and your own valet rather than either of us."

Edgewood's jaw ticked. "Not that I am admitting to anything, but I couldn't have been the one who tried to kill you in India. I was already on a ship. I can't say I'm pleased to see you survived, though."

Nick turned to Marcus. "We don't have any Maratha mercenaries here to do our bidding — but how many shots do you think you would need to kill Edgewood yourself?"

Marcus leveled his pistol. "One."

"You have no proof whatsoever," Edgewood said, baring his teeth.

"I would wager that a judge might not see it that way, not with what I've learned about you. I may have no class, but I am a marquess, and I'm richer than your petty little schemes ever could have made you. Do you really think you can keep yourself from swinging from a noose? Take the trip to Van Diemen's Land. I've heard it's cooler there than India."

"Funny. I've learned a lot about you as well, you know. If I were to stand trial, the newspaper men would love to write all of my testimony about how you obsessed over your dead cousin's wife, wouldn't they? I saw everything you bought for her. I heard all the rumors of how you used to call for her when you were sick with fevers. Makes your decision to share a house with her seem a bit lewd, doesn't it?"

Nick shrugged, but didn't drop his pistol. "Lady Folkestone is no concern of mine."

"Hmm," Edgewood said. He turned his focus to Marcus. "Or your lady friend...Mrs. Grafton, she calls herself? A shame that she was injured last night. Of course, from what I've learned about her past, this isn't the first time that little whore..."

Marcus snapped. Nick felt it happen, felt the atmosphere in the room pull in on itself, then explode. "You bloody bastard," Marcus snarled as he rushed around the table.

Edgewood stood up faster than should have been possible, as though he'd been waiting for his chance. Marcus set aside his pistol and punched Edgewood square in the mouth, but Edgewood didn't back away. He drove his fist into Marcus's midsection and followed it with a knee to the groin — a dirty, dishonorable trick, but it did what he wanted it to do.

Marcus dropped to the ground in agony. Edgewood dove over him, reaching for the pistol on the table...

Nick didn't hesitate. He braced his feet and fired.

CHAPTER THIRTY-SEVEN

By midnight, Ellie wanted nothing more than to be alone with Nick. But she didn't want to draw attention to him by seeking him out — not while her guests were chirping like magpies over the best gossip of the season.

The aftermath of Edgewood's death had taken hours to resolve. The magistrate was shocked to learn that the Marquess of Folkestone had shot a man after being in the country less than a fortnight. But even though the story would raise eyebrows for months, no one would question that it was self-defense.

More shocking was that Edgewood would be buried in unconsecrated ground just outside the family plot. He wasn't their cousin any more than Napoleon was. But if people knew that Christabel had shared a house with an unrelated stranger, she would be utterly ruined. So they had all lied, with depraved fluency, and claimed that Edgewood was indeed their cousin — and that he had tried to kill Nick and Marcus in order to inherit the title himself.

It was a flimsy excuse, but the magistrate accepted it gracefully. If a marquess, an earl, a duke, and a marchioness closed ranks around each other, there was little he could do to disprove their statements. Her excuses to Norbury, however, were more difficult to offer.

"Don't tell me you knew Folkestone was going to accuse me of murder," Norbury had demanded that afternoon, when she had finally returned from the dower house.

Her wince was the only answer he needed.

"And you believed him?" Norbury asked. His voice was hoarse from coughing, which only made it worse.

Ellie sighed. "I am sorry, Norbury."

"But we've been friends for half a decade. You know I'm not nearly dangerous enough to shoot anyone."

"I think you give yourself too little credit. Haven't I always found you interesting? Perhaps not dangerous — but certainly capable of daring deeds."

He drew his shoulders up. The heroic effect was diminished when he sneezed. "You are stroking my ego, Lady Folkestone."

She shrugged. "That's what friends do. But I'm glad you're not the killer."

"As am I. Folkestone, however, owes me an apology."

Nick had disappeared as soon as they had returned, although he had promised to rejoin them for dinner. So she knew he wouldn't overhear when she leaned in to Norbury's ear. "You should tell him you expect to spend two weeks hunting with him. He hates the country — it might be punishment enough."

Norbury laughed. "Only if you're there to organize the entertainments, my lady."

There was a sly look in his eyes, but she didn't acknowledge the lurking question about her future. She was just glad that he seemed willing to accept her apology, even if there would still be some awkwardness over what had happened in her breakfast room.

But as the afternoon and evening wore on, Ellie struggled with how to entertain her guests — particularly since all she wanted to do was talk to Nick. There was no clear etiquette for how to handle what had happened. The party should have dispersed after such a shocking development, but no one had left — they were too busy tittering and writing overwrought letters to their friends to bother with making travel arrangements.

When the clock finally tolled midnight, Ellie was still in the drawing room. Sir Percival sat beside her, scrawling something on a piece of paper. From what she could see, it was the start of an awful poem about Folkestone as Odysseus, come back to kill the intruders in his house.

She didn't fault him for it. At least Percy would take some inspiration from what had happened, rather than dining out on the *on dit* for the next month as most of her guests planned to do.

She wasn't being fair to them. The ones who cared about her weren't spreading tales. The rest didn't particularly matter.

All that mattered was whether Nick was all right. He had come down for dinner, but he hadn't joined the ladies in the drawing room afterward. Marcus had told her that Nick had retired early. She couldn't go to him without being noticed — but by midnight, she was ready to find him no matter what anyone thought.

Just as she stood up, a footman appeared with a note on a silver salver. She took it, trying not to blush as she slid her nail under the wafer and opened it.

E. - Conservatory, ten minutes. - N.

She stopped blushing. Where was the wildly evocative description of what he would do to her?

Surely he wasn't having second thoughts?

She was in the conservatory in seven minutes, not ten. She couldn't wait any longer. But it seemed Nick couldn't wait either.

He lounged against a pillar near the entrance, half-concealed in the shadows.

The conservatory wasn't as cold as the outbuildings. The gardeners built fires during the day to keep the plants warm, and the heat hadn't been lost overnight. But she still shivered. "I was beginning to think you wouldn't send for me."

She winced at the plaintive note in her voice. He unfolded himself and came over to her. "I couldn't make polite conversation with all your guests tonight. But I couldn't wait any longer to see you."

He grabbed her hand and pulled her deeper into the conservatory, moving down the paths between the plants like a man rushing headlong into battle — all nerves and energy, abandoning all caution so that he could keep pushing forward.

She kept up with his pace, but her worry grew. "Are you feeling well? I know you had a shock today — should you perhaps be resting?"

He shook his head and didn't slow down. "I don't want to talk about it."

His voice was a closed door. But it wasn't a locked, barricaded, impassable door — more like a gate that he wouldn't open today, but might open tomorrow.

She would ask him about it again. The speed in his stride and the thrum of energy in his voice distracted her, though. She'd heard that men were sometimes…voracious after battle, as though the stress of surviving needed an equally strong release.

This might not be a night for conversation. But she would help him however she could.

He cast her a backward glance, one that managed to look both amused and sardonic in the dim light of the waning moon. "When was the last time you let a challenge like that go unanswered?"

She made a wry face at him. "Since I realized how much you like to bait me. You'll have to try harder than that."

He stopped suddenly, near one of the back corners of the conservatory, and pulled her into his arms. "Would you take this bait?" he murmured.

She was pressed fully flush against him. She felt him hardening for her, felt herself melting against him. She tilted her face up to look into his eyes. "I might consider it," she whispered.

He dipped his head and grazed his lips against hers. "And this bait?" he asked.

"You win," she said. She draped her arms on his shoulders and kissed him thoroughly, consumingly. Her mouth wanted more of him. Her hands wanted to touch him, everywhere, but she contented herself with his broad shoulders and the silky hair that brushed across her fingers. The tempo of the kiss matched the thudding of her heart — and they came together without hesitation, without regret, as though all the walls between them had crumbled into dust.

When he pulled back, she sighed as she lost him. "What shall it be tonight, Nick?" she asked. "Do you want me as a woodland nymph? A gardener? A lost princess trapped in the woods?"

He shook his head. Then he gestured to the bed of plants behind him. "Do you know what these are?" he asked.

She squinted into the darkness. "Strawberries?" she guessed. "But it's too early to pick them. The chef will have your skin if you interfere with his produce."

"I will not commit any crimes against the chef," Nick vowed. "But I'm disappointed there are no blackberries in the conservatory. I cannot find a blackberry in Surrey at this time of year to save my life."

"Why do you want blackberries?" Ellie asked, bewildered. "Surely the chef has some blackberry liqueur. He might make something with it for you."

"You don't understand, do you? I'd hoped you would, but you may not remember that day as I do."

"That day…?"

He frowned as though willing her to share his memory. "The day we picked blackberries," she said suddenly. "I think it may have been the best day of my life."

It was a dramatic thing to say — but then, it had been a dramatic day. Everything was bright, cloudless. The berries were sweet; Nick's laugh was sweeter still. He had only just started laughing for her then, and she had treasured each time he sparked a smile for one of her jests. And when he had kissed her…

"It may have been the best day of my life, too," he said. "So perfect that I sometimes wondered what the purpose of life was, if that day could not be bettered."

Then he took her hands into his and stripped off her gloves. "Can you guess why I brought you here?" he asked.

She shook her head. She hoped she knew why he had brought her there. But she wasn't going to rush him. "If it's to tell me you are going back to India, I shall murder you."

He stuffed her gloves into his waistcoat and twined his fingers through hers. "No trips to India in my future. But I have thought a lot about beginnings."

Nick paused. Ellie held her breath. It seemed the whole conservatory held its breath — in the cool mist of the greenhouse, they were utterly alone, utterly able to focus on each other.

And what Ellie felt in Nick's grip on her hands made her heart flip.

He drew a breath. "I have thought a lot about beginnings. That blackberry patch was a beginning. And it felt right, tonight, to revisit it — not with the girl you were and the boy I was, but with who we are now."

She squeezed his hands, but she didn't speak. And for once, Nick didn't need to be drawn into laughter. He smiled at her. If there was awe in his eyes, it wasn't the worship she hated — it was the same awe that she felt, that they could be together, in this moment, and it could feel so right.

"I never thought I would have to make this speech, you know. It was always you, Ellie. Always, always you. There would never be anyone else for me. And I suppose my stupid revenge was an attempt to convince myself that I could let you go. But I can't. Everything I am, everything I want to be, is for you."

"It was always you, too," she said, in a voice that was suddenly hoarse. "And it always will be. No matter where this leads."

She could have let it go at that, at least for that night. But Nick didn't stop. "I know where this leads. It will always lead back to this moment. Don't you see? Our lives aren't intersecting paths. This isn't a crossroads. This moment is a mirror of that day in the blackberry patch — and there will be another moment someday that is a mirror of this one. No matter what happens, no matter what we do to each other or how we fail ourselves, we will always circle around to this moment and start again."

Start again. It sounded so much better, so much kinder, than all her exhortations to stop being dramatic and find a purpose. She sighed wistfully. "I would like that, Nick."

He smiled. "I know."

"Not lacking in confidence, are you?" she said with a laugh.

He grinned in response, but it looked a little shaky. "Only about one thing."

Then he shocked her, utterly, by dropping to his knee.

"Ellie, I love you. I've always loved you. Granted, I used to love your passion, and your laughter, and your hair." He laughed, a little self-deprecating. "But we're both more than that. I know what we are now, and I know what I'm offering when I say that I want to share forever with you. I still want your passion — but I also want to sit beside you and breathe the same air and know that, in this world, we're together. Can you give me that, Ellie? Will you marry me? Can we grow old together and discover whatever it is we might become?"

She had laughed when he mentioned her hair, but her laughter was overwhelmed by tears. In another life, she might have wiped her tears away — but in that moment, she chose to let them overflow, to give them to him so he might see the heart their love had opened up and knit back together.

"I love you, Nick. Beyond all rationality and comprehension, I love you. And I know what it means now, too. It's not because you're persuasive or because I want to please you, but because you give me the courage to stay even when I'm scared and even when it hurts."

She dropped down to her knees in front of him, looking him dead in the eye. "There could be no greater joy in my life than to marry you, Nicholas Claiborne. And I will love you no matter how many times we begin again."

Their kiss was like the first time — wondrous, magical, a meeting of two people who could hardly believe their luck. They could be slow. They could explore each other rather than merely devouring. Their love wasn't perfect. There were lumps and bruises and scars — memories woven into their fabric that would never fully fade.

But it was *real*, not a dream.

Nick pulled away first. He lifted her hand and kissed it — right over the ring finger, where she would soon wear his wedding band. The thought filled him with some swell of pride he'd never thought he would feel. He was already thinking of the wedding night, and children, and the life they would have…and the wedding night again. He forced himself to take a breath. "Don't change your mind this time," he said. "Or I will take you to Gretna Green without a second thought."

She gave him a wicked grin. "I won't. On one condition."

Her conditions didn't worry him. Perhaps they should — but the grin she used now said he would like whatever it was she wanted. He leaned in to nibble her ear, wondering if he could distract her as much as she distracted him. "And what is that?" he murmured, after a long moment.

She paused, and he grinned into her hair; she was just as susceptible as he was. Finally, she said, "Promise me we'll share a bed. Not that I'm opposed to the occasional floor or chaise," she said, with another grin that made his heart stop. "But I rather liked waking up with you."

That was a demand he would happily fulfill. He stood abruptly and scooped her up into his arms. "I'll keep you in bed for a week if that's what you want. You may break me after all, goddess."

Ellie laughed. Then she rested her head against his chest. "I'm glad you came home."

Home. He still barely knew his way around his house, but it didn't matter. Ellie was the only direction he needed.

He strode for the door, dodging plants and pillars. The future waited for them, as it always had, and they finally had the courage to seize it.

"I've half a mind to carry you through the drawing room just to make sure you can't get away after tonight," he said as he nudged the door open.

"My last scandal as Lady Folkestone…or my first scandal as Lady Folkestone?" Ellie asked. "There's an advantage to this wedding — I won't need to order new calling cards."

Nick laughed. "There will be time enough for scandals when you're my Lady Folkestone. Tonight, I want you to myself."

"I've always been your Lady Folkestone," she said. "But if you want to impress that fact upon me…"

"I do. I think you will like what you will wake up to in the morning, Ellie my love."

She smiled, a seductive little grin that added speed to his steps. "If I don't, we shall just have to begin again. But I trust you'll make it good, Claiborne."

He brushed a kiss against her hair. "Always."

THE END

Books by Sara Ramsey

<u>Muses of Mayfair</u>

Heiress Without a Cause
Scotsmen Prefer Blondes
The Marquess Who Loved Me
The Earl Who Played With Fire

Author's Note

Thank you for spending a few hours with Nick and Ellie! I'm so grateful for your purchase, and I hope you enjoyed it. If you have a few moments, please consider leaving a review on your favorite reading or retail site — whether you loved it or loathed it, I appreciate your thoughts.

The next book in the series, *The Earl Who Played With Fire*, features Miss Prudence Etchingham. It should be out near the end of 2013. Beyond that, I have vague plans for novels or novellas featuring several other women from the series. If you have a favorite character whose story you want told, feel free to lobby me on email, Twitter, or Facebook — I can't guarantee I will write them all, but I plan to stay with the Muses world as long as there are interesting stories within it.

Thanks again for picking up this book, and happy reading!

Best wishes,

Sara Ramsey
San Francisco, California
February 2013

Stay in Touch

Do you want to be the first to hear about new releases, special content, and giveaways? Sign up for Sara's newsletter at: http://www.sararamsey.com/newsletter

Sara loves to hear from readers and usually responds quickly, barring deadlines. Please send questions, criticisms, or compliments to dearsara@sararamsey.com

If you want to share this book with your book club, Sara is happy to talk to groups in person or via Google Hangouts/Skype. Please send Sara an email to discuss possible options.

You can also find Sara on Twitter (@sara_ramsey), Facebook, or Goodreads.

Photo by Misti Layne

Sara Ramsey writes fun, feisty Regency historical romances. She won the prestigious 2009 Romance Writers of America® Golden Heart® award with her second book, *Scotsmen Prefer Blondes*. Her first book, *Heiress Without a Cause*, was a 2011 Golden Heart finalist.

Sara grew up in a small town in Iowa, and her obsession with fashion, shoes, and all things British is clearly a rebellion against her hopelessly uncool youth. She graduated from Stanford University in 2003 with a degree in Symbolic Systems (also known as cognitive science) and a minor in history. She is currently living the hip romance writer life in San Francisco, California. Read all about her Regency obsessions and upcoming works at www.SaraRamsey.com.